For Crying Out Loud

David Richard Chaloner

Foreword

This book came about because of many requests from family members to tell the story of my father George Robert. He was known as Bob to everybody except for his mother and siblings who called him Robin.

It is impossible to tell anyone's life story on the basis of a collection of short stories and in truth, that is all we have. Even the stories vary considerably according to who is relating them. My father's original telling of them probably varied according to who was listening.

This book is a work of fiction that attempts to bind together these stories that have floated around within our family for years. In the fictional parts of this story I have tried hard to be true to Dad's character. His reactions to the fictional people and events in this book are my best guess having actually been present at some similar events later in his life.

I apologise to anybody who feels that they, any of their family members or friends, have been misrepresented or inaccurately portrayed in this story. Please remember that it is offered as a work of fiction and even the parts that include Bob's family are put together from his stories and point of view and may not exactly match those of others.

It could be argued that he was a rogue, certainly he didn't always stay on the 'straight and narrow' and some of the things he did were decidedly 'dodgy.' However, I believe him to have been a gentle, kind and generous man and this book is written with great affection that I hope will come through to the reader.

Thank you to my sister Sue for her invaluable information and reminders of forgotten stories. Thanks also to my colleagues at Forest Talk (Forest of Dean talking newspaper) who encouraged me to tell the stories. Finally, I must thank my wife, Anita for her proof reading and for her patience as this has slowly taken shape.

Apart from family members all the characters in this book are fictional and any similarity to any person or persons living or dead is purely accidental.

David Chaloner

Chapter 1

The authoritarian public-school voice rang out loudly, rousing those who had dropped off in the warmth of the Church and regaining the attention of the rest who, for the most part, were still trying to decide whether they had listened to a sermon or a campaign speech for the Labour Party.

"The collection plate will now be passed round, those who are able to should put something in and those who are in need should take something out" called the lay preacher. He moved down the aisle with a confident and reassuring manner, a hand on a shoulder here a helping arm offered there, his manner that of someone much older than his twenty-two years.

Eventually alone in the Church Bob reflected on what he had been saying to the congregation and wondered, not for the first time, whether any of them had even listened much less taken anything from it. They had certainly taken something from the collection plate though as yet again, just one single penny had been left. Bob thought that nobody quite had the nerve to take the last coin and anyway it could be worse with the last coin being a half-penny or even a farthing!

Bob had actually been Christened George Robert but after being called Bob by school friends the name had somehow stuck with him and anyway, he certainly preferred it to George and now always introduced himself as Bob.

He left the chapel and hurriedly made his way down several side streets until, as he was passing a lady scrubbing her front step she looked up and said "he's in't ginnel" nodding towards a gap in the terrace. 'He' was Tommy, a lad of about ten or twelve who as a 'runner' took horse racing bets from the locals and carried them to the Bookmaker whose whereabouts was only ever known to his 'runners'.

Bob found Tommy loitering in the alley and passed him the slip of paper with the name of the horse and time of the race at Manchester race course plus, of course the money which in this case was ten shillings, a large amount to gamble but not unusual for Bob. This was most likely the only reason that Tommy was allowed to take the bets from him. Bob not being local and wearing a suit and tie would normally be enough reason for distrust. Tommy had told the Bookmaker that he looked a bit of a toff.

The whole business of placing a bet and collecting winnings, should there be any, was conducted on trust. If the Bookmaker didn't pay out then nobody would bet with him, it was illegal and this meant that everybody involved would have to take great care who they dealt with. It wasn't uncommon for people to be reported for the *heinous* crime of gambling and if found guilty in Court then a prison sentence was almost inevitable.

Bob walked back to his lodgings, ever the optimist he mused over what he would spend his winnings on when his horse was a winner in tomorrow's race. The newspaper had put the odds at ten to one but the 'Bookies' never paid out what the papers said. It was likely to be seven or eight to one which would still give him a pay-out of around four pounds, if it won.

He thought about some luxuries that might come his way if his horse won. The truth was that he would be spending it on food and clothes for the so called 'drop outs' who being homeless, sheltered under various bridges or made rough shelters from whatever they could find on waste ground.

He had first encountered these men when, walking aimlessly one day with his mind elsewhere he found himself completely lost and in the midst of some pretty wild looking men. His polite request for directions had been met with much amusement but maybe they sensed that he was sympathetic to them. They found him not at all condescending and so, after chatting for a while, they told him how to get back to '*civilisation*' as they called it.

He found his way back to see them quite often and that was how the spending of his winnings on them had started. He couldn't quite work out why he did this, the men were always grateful for what he gave them but he never felt any sense of satisfaction or achievement. The socialist side of his nature meant that he was alternately depressed and then angry that nothing really ever changed for them.

Many of these men were ex-soldiers that had returned as heroes from the so called 'great war' and then found that there was nothing waiting for them other than to beg and steal and survive any way they could. Bob had listened to their stories often enough and was always left with a nagging feeling of doubt about what God and the Church was actually doing to help anybody except the well off.

He lived relatively comfortably himself, being paid a small amount of money for his preaching and pastoral work and also receiving regular money from his parents. He had mixed feelings about the money he got from his parents. Admitting to himself that the feelings about *not* taking it were stronger just after he had spent one lot and then faded somewhat just before receiving the next.

His mother and father had no mixed feelings about sending him money. They were simply delighted that after a very unpromising start, he had somehow managed to negotiate Public school and University without gaining any tangible qualifications. He now seemed to be settling into something that they thoroughly approved of as they were both very devout Christians.

For as long as he could remember Bob had not been comfortable with his parent's religious fervour but had learned quickly, especially where his mother was concerned, that it was easier to go along with it than not. Once freed from the family home he had adopted a much more relaxed approach to being, as he thought of himself, a believer.

He returned to his lodgings, stopping on the way to buy a paper and a pack of Players Navy Cut. He had a room with Mrs Cahill a widowed lady who had "lost my Fred god bless his soul" in the war and seemed to him to be always on the verge of tears.

Most evenings he would eat the meal she prepared for him and retire to his room as quickly as he could without seeming rude. He wasn't unsympathetic toward her but occasionally the way she looked at him made him very uncomfortable.

His room was sparsely furnished but adequate for his needs and did include the luxury of a small gas heater so he was never cold and on this particular evening he lit the heater as soon as he made it to his room. He took off his shoes, jacket and tie and stretched out on the bed to read the newspaper. This was one of his great pleasures and he would read every article, even re-reading some to make sure he really understood them, before finally studying the racing information on the back page to decide on his next wager.

He had just begun to read when there was a knock on his door, he ignored it at first thinking maybe it was just a noise in the house somewhere but the next knock was louder and definitely on his door. He was surprised because in almost a year since he had been there this had actually never happened before.

He opened the door to find a scruffy lad thrusting a piece of paper toward him and saying "he told me you'd give me a tanner for bringing it" Bob was still so taken aback at someone coming to his door that without thinking he dug into his trouser pocket and found a sixpence which the boy snatched from his hand and was gone in a flash.

The sound of the outer door slamming brought him back to reality and he then realised that the boy would never have agreed to take a note with being paid first and also that he hadn't even asked who had given it to the boy to deliver.

The note was addressed to George. R. Chaloner and simply said

I and the Elders will be pleased if you would present yourself at the Church at 9.00am tomorrow promptly   Reverend. B. Pritchard

Bob was puzzled by this and a bit concerned, it was odd, after many months the Minister had finally stopped calling him George and was lately addressing him as Robert which he minded a bit less than George. Also, the Minister was always somewhat flowery in his speech and much given to repeating himself, three times was not unusual.

Bob thought the note was very formal and rather curt but having never before received a note from the Rev, as he thought of him. There was nothing to compare it with really and so he put it to one side and tried to settle down with the newspaper again.

It was no good, he could not concentrate and his plan of a nice evening with a small drink and a couple of cigarettes while reading the paper was not to be. Having an earlier start than usual in the morning, he got ready for bed, turned off the heater and set his alarm clock for 7.00am.

He had fallen asleep thinking about the note and it was the first thing on his mind when he woke up to the alarm. He used the jug and bowl in his room for a wash and a cold shave and tried unsuccessfully to put the note out of his mind. He retrieved his trousers from being pressed under the mattress and dressed quickly. He remembered to leave a note explaining his absence from breakfast and quietly left the house.

It was a thirty-minute walk to the Church so Bob had plenty of time to pick up the morning paper and detour to the State Cafe where he could at least get a cup of tea and ready himself for the meeting.

He had thought that it might be to do with his gambling but most of the male members of the congregation used the same bookie as him. He got his best tips from some them and since he also suspected that the 'Rev' did as well, he dismissed that as a possibility.... it couldn't have anything to do with him directly could it? He would just have to wait and see.

Bertram, the Reverend Pritchard, arrived early but he was surprised to find the two church elders already there. Mr A Edgerton and his brother Mr C Edgerton were both in their seventies or possibly older and both wore suits that would have been popular thirty years earlier. They each carried a walking cane, obviously just for effect as neither of them appeared to need any assistance as they walked briskly into the church and headed for the Vestry. Mr A the older of the elders made a show of consulting his pocket watch; he was rather hoping that young George Robert would be late; more ammunition to add to what was, in his mind, already quite a considerable catalogue.

There were only two chairs in the Vestry so Bertram went quickly to get just one more... he would enjoy them being seated while Robert... he corrected himself, *a person should use their given name* he thought....while *George* remained standing.

Try as he might Bertram could not stop feeling a little pleased that the confident, self-assured young man was to be taken down a step or two, in quiet moments of self-examination he could admit to himself that he was a bit jealous. The easy way Bob had with people and the popularity that he had gained was something that he knew he would never achieve himself.

Bob arrived at the Church and made his way to the Vestry; he was called in and told by the 'Rev' to close the door. Something about the musty smell of the Vestry reminded him of school store cupboards and always made him feel slightly uncomfortable. It was obvious that he was to be left standing and that he was, in fact, in some trouble. That was confirmed by Mr A's first words. "We have had serious complaints" he said, Bob looked from one to the other and it seemed to him that they all looked just a little smug.

There was a silence as if they expected him to respond but he just stood and waited. The Reverend Pritchard had obviously chosen or had been chosen to lead the 'interrogation', as Bob was now starting to see it. "The amounts from the collection plate have been considerably lower over the last few months" said the Rev. Bob remained silent.

The Rev knew about his allowing those in need to take money from the plate. He knew strictly speaking it was not Church policy but had allowed Bob to persuade him that the Church should be helping out while things were so bad for some of the congregation.

Having had no response, the Rev continued "You have been seen giving food and even clothes to drunkards and beggars"... Finally, Bob spoke. "That is correct" he said. The Rev and the elders exchanged a look and then the Rev actually asked a question.

"Where did you get the money to buy the food and clothes that you are so generously giving away?" Bob began to realise where this was going and also that he was in more than a little trouble. He could not say where the money came from without admitting to his gambling. "I have only used my own money" said Bob.

The elder Mr C spoke for the first time now "We know how much money you receive from the church and we know how much you are sent from your father. We know the cost of your food and lodgings and how much you spend on Cigarettes and other comforts so there is simply not enough left over for you to spend on buying food and clothes for your *friends*".

Bob was staggered; they had asked his father how much money he was sending!! They had checked up on his spending!! He was speechless....Of course he knew that his father had contact with the Elders, that was partly how he had arrived in the position....but this!

The Rev was speaking again now "the only way that you could be spending that money is if it is you taking the money from the collection plate and not the needy in the congregation as you would have us believe". Bob had still not spoken since his three words earlier.... the Rev continued. "We have decided not to call a Constable and you are to continue with your preaching and pastoral work. However, you will no longer encourage anyone in the congregation or otherwise to remove money from the collection plate. They will be arrested for theft should they do so and I will be overseeing the collections in future."

He looked to the brothers and they both nodded, encouraging him to continue. "You will not visit the beggars and vagabonds again and you will restrict yourself to doing the Lords work among those who appreciate it and not waste any more time on those who don't."

Bob was still stunned by the revelation that they had delved so deeply into his private affairs. He was lost for any words that would adequately convey his feelings about the intrusion or the injustice.

He was also beginning to realise that nothing he could say would have any effect on them so he just stood thinking of all the words that he could use to describe them which included pompous, self-righteous and a few more unrepeatable ones.

The Rev and the Elders obviously mistook his silence for penitence and when Mr A spoke again it was a little less harsh. "You will return to your lodgings where you will stay for two days while you reflect on this meeting, Mrs Cahill has been made aware of this, you will then return to your duties in a proper manner supporting Reverend Pritchard with the Lord's work"

Mr C spoke up now. "Be very clear Mr Chaloner, should you indulge yourself with any further behaviour of this kind it will be dealt with much more harshly", Reverend Pritchard stood up and faced Bob. He couldn't quite hide the look of triumph on his face. "You obviously have nothing to say for once, you may now leave". He turned his back on Bob and said to the Elders "Now I think there may be some *important* matters for us to discuss as you are both here".

Not knowing what else to do Bob simply left.

He was still seething when eventually he got back to his lodgings, he was slowly making his way upstairs when Mrs Cahill called up to him. "You'll be needing more food and everything for a couple of days". He heard something in her voice that wasn't quite as friendly as previously "It will cost more you know" he wasn't too sure what the *'everything'* was but thought maybe she meant extra gas for the heater?

Bob stretched out on the bed, not even taking his shoes off and not caring about the creases that would be in his jacket and trousers. He could hardly believe what had happened at the Church. He was now thinking of all the clever things he could have said but in his heart, he knew that nothing would have made any difference.

They had decided and that was that. He lay there thinking now about who it was that had complained. He couldn't imagine any of the people who attended the Church going anywhere near the areas where the homeless men hung about.

Bob recalled a remark that the 'Rev' had made a few weeks earlier about his *poor friends.* He had not thought much of it at the time thinking that the 'Rev' was referring to some in the congregation but now he thought perhaps it was something different and he began to wonder whether there had actually been any real complaints at all.

That evening he ate his meal alone. Mrs Cahill didn't join him as she often chose to, and he soon returned to his room.

He took some writing paper, a pen and some ink from the small cupboard under the window and, using his small suitcase as a desk top he started to write.

Chapter 2

ob was jolted awake as the train switched tracks several times in getting past what had once been Macclesfield station. He'd been alone in the carriage since getting on at Manchester London Road and it would most likely stay that way until the train reached Stoke on Trent when even a mid-day train might start to fill up. His thoughts inevitably drifted back over the events of the past three weeks, his life seemed to have changed so dramatically in such a short time.

While still on the two day 'period of reflection' he had written a note to the Reverend Pritchard, he wasn't 'Rev' any more. The note had said that he wished to meet with the Reverend and the Elders on the day of his return as he had something to say that he was sure they would want to hear. He knew that they would be there, ready to enjoy what they assumed would be a repentant apology. He couldn't help grinning as he recalled their faces at the meeting.

They had met as before in the Vestry but this time Bob had swiftly moved the chair that the Reverend was about to use and sat on it himself, saying "I think the Reverend may need to get himself a chair." The Reverend hesitated for a moment and then angrily stalked off to find a chair.

He grabbed the first one he came to, only realising as he brought it in and sat down that this was the chair that the previous Minister had had specially made for a church member who was what was then known as a dwarf. This little man had long since passed on and these days children would fight over who used the chair as whoever won would not then have to sit still in the pews.

Looking at the Reverend who had his knees up quite close to his very red face and with a vein visibly throbbing on his forehead Bob had struggled to keep a straight face but turning to look at the faces of the Elders made this particular problem go away. Reverend Pritchard stood up then sat down again, this time on the edge of the chair with his legs splayed outward trying hard to regain some dignity.

"Well young man... you have us assembled here at your pleasure, at *your* pleasure I say, at *your* pleasure" he said gesturing impatiently for Bob to speak.

Bob imagined that they all knew by then that this was not going to be an apology but he had told them that anyway, going on to say that, "if there were a God, which I now doubt, then God would surely not want scheming, self-important, self-gratifying people running his Church and he definitely wouldn't want liars either," looking straight at the Reverend as he said it. He had gone on to say that, "if there *were* a God, he would want the Church to actually help the needy and not to punish people for trying to do just that."

He had continued in this way until he eventually ran out of steam and he had been getting a bit concerned that the Reverend might soon need medical assistance with his mouth opening and closing like a fish and making odd squeaking sounds. He ended by wishing them luck in finding their next preacher as they would not be seeing him again and left the room.

Having given them no opportunity to reply he walked briskly out of the Church. He had realised at that moment that what had been troubling him for some time had taken form and been confirmed. He no longer believed in God *or* the Church.

His thoughts turned to his family; he had four older brothers and two sisters, only his sister Margaret was younger than him. He had never felt close to any of them really with the exception of James (Bob always called him Jim) who shared his sometimes odd 'cartoonish' view of things.

Although being three years older Jim allowed Bob to lead him into all kinds of trouble. Their pranks were often extremely elaborate and quite often aimed at their mother. They had managed, a couple of times, to completely fool their mother with Bob providing the words for an outrageously rude letter purporting to be from one of her friends with Jim doing a remarkable job on the forgery.

He looked back on it now as being quite cruel but at the time he and Jim would be in uncontrollable fits of giggles, which on each occasion had been their undoing. Their mother was a forceful woman and was one of the founder members of the new Band of Hope, campaigning vigorously for the abolition of alcohol. She would brook no argument when in the Church, or when out campaigning, however in the home or just in the company of their father she employed a different tactic.

Whenever it seemed that there was the remotest possibility of her not getting her own way with something she would 'faint' completely away, though never once actually hurting herself as she sank gracefully to the floor. Apart from the immediate administering of smelling salts and much hand patting by Mary, the eldest daughter, the only thing that would completely revive her was the assurance that she had got what she wanted.

She used her 'fainting' to ensure that Bob and Jim were "properly punished" by their father on his return home at which he would order them into his study to wait while he heard of their misdeeds. The first time this happened both Bob and Jim were more than a bit worried not knowing what to expect and still hearing their mother outside demanding the most serious punishment.

Their Father had entered his study, closed the door and stood looking sternly at them for a moment before saying in a very loud voice "both of you will bend over on my desk and receive your punishment, James you will be first". Jim started toward the desk but their father gestured for him to stay where he was and started to hit the desk with his hand, after the first couple of hits he said quietly to Jim "make some noise, you're being punished". When he hit the desk again Jim cried out, "louder please" said their father.

By the time it was Bob's turn to be punished he had got the idea and did a great job of crying out after each blow, they were then told to go and apologise to their mother, which they did, after limping theatrically out of the study.

They realised that these 'let offs' would only happen if their father was also amused by what they had done and that they should be careful with any future pranks.

Bob thought fondly of his father, in spite of his always appearing stiff and formal. He was a well-respected and successful business man as well as a leading figure in the Church and the local community. However, Bob had occasionally glimpsed a warmer and more humorous side to him which he liked to think of as his father's real character.

Bob had been so lost in his thoughts that he was surprised to discover that he had been joined in the carriage by a young woman with a small boy that he assumed was her son. There had been no stops so she must have used the corridor and he wondered why she had moved.

Encouraged by his smile the small boy immediately moved to sit beside him. He didn't mind at all, he was always being told that he was good with the very old and the very young.

He often wished that he could be as well received by people nearer his own age, particularly ladies. Bob was a little over six feet tall, slimly built with a shock of black hair which he brushed back in the style of the time and he knew that, at worst, he was not unattractive to women but even being the slightest bit attracted to a woman meant that his normal easy eloquence simply disappeared.

The little boy was now chatting away with Bob understanding virtually none of what he was saying. The young woman was apologising for her son disturbing him which Bob dismissed, saying that "he is no trouble at all, a lovely little lad" which elicited a smile from the woman and now Bob noticed how pretty she was. She had dark hair curling in ringlets around her face and big brown eyes with slightly a distant look which Bob found most appealing.

A few moments later the woman moved to sit next to Bob, scooping up her son and plonking him on her lap. She was now sitting very close to him and Bob was unsure if he should move away slightly but decided to stay put. After all, this forward young lady had put herself there. She offered Bob her hand and in doing so moved even closer.

Now he was experiencing some feelings which he knew that he should put aside. She introduced herself as Lucy, quickly adding, Mrs Lucy Braithwaite that is. As he turned away after shaking hands Bob thought he saw her smile fading when adding the last bit, or did he imagine it? He was feeling strangely disappointed finding that she was a married lady, but he didn't quite know what he was thinking anyway with having just met her, and her having a small child.

An hour later, and with only about twenty minutes or so of the journey left Bob realised that he had told her everything that had happened to him over the last few months, including his recent conversion to what he now thought of as Atheism. Lucy had a way of listening, smiling and nodding, which had encouraged Bob to keep talking about himself but now he wanted to know at least something about her.

He instantly regretted his first question about her husband, her smile had faltered and although she recovered quickly he knew that he had chosen the wrong subject. Bob apologised but she insisted on going on, saying that after all he had just confided so much to her, and so, gently moving her now sleeping son to a more comfortable position, she began.

Lucy had met and married Thomas the only child of Clive and Evelyn Braithwaite, Clive Braithwaite owned and ran C.R.Braithwaite Estate Agents which, she said quoting him, was "very successful in selling the more desirable properties in the outer London area." Thomas had joined his father in the business and, although quite young, had proved to be very good with the prospective buyers, moving sales to a much higher level in a very short time.

This increase in sales had convinced Clive Braithwaite that the time was right for expansion. He had harboured thoughts of having more branches for a long time but was wary of creating competition from the larger firms and had decided that it would be better to open a new branch in Birmingham or Manchester.

Thomas was only a little younger than Clive had been when he started the business and so it was decided that it would be Thomas who would go and find suitable premises. Manchester was chosen and plans were made for Thomas to go and set everything up to start the business. Thinking that it might take him a year or more to reach a point at which they could hire a manager and for him to then return to London Thomas had rented a house and he, Lucy and young Thomas moved in and began to make it home.

Lucy stopped and seemed to gather herself before going on. "It was the day he had found the perfect shop to rent. Thomas was very excited and said he could hardly wait for me to see it." Lucy had become visibly upset and Bob was at a loss as to what to do, in the end doing nothing. "He must have had his mind on the new shop because the tram driver said that he had just stepped straight in front of the tram."

Mr and Mrs Braithwaite had Thomas returned to London and the funeral took place at their church in Norwood. A week after the funeral Lucy insisted on returning to their home in

Manchester. After just a month she realised that it was not really practical and the Braithwaites, as she referred to them, were insisting that she came to live with them for the sake of young Thomas if nothing else.

Bob and Lucy sat in silence for a few minutes mainly because Bob had no idea what to say. His recent experience in pastoral care was of no use to him at all. It was Lucy who started talking again. She had quickly regained her cheerful manner and asked Bob what his plans were for work now that he was no longer a preacher? He just had no idea about what he could do next. He had given a great deal of thought to what he was *not* going to do but not much thought beyond that.

He had written a long letter to his father explaining what had happened in Manchester and giving a very honest account of his part in it including his actions when leaving and his conclusions regarding God and the Church. He had written that letter almost three weeks earlier but had not received a reply up to leaving his lodgings earlier that day. He had also written to his brother Jim telling the story again and Jim had written a very sympathetic reply.

Jim had moved to Maidstone in Kent after his marriage to Winifred and was working in a business owned by her father doing something of which Bob had no idea. Jim apparently was not that keen on the work but it was a job. Jim's reply had arrived a week later, amazingly quickly, and had included the names and address of some "good people" in Coulsdon where Bob would be able to stay if he wished. Bob wrote thanking them and giving a date when he would arrive, it was a relief to have somewhere to stay.

Jim's letter had gone on to say that Bob was "persona non gratis" at the family home, nobody was allowed to talk about him and his mother was in such a state that the smelling salts were in almost constant use!

Lucy nudged him and he realised that he had not answered her for several minutes, "I honestly haven't the faintest idea" he said, "I have a few pounds and somewhere to stay but I'll have to find something soon." Lucy had moved from being next to Bob and was now seated opposite him and was holding on to Thomas quite tightly with a worried look on her face. Bob was immediately concerned and asked if he had said something to upset her.

She assured him that it was nothing that he had said and explained that on one of her return journeys the train had not stopped in time and crashed into the buffers at Euston Station. Luckily, she had not been hurt and only suffered from shock. However, a number of passengers seated nearer the front of the train had been injured, some quite badly. She now made sure that she was seated with her back to the engine and had a good hold on young Thomas who was now awake and smiling at Bob.

As he smiled back at Tommy, (he was already calling him that in his head), he recalled his last meeting with Tommy the Bookie's runner and thought how different the lives of the two Tommy's were now, and likely to be in the future. With all that had happened Bob had almost forgotten to collect his winnings; the horse had won!

The day before he was due to catch his train, he went to find Tommy the runner and was surprised to receive five pounds and ten shillings, his biggest ever pay out from the Manchester Bookie.

After giving a very happy Tommy ten shillings he had thought about giving some, if not all, of the rest to the homeless men but in the event he ran out of time to go and see them. He was glad of that now as all he had left after paying for the train ticket was ten pounds two shillings and sixpence including his winnings which was going to have to last for a while. Just how long he had no idea.

The train came to a stop and Bob helped Lucy to get down to the platform. She only had one case with her but a porter was there in a flash to put it on his barrow. The porter reached for Bob's case but Bob said "No, we're not together". There was a slightly awkward moment and then they both laughed, Lucy produced a card from her handbag and gave it to Bob saying "I hope we can meet again, perhaps for tea at some time?"

She saw Bob glance quickly at what was a Braithwaite Estate Agents business card, and added "You can contact me through the Braithwaites if you want to" and then, picking Thomas up and signalling to the porter, she walked away. Bob stood watching her walk off, wondering again why she had moved to his compartment. He hadn't asked her that. He shrugged his shoulders and pocketed the card.

Then left the station and went to find a bus to Coulsdon.

Chapter 3

Dick and Brenda's flat occupied half the ground floor of a large Victorian house in a nice tree lined road. Once home to just one family the house was now divided into four large self-contained flats.

This was becoming more common and as Bob walked the last half a mile or so from the bus stop he noticed the signs of building work going on in at least six large houses along the way. He wondered whether the flats would be rented or sold, he didn't actually know whether *parts* of a house *could* be sold.

Lucy might know something like that; he would ask her if they met up again. Not that he was in a position to buy one now, or even in the foreseeable future, but he was interested to know anyway.

Bob always took a keen interest in politics and even more so recently as things were getting worse for people with the economy struggling and unemployment staying at a high level. As 1929 approached all the predictions were for it only to get worse. He thought that this must be the reason for the house conversions he was seeing, but surely *four* families housed where there was previously only one was actually a good thing, wasn't it?

Dick must have been looking out for him because as Bob walked up the short path the front door opened and Dick was there with a welcoming smile and showed Bob down the hallway to the door of their flat.

The flat was larger than Bob had expected but was warm and had a cosy feel. The smell of cooking added to pleasure that Bob felt as Dick showed him round, taking Bob's case as he did so and putting it onto the bed of what was to be Bob's room. The quick tour ended at the kitchen door. The kitchen was surprisingly large and had a cooker and a sink on one side and a number of cupboards on the other. In the middle of the room there was a large table and four chairs in a very modern 'boxy' style.

Brenda turned from the cooker as he entered, Dick had pushed him forward, "Hello Robin" she said, "James has told me of your difficulties" turning back to stir something on the cooker she said "I'm glad that we can help you for a short time while you find somewhere of your own".

The message was clear and Bob replied "Yes, thank you Brenda, I'll be gone very soon." He disliked her use of 'Robin,' but that is how Jim and Winnie would have spoken of him. As far as he was concerned, he had stopped being 'Robin' when he left the family home.

Dick seemed blissfully unaware of any tension between Bob and Brenda. He went with Bob to his room and talked non-stop as he 'helped' him unpack his case. It was clear to both of them that they were to be friends.

Brenda called to them that the meal was ready. Once they were seated she and Dick bowed their heads and she said Grace, adding "In this home we respect Christian ways". She obviously objected to Bob staying with them and could barely contain her disgust at his declared Atheism. In spite of this she had obvious gone to quite some trouble to prepare the meal. They had braised beef with vegetables, including Asparagus which Bob found a bit odd, followed by delicious homemade Apple Charlotte. Dick earned himself a glare from Brenda by telling Bob the apples were from a tin; nevertheless, they all spent some time talking about all the things that could now be bought in tins. "Canned food" said Dick, "Our neighbours across the hall say canned", "They're Americans" said Brenda, making it sound like a disease.

"We've been in to see their refrigerator; it's all very good if it works as they say." Brenda seemed quite put out, "I invited them to join us to listen to the BBC Daily Service on our Bush Wireless Radio but they haven't been yet." *Not for a year or two yet* thought Bob, then immediately chastised himself, having just enjoyed a nice meal cooked by Brenda.

The next week or so passed by without incident and Bob had time to explore the local area which he found he really liked. He was aware though of how little money he had left and the pressing need for some income. He wasn't expecting anything from his parents, there was still no contact between him and any of the family apart from Jim and Winnie. He had a suspicion that Jim was somehow keeping the family updated. He liked to think that they would want to know that he was alright.

It was a bright but cold December morning and Bob got up early and left the flat before seven and, lost in his thoughts, he walked for almost three hours. He looked for a street name to help him find out where he was but not finding one, he went into a shop to ask, he was in Norwood High Street.

He searched through the odd bits of paper that he habitually stored in the top pocket of his suit jacket and eventually found the card that Lucy had given to him almost two weeks ago. As he had thought, the Braithwaite's shop was in Norwood, the address on the card was Norwood Road.

He popped back into the shop and asked the shopkeeper for directions to Norwood Rd, the shopkeeper gave him directions and asked him whereabouts in particular because it was a long road. Luckily the man knew the Braithwaite's shop and told Bob that once he was in Norwood road it was not far along and to look out for the new Cinema that had been built. The shop was close to that.

Bob found the Cinema, the building work was not quite finished but he stood admiring the Art Deco style building...... "Bob...Bob, it is you isn't it" he turned to see Lucy with a big grin on her face and before he could say anything she was giving him a hug. She let him go and said "I knew you would come. "Bob had still not spoken, "You did come to look me up didn't you?" "Yes, of course I did" said Bob.

Lucy took Bob's hand and practically pulled him along the road to the shop. It was double fronted with the sign written fascia **C.R.Braithwaite Estate Agent** above. Both windows were clear of any advertising and allowed a view inside of two desks facing the front. One of the desks had a typewriter on it, the second had a telephone on it and a rather sombre looking man behind it.

The man smiled as Lucy entered the shop, the smile disappearing as he realised that Bob was following her in. "This is the man that I told you about" she said, Bob noticed how her voice had changed and she was straight away quieter and more serious. He was introduced by Lucy as Bob but the man simply introduced himself as "Braithwaite"as they shook hands.

Very quickly it became obvious to Bob that Braithwaite was not the man that he must have been before the untimely death of his only son. He was obviously grieving and it looked to Bob that he might be for some considerable time to come.

Braithwaite patiently answered Bob's many questions about the business until Lucy reminded him that she had come to walk with him back to their home for lunch. The old Clive Braithwaite would never have closed for lunch but since his son's death he was opening later, closing earlier and business was really falling off.

"I thank you for your kindness to my son's wife," he said, "You must join us for lunch, I'm sure Mrs Braithwaite would like to meet you." "Yes, he will join us" said Lucy. Braithwaite turned to her "I'm sure Mr.....?" "Chaloner" responded Bob, "I'm sure Mr Chaloner can make his own decisions" Bob said that he would love to join them and so, after locking the shop they all walked to the Braithwaite's house barely ten minutes away.

Mrs Braithwaite was pleased to meet Bob, who was introduced as Mr Chaloner. She didn't seem at all bothered by having one extra for lunch. She had obviously been playing with young Thomas, who was now having a nap, and she swept the toys to one side with her foot as they walked through to the dining room.

A nice lunch was produced and eaten and in what seemed like no time at all Bob was left alone with Braithwaite. (Bob couldn't think of him as anything but just Braithwaite). He was enjoying an after-meal cigarette and Braithwaite, without asking, had given him a small whisky. He noticed that Braithwaite's whisky was considerably larger.

It became obvious to Bob that Lucy had told the Braithwaites much of what he had told her on the train. He didn't mind, he hadn't told her in confidence, but it was a bit disconcerting to hear it coming back from someone who was really still a stranger. As if reading his mind Braithwaite said "I know we are really strangers" he paused, and then continued. "Knowing that you are at a loose end at present, and in need of some money I should think, I wonder if you would consider helping me in the business for a short while?"

Bob was a bit taken aback saying "We don't actually know each other at all" it sounded sharper than he intended but as he was about to add something else Braithwaite cut him off, saying "look, I hope that you realise that I am a well-respected member of the local business community and indeed our local Church." There was a pause then Bob replied "It was more about you not knowing much about me really". "Lucy says that you are a good man and I trust her instincts". Braithwaite finished off his second whisky in one go "After all she chose to marry my son".

They sat in silence for a few minutes until Braithwaite started to tell Bob what he had in mind. He admitted that he had not had his mind on the business since his son's passing. Things were piling up and there had been no property sales for weeks.

Bob protested his ignorance of anything to do with Estate Agency business but Braithwaite just waved this off. He would soon learn enough to be helpful and anyway, Braithwaite said, he wouldn't be able to pay him very much at all.

Mrs Braithwaite, Lucy and young Thomas joined them in the dining room. On hearing that Bob was to start on Monday morning 'helping' in the shop Lucy smiled broadly and clapped her hands getting a stern look from Mrs Braithwaite. "Thank you, Mr Chaloner, may I call you Bob?" Bob replied "of course" she could. She offered no name in return so it looked like she would remain Mrs Braithwaite to him.

Bob left the Braithwaite's house still wondering about the sudden turn of events and whether he had been right to agree to work for Braithwaite, or 'help out' as it was referred to. He was facing a long walk back and so, as he now had the prospect of a little money coming in, he decided to find a bus for at least part of the journey.

He arrived back at the flat much later than he had intended and long after his meal had been consigned to the dustbin. He apologised to Brenda and explained where he had been and what had happened. Dick was really pleased and cross examined him for all the details, particularly where *Lucy figured in the whole thing*? Bob assured them that there was definitely no romance on the horizon while wondering if that was actually true.

Bringing it back to a more practical level Brenda asked how long it would take him to get there and back, pointing out that it was a journey he would be taking every day. On hearing how long it had taken him to get back this time she said "surely it would be better for you to find somewhere to stay that's nearer to the shop."

My word, thought Bob, *she's got me moved out already!* He explained again that it was just helping out and that it might not come to anything permanent even if he wanted it to. "Well, let's hope it works out well for everybody" said Brenda, going off to find some things to bang around in the kitchen.

Chapter 4

ob was startled by the telephone ringing. The bells on the wall box were very loud and it had only happened once before since he had started on Monday. It was now Wednesday morning and the first time he had been on his own in the office. Monday and Tuesday had consisted of a 'crash course' in Estate Agency operation. Bob was a quick learner and Braithwaite had been impressed.

He picked up the receiver and then realised that he didn't actually know what to say, the 'crash course' hadn't covered that. While he was still thinking about what to say a voice said "Braithwaite, is that you?" Bob had recovered sufficiently and said "Mr Braithwaite is not here at present, my name is Robert, and I am helping out at the moment"

He couldn't think why he had called himself Robert and not Bob, it may have been something to do with the rather 'upper class' sound of the person calling. "Well Robert, perhaps you could *help out* by telling me when I'm *actually* going to see the house that I am still interested in purchasing?"

Bob quickly settled into a more business-like manner, "If I can take your name please and which property you wish to view, then we can arrange an appointment" Bob wasn't at all sure that this is what was supposed to happen but was in confident 'sales' mode now. Actually, it was 'preacher' mode, but as he soon learnt, there was no real difference.

He had the name of the client and the address of the property and searched quickly through the filing drawer, relieved to find the property details if not the client's. "When would be convenient for you to view the property Mr Duncan? "There was a pause followed by a chuckle. "Duncan is my first name, Duncan Walding," Bob apologised but the client said "No, Duncan is fine. Can I call you Bob?" It was Bob's turn to laugh. "Everybody does" he said.

Arrangements were made for the viewing. Duncan, accompanied by his wife and their two daughters, would meet Bob at the house at 3.00pm the following day.

It was nearing 5.30pm and there was no sign of Braithwaite, Bob was wondering if he should walk to the Braithwaite's house to get a key for the shop...He corrected himself, Braithwaite liked it to be called the office. Just as he had made his decision to go Braithwaite came through the door looking more than a little dishevelled. Bob soon realised that the whisky bottle had been in use. In the confines of the office the smell was a bit overwhelming for him. He wished Braithwaite a good evening and left quickly, giving no him opportunity to say anything at all.

The following morning he arrived little earlier, having worked out that with a couple of changes he could do almost the whole journey by bus. Braithwaite was already there doing something *busy* at his desk. He looked up as Bob came in. "Nice and keen, I like that" he said. "How did you get on yesterday, any problems?" Obviously his absence was not going to be mentioned.

Bob told him all about the phone call and what he had arranged with Duncan. Braithwaite was looking at him with an odd look on his face and was slowly shaking his head. "Have I done something wrong" said Bob, "is that not what should happen?"

Braithwaite explained to him that his new 'friend' Duncan was an extremely wealthy man with interests in all kinds of businesses and that the house he was going to view was one of the highest value properties on their books.

During the course of the morning Braithwaite filled Bob in on what was normal practice for dealing with viewings. He pointed out that because they were dealing with what he called the 'upper end' of the property market prospective buyers usually expected to have transport arranged for them or indeed be picked up by the person taking them to the viewing. Obviously, Duncan Walding was not one of the usual clients thought Bob.

As the morning went on Braithwaite confided to Bob that he had forgotten to get back to Mr Walding the week before. He had been letting things slide quite badly since the loss of his son. "I really do appreciate your being here" he said and Bob realised then that this might turn out to be more than just helping out.

From looking a bit careworn Braithwaite suddenly brightened up. "Do you drive motor cars?" he asked, Bob said that he never had. After a little thought Braithwaite said that he would drive them to the viewing but, he said, "you will be conducting the viewing" he also said that Bob should watch him in the car as it wasn't difficult and he might have to drive at some point.

Bob hadn't realised that Braithwaite owned a car and it was only now when arriving at the house that he noticed there was a garage at the side of the house. He had been invited for some lunch and as he went in Mrs Braithwaite greeted him with a smile and a hug. "Lucy will be upset to have missed seeing you, she's gone to visit her parents."

They had a nice lunch during which Braithwaite told his wife all about the viewing and how it had come about. She was really pleased and said "I knew Bob was going to be helpful to you". They finished eating and Braithwaite told Bob that they should be going. It was not yet 2.00 a clock but he said that it would take some time to warm the car up before they could go.

It was twenty past two by the time they were ready to drive off. Bob had watched as the choke was pulled out, the starter button was pushed and the engine turned over. It started with a cough and a bang, a rather large cloud of smoke hung behind them and eventually it settled to a regular beat. Apparently he was in a Hillman 14, purchased the year before and having all the latest innovations though he wasn't actually told what they were.

They finally moved off with Braithwaite showing him how press the clutch down to move the gear stick to neutral and then press it down again to put it in the right gear. Bob was thrown about all over the place and had to hang on to whatever he could with the car 'kangarooing' down the road while Braithwaite was explaining to him the importance of smooth gear changes. At last the driving steadied up a little and they made their way, very slowly, to the viewing.

The house was a very large detached place in substantial grounds, surrounded by a high wall and with imposing double gates. It was situated in a rural spot to the west of Norwood. Although quite a lot of house building was going on it hadn't yet reached that area, which still had a nice village feel to it.

Bob got out and opened the gates and Braithwaite drove up the short driveway and parked in front of the house. He told Bob that he was going for a walk and would be back in an hour or so by which time, he thought, the Waldings should have decided whether they liked it or not and gone.

Bob was totally unprepared for this, he had assumed that Braithwaite wasn't really just driving him there and would in fact take over dealing with the clients. He was still wondering what he was actually supposed to do at a viewing when a large car drove in and stopped just inches from where he was stood.

On the top of the large chrome radiator grill was a badge which said Lagonda, on each side of the grill there was an enormous chrome headlight. Without thinking Bob put his hand on the grill.

Duncan leapt from the driver's seat and was beside Bob in a flash, who withdrew his hand quickly, but Duncan said "no...you can touch her, I find I can't keep my hands off her" he was smiling at Bob now and went on "she's a beauty isn't she, Lagonda sixteen sixty-five, two point seven litres, four speed gearbox" he'd lost Bob completely with this but just then Mrs Walding appeared from the other side of the car.

"You must be Bob" said Duncan, and without waiting for a reply "This is my wife Muriel and the two horrors in the car are our daughters Annie and Gloria." The 'horrors' escaped from the car and dashed off out of sight around the side of the house.

Duncan looked at Bob expectantly, "We're ready to see the inside" he said. Bob had been thinking quickly about what he should do next, he'd realised that if you were going to show someone round a house then you really should know something about it. He wondered if this was why Braithwaite had left him alone, as a lesson. If he ever did this again, he would be well prepared.

"I think it would be nice if you and Mrs.." "Muriel" she said, "You must call me Muriel" "I think it would be nice if you and Muriel went and looked on your own without me hovering around trying to convince you to buy it." Duncan laughed, "Meaning you don't know the first thing about what's in there" he said with a grin. Bob owned up and they all laughed. He really did like these people. Despite their obvious wealth they were open and friendly and appeared to have none of the 'airs and graces' that so many adopted.

"Ok Bob, you stay here and relax, have a smoke eh?" He was still smiling. "If the horrors ever come back, send them in please." He grabbed his wife's hand and took the keys from Bob "Come on then Muriel, let's go exploring!"

Half an hour later and Bob was on his second cigarette when they all came out of the front door. The girls had obviously found another way in because they hadn't passed him. They were all talking at once and again Bob noticed how relaxed Duncan was about everything. He couldn't help but make comparison with his own family experience which had been very stiff and formal in the main.

Duncan came over and put his arm across Bob's shoulders. "We're going to buy it" he said. "Tell Braithwaite that you've made a sale." Bob was quite taken aback but kept his wits about him "We haven't talked about the asking price" (He was now recalling the 'training' that Braithwaite had been given him earlier in the week) "There may be a little room for negotiation" he said.

"The asking price is very fair, maybe even a little low, so I'm fine with it" said Duncan giving the keys back to Bob. "My solicitors will be in touch tomorrow, don't forget to lock up". He got in and started the car. It ran nicely straight away, seemingly without any of the fiddling around that Bob had witnessed with the Hillman. Duncan turned the car round expertly and was through the gates and gone in no time.

It was well after four o clock when Braithwaite returned. He seemed almost disinterested as Bob excitedly told him that they had sold the house. They drove back to the office in silence until finally, once they were inside, Braithwaite asked him what Walding had said about the purchasing of the house. Bob said that Duncan's solicitor would be in touch in the morning. "He's in a hurry then, knows it's a bargain" said Braithwaite.

He explained to Bob that the house had been repossessed by the Bank because the previous owner had defaulted on the loan secured on the house. The man's business had collapsed following the Stock Market crash and, in spite of efforts made by the bank and other creditors to find him, he had not been seen or heard of since.

Sadly, this was not uncommon said Braithwaite. "Everybody is feeling it now and it's set to get even worse." During the last year or so Bob had read many articles in the newspapers about the economic depression, the rising unemployment and the hardships that followed it. He had not been touched by this directly and although the sale of this house was ultimately to benefit him, the reason for the sale did serve to bring it closer.

Braithwaite apologised to Bob for his earlier lack of enthusiasm, saying that it was the first house sale since Thomas had died. He promised that he would be with Bob the next day in order to show him what paperwork needed to be completed and also what the solicitors would require from them.

It was quite late when Bob finally left the office. Braithwaite had obviously decided that Bob was going to be useful and had broached the subject of payment. He had suggested a weekly payment of two pounds and five shillings which was in fact well below the rate at which even a shop assistant would be paid. Bob had been about to protest when Braithwaite said "I know that is not much but I would also pay a commission on every sale that you make"

He went on to say that he charged two and a half percent on sales and that he would pay Bob one percent on any sales that he made on his own. "Starting" he said, "With the sale that you made today".

Bob's excitement was short lived as Braithwaite explained to him that it was often weeks, sometimes months, before the commission actually came in as it was never paid until the sales reached completion.

Bob quickly worked out what he would be getting from today's sale. The house was priced at £2,250 and so he would eventually be receiving £22.10.0 which would definitely improve his finances! He agreed to continue 'helping out' until such time as Braithwaite felt he was no longer needed.

Sitting on the bus Bob was working out what he could earn in commission if he sold just one house every couple of weeks. Of course, most of the houses on the books (as Braithwaite called it) were valued at below a thousand pounds but some were considerably higher as with today's sale.

He was sat behind a large lady wearing a wide brimmed hat covered in silk flowers and with two long ribbons hanging down from the back. He watched the ribbons swinging around and wickedly thought about tying them to the stanchion on the rear of her seat. Eventually he couldn't resist the temptation any longer and very carefully reached forward and tied the ribbons together around the post. Three stops later the lady prepared to leave her seat.

Bob was already regretting what he had done but it was too late.... Nothing happened immediately. As she rose from her seat the ribbons just slid up the pole but as soon as she moved forward her hat was wrenched off but not completely. The long pin that she had used to keep it on was doing its job; she was still attached by her hair.

Eventually she got free and with her hair sticking out in all directions was now glaring at Bob. "I think they've got tangled round the pole" said Bob, frantically trying to untie them. She looked at him with suspicion but as soon as he had untied them she just snatched her hat and left.

A voice from behind him said "That wasn't funny; you should be acting your age." It was only then that Bob realised that he was a year older, today was the 16th of December and it was his birthday!

He made his way back to Dick and Brenda's and as he entered the flat, he was aware of an air of excitement. He had a thought about his birthday but immediately dismissed it; how would they know about a thing like that.

Although he arrived back very late there was still a meal waiting for him which was odd and as he sat at the table to eat, Dick and Brenda sat with him.

"We have some news" said Dick. "We're pregnant." "Well that is to say, I'm pregnant" said Brenda, laughing. Dick was grinning, "I meant to say that we're expecting." They all laughed and Bob congratulated them both.

He thought that it must be time for him to move on but he had grown to like Dick and Brenda had tempered her dislike of his non-belief. He would miss Dick and also, he realised now, he would miss Brenda.

"It's my birthday today" said Bob.

Chapter 5

Christmas had come and gone. Bob had spent a really nice Christmas day with Dick and Brenda. Apparently it was the first Christmas that they had not been with their in-laws. The three of them had eaten a little too much, drunk a little too much and the conversation over a haphazard game of cards had been gentle and humorous. Brenda had suspended her hostility toward Bob and, apart from a couple of jibes about it being *Christmas*, was as nice to him as she had ever been. They exchanged presents, he had bought them a table lamp and they had given him a fountain pen which he was really pleased with. He had used it a lot already.

The New Year started with him moving into two furnished rooms in a house less than 100 yards from the office. Lucy had come up with this within two days of his mentioning to Braithwaite that he needed to find somewhere. He would have much rather found somewhere himself but Lucy was so keen to help and the rooms were really handy for the office as well as being very cheap to rent.

The sale of the property to Duncan Walding had completed, remarkably quickly in Braithwaite's opinion, and Bob had been paid the commission. Receiving a cheque meant that he needed to open a bank account and Braithwaite had introduced him to the local National Provincial Bank manager.

Bob thought that the bank manager looked like he had stepped straight out of a Dickens novel but he proved to be friendly enough though. Soon his cheque was paid in and he was told that the account was now open and a cheque book would be ready in two to three weeks, in the meantime he could go into the bank if he needed money. *That would not be far off* he thought, he had had to pay in 10 shillings as well as the cheque in order to open the account and would be drawing out 9 shillings and sixpence in no time at all!

It was a cold January Monday morning and he was sat at *his* desk in the office wondering what he should be doing. There had been lots of people passing by but no one had so much as glanced in the windows. The telephone had not rung all morning.

He began to think back over the last few weeks, so much had happened it seemed like more than just a few weeks. Leaving Manchester after all the unpleasantness. His chance meeting with Lucy. Moving in with Dick and Brenda. Bumping into Lucy again and then meeting Braithwaite. 'Selling' the house to Duncan Walding. And now moving into his rooms and working as an Estate Agent. "Thank you Reverend Pritchard" thought Bob, "It seems you did me a favour."

He pulled opened the drawer that held details of all the properties. He was about to start going through them for the second time in as many hours when the door opened and a smartly dressed middle aged man entered the shop. Bob judged by his demeanour that he was obviously a man used to getting respect from others but he did seem a little uncomfortable, even nervous.

After starting rather hesitantly he soon became more comfortable talking to Bob and explained what he had in mind. He had suffered greatly with the stock market crash a year or so before with the value of his shares being slashed and some of them becoming almost worthless. With the income from his shares virtually gone and his business not doing well he had found himself "In a pretty awkward spot."

He confided to Bob what he thought might be a solution. His idea was to sell his large house, albeit very cheaply for a fast sale and then purchase a smaller, cheaper house. He would then have some urgently needed capital to *see him through*, as he put it, *until things picked up.*

Bob took as many details as he thought necessary from the man and made an appointment to visit the house on the following day. Before the man left Bob was sworn to secrecy and told that if anyone should ask what he was doing at the house he was to say that he was a surveyor. "Must keep up appearances eh," he said. Further instructions were that the *new* house must be priced at around £500 or less and should be at least five miles distance from the old one.

There were two things bothering Bob, the first was that he had very little idea about valuing a house and secondly, they had no houses on their books for sale at less than £950.

Braithwaite had always concentrated on the higher value properties, reasoning that there was less competition from other agents. There were also fewer sales to deal with and much more money coming from each of the sales.

Bob decided that he once he had gathered some details on Mr Brady's house, he would then compare them with anything similar that they had on the books. He would then deduct an amount that would, he hoped, make it cheap enough for a quick sale.

He gave a great deal of thought to the fact that they simply had not one house on the books which they could show Mr Brady, however he had agreed to deal with the whole thing in confidence. The solution, he hoped, was to approach the nearest Estate Agent that was dealing with properties of the right value. He would ask if it would be possible for him to show his client one or more of their houses and, if he made a sale, would they share the commission.

On visiting a nearby Estate Agent, he was surprised to discover that sharing property details and sales was actually quite normal practice among many Agents. He also discovered that Braithwaite had refused all offers of any sharing and was, in fact, known amongst other Agents as being 'high handed' and very much a 'loner'.

Bob left the Estate Agent armed with details of a dozen or more houses all valued between £400 and £525 and all sufficiently far away from Brady's house. The two houses at £525 were newly built semi-detached and he was told that a cash offer around £510 might be successful.

The next day, after lunch, he locked the shop and left for his valuation appointment. He arrived in plenty of time and was quickly ushered in by a lady who he took to be Mrs Brady. He wandered around the house and garden making a few notes, more for show than anything else, with Mrs Brady hovering close by all the time.

In no more than ten minutes he was ready to leave. He offered a card to Mrs Brady saying "If Mr Brady would be good enough to contact me at his convenience, I will have the valuation ready" Mrs Brady took the card and said "Thank you Mr Braithwaite, I'm sure he will telephone you tomorrow." Bob thought that he really must remember to ask Braithwaite if he could have some cards of his own.

It was close to 4pm by the time he arrived back at the office. He just seemed to choose 3pm for appointments with no idea why, but it had worked for him so far. As he was about to unlock the shop door Lucy appeared carrying two large bags, "I have a few things for your new place, to make it feel more homely I hope" holding out the bags to Bob. They were still stood in the doorway, "Let's go now" she said, and with a cheeky grin "I don't see a queue of people waiting to see you" I was quite late in the afternoon so Bob agreed to go with her to his rooms.

The next two hours seemed to go by very quickly and he suddenly aware of being very hungry. It was after six and he was in bed enjoying a smoke but he hadn't eaten all day. Lucy had leapt out of bed ten minutes earlier and dressed very quickly saying that she should be home by now.

She kissed him lightly on the forehead, thanked him for "a lovely time" and headed for the door. "I never asked why you came into my carriage on the train" he said. "I just liked the look of you" she replied and dashed off. He was still slightly bemused by the speed at which this had all happened and was wondering where it would lead. The bags with things Lucy had bought for him were still by the door untouched.

It had been immediately apparent to him that Lucy was much more experienced and so he had happily let her take the lead until they were undressed and in bed. Lucy had made it clear that from this point on neither of them would be taking a leading role. Bob quickly adjusted to the fact that Lucy was totally uninhibited and they had both enjoyed themselves very much, he just hoped that they hadn't disturbed anyone in the house!

The next few days were very busy. Mr Brady had called and, surprisingly, agreed to the valuation of £925 but only if it resulted in a very quick sale! Bob typed up the details in the style that was used for other houses on their books and then filed the sheet in the drawer.

Braithwaite had a regular advertisement in the local papers and so all that Bob needed to do was to send them an updated list of houses for sale. Although Brady's house did look like good value compared with others on the list, he was not at all confident that this would get the quick sale Mr Brady was hoping for.

Bob got to thinking, he now had details of many more houses to sell albeit that they weren't the type that Braithwaite normally dealt with. Two things struck him, one that surely there were others in the same position as Mr Brady in needing to 'downsize' and secondly, the many people passing by the shop every day might be interested to see details of houses that could be within their reach to purchase. Even in these hard times he reasoned, there might still be some people doing well.

The week-end arrived and Bob decided to go and see Dick and Brenda. They were really pleased to see him and Brenda gave him a big hug which took him by surprise. He spent the day with them and enjoyed nice meal in the evening after which they started to question him about Lucy.

"Don't you want to know how the Estate Agency business is going" he asked. "I'm sure that's all going very well" said Brenda. "When are you going to bring Lucy for a visit?" Bob promised that he would ask Lucy when they saw each other next. He had a suspicion that Brenda thought Lucy might be the key to his salvation! Bob made his excuses, saying he needed to go in order to catch his bus but promised to visit again soon with Lucy if she agreed.

When got back he sat down to write to Jim, he wanted to know how they were of course, but he also had something else to ask. He had made a sketch of a holder that could be stood in a window or on a shelf and could be used to display A4 sheets of paper containing property details. Knowing that Jim was very good at making things Bob asked him if he could 'knock something up' for him to collect in a week or two if he was able to visit them.

The following week passed without much happening. Braithwaite had not appeared at all and apart from Mr Brady ringing to find out how things were going, there had been no calls. Bob had told Mr Brady that they had had some interest and he was sure that the house would sell quickly. The Newspaper advertisement was not due out for a few more days, Bob was hoping it would produce some interest.

The one interesting thing that happened that week was that Lucy had popped in with little Thomas. She had given Bob a peck on the cheek saying that she had just come to make sure he was alright and did he like the things she had bought for him? Bob said he was ok and yes, he loved the things she had bought.

He was thinking that he really should see what was in the bags that were still by the door to his rooms. "I'm so pleased you liked them" she said, "I must visit soon to see where you have put them." "Yes, you must" said Bob. Lucy waved her long cigarette holder in his direction and said "And then we can have a lovely time again"

With a big smile and a wink, she was out of the door and gone with little Tommy waving to Bob through the window. Bob was seeing a very different Lucy to the one that he had met on the train.

The week-end was quiet and Bob spent some time making himself at home in his rooms. The bags that were left by the door had contained, amongst other things, an ashtray with a lid that could be opened with a button on the top and a table lamp in the form of a naked lady holding the shade above her head, people were calling this style Art Deco and he loved it. He finished fiddling around making his rooms 'homely' and then popped out to a nearby restaurant where he enjoyed a very good meal to round off a nice week-end.

Although he had some concerns about the week ahead Bob was quite calm and relaxed as he opened up on Monday morning. He had received a reply from Jim to say that he was working on the holder and also saying that they would love to see Bob the following weekend if he could make it.

That calm lasted about ten minutes until Braithwaite burst into the office and started banging the desk while shouting "What the hell do you think you are doing!? Do you think this is your business to do as you like!?"

Bob tried to say he was sorry, he didn't understand what the problem was but he only got as far as "sorry" before Braithwaite was off again "You might well say you're sorry" he shouted. "It's taken me years to make this business what it is and you've ruined it in weeks" At this point Braithwaite picked up the pile of house details from the other Agent and threw them up in the air. As the sheets had fluttered to the floor Braithwaite slammed out of the door shouting that he would "Have to come back and take over!"

Bob had absolutely no idea what to do; he gathered up the sheets of paper from the floor and sat at the desk trying to make sense of what had just occurred. He decided that he would lock the office and take the key to the Braithwaite's house, if necessary, he would just post the key through the door, after that he really hadn't a clue.

Halfway to the Braithwaite's house he met Mrs Braithwaite who said that she was on her way to find him. She was in a very distressed state and asked him what had happened. He relayed to her exactly what had taken place. She told him that he needed to come to the house and when he said that he was coming to return the key she said "Whatever, please just come to the house now.

When they arrived at the house the Doctor met them at the door. "I have given him something to calm him down, he might well sleep for some hours now" he said. "Is he going to be alright" asked Mrs Braithwaite. "He'll be 'right as rain', back to normal in no time, I've seen this before" then gently he said "how long is it since your son died?" she didn't say but he continued "It's the anger finally being released, it has to happen at some point, I wouldn't be surprised if he was back to his old self as soon as the morning. "I thought you said he would be normal" said Mrs Braithwaite. There was a pause and then they all laughed.

The doctor said that he would look in the next day and Bob agreed to go back to the office and see what happened over the next few days.

Bob got back to office in time to hear the phone ringing; he quickly unlocked the door, went in and grabbed the phone. Apparently, this was the third time that the caller had rung, Bob apologised telling the man that they were a very busy Agency.

The caller said, impatiently, that he wanted to view the property that was advertised in the newspaper. It turned out to be the Brady's house and he wanted to see it as soon as possible. Bob took the caller's name and asked him if he was happy to meet at the property (He liked to use the word 'property' he thought it made him sound more professional). "If that's the only way that I can view it quickly then I suppose I can find my own way there" said the man and took down the address.

"Would three o clock tomorrow suit you?" said Bob.

Chapter 6

ob was sat in the car with the engine running to keep it warm but none of that warmth was reaching him. He pulled his overcoat round him and turned up the collar trying, unsuccessfully, to retain a bit of warmth while he continued to wait.

He thought back to the day that he had got the overcoat, Lucy Braithwaite had taken him shopping, well... dragged him from one shop to another as he remembered it. She had insisted on buying the coat for him as well as lots of other clothes in order to "Modernise him" as she put it. He had not been comfortable with her paying for everything that day but she had told him, quite forcefully, that she was not short of money and it was hers to do with as she chose! He had learnt that in all areas of her life Lucy did what she wanted, when she wanted.

He couldn't believe that almost two years had passed since that day and how much things had changed in that time.

He had suddenly found himself not 'helping out' any more but totally running the business. Braithwaite had come to the shop a few days after his breakdown, as it was now referred to. He had apologised for his previous behaviour and went on to assure Bob that he was doing a good job. He spoke at length about how he knew the business needed to change and Bob was obviously the person to do it.

It was after Braithwaite had left the office that Bob realised that he had effectively been handed the business to run as he wished. This was further confirmed the next day when Braithwaite told him that he and Mrs Braithwaite were going to stay 'with family' in Devon for a few weeks and handed him the key to the Hillman.

Bob had paid the five shillings fee to the local Council and received his driving licence. He had collected six display holders from the Post Office sent by his brother Jim, he still had not visited. He had put house details in the holders and placed them where they could be read through the windows of the shop. They had been pulling in prospective customers ever since. He had sold Mr Brady's house quickly and also managed to find them a new house, earning commission on both sales.

The weeks and months had flown by and, despite the 'Doom and gloom' in the press about the deepening economic depression and rising unemployment, business was very good. Bob had succeeded with two more 'confidential' deals for colleagues of Mr Brady and sales on the lower value houses were very steady. Bob treated the buyer of a £400 house exactly the same as the buyer of a £1000 house and it was this, he had been told by one of his clients, that was bringing people to him.

He had soon needed to increase the size of the advertisements in the local paper in order to list all the properties. He had also taken on a young lady to answer the phone, type whatever was needed and generally look after the office. He was spending more and more time out of the office doing valuations and viewings.

Braithwaite's *few weeks away* had turned into three months after which, for the rest of the year, Bob had seen him no more than half a dozen times and they were just fleeting visits. Not that he minded at all, it gave him complete freedom to do whatever he wanted.

He was now very cold, even with gloves on he was starting to lose the feeling in his hands.

At last the front door of the house opened and Lucy appeared accompanied, to Bob's surprise, by a tall smartly dressed man, in his twenties Bob guessed. Lucy got into the back of the car and the man got in beside her, "This is Trevor" she said to Bob and to Trevor she said "This is Bob, he works for my Father-in-law." Bob was immediately angry and was going to say something but then he thought "well, I suppose I do really." It just wasn't the right way for Lucy of all people to describe what he did.

"Would you be a sweetie and take us to the Regal please" said Lucy. Bob was still angry and this did nothing to calm him down. "I am not a taxi service for you and your friends!" he said. When Lucy had asked him if he would pick her up from her friend's house, he had understood it to mean that he was collecting her from one of her many Women's League for Freedom meetings as he had done a few times before.

Looking in the rear-view mirror he could make out that Trevor was sat sideways on the edge of the seat facing Lucy. He was driving a lot faster than his normal style and realising he was passing the Regal Cinema he stamped on the brakes throwing Lucy forward from her seat and causing Trevor to slide off the seat onto the floor of the car where he became wedged between the front and rear seats.

Lucy got out and once she had helped Trevor free himself from between the seats, they just walked away without another word.

It was about a week later and Bob happened to be in the office when Lucy came in. Beryl had told him earlier that she had seen Lucy walk past several times when he was out. "Do you have a moment for a chat?" Lucy asked. "Of course," he said. "Let's go for a walk" she said.

As they walked along Norwood road, she told him that she was sorry about the misunderstanding with Trevor and asked if he was ok. Bob didn't reply, he was thinking about how things had been between them since that first time in his rooms.

They had seen each other fairly regularly. Every two to three weeks Lucy would appear at the shop just before he closed and they would go off somewhere together. Sometimes they would go to the Cinema, other times they would go to a restaurant to eat, occasionally they would go back to his rooms for, as Lucy put it, some fun.

The times for going out and the times for 'having fun' were always decided by Lucy and he didn't mind this, he was busy and anyway, by his own admission, was lazy when it came to social things. He had long since got used to the idea that they would never be more than good friends and was also accepting of her increasingly 'bossy' ways.

"You're doing it again" she said. "What am I doing?" Said Bob. "You're thinking about something else while I'm talking to you." Lucy didn't seem her normal self. "Actually, I was thinking about us" he said. "There's never really been an 'us' has there." She made it a statement not a question.

"Trevor has asked me to marry him" she said quietly. "Good heavens" said Bob, "You've only just met him." Lucy turned to him, "Actually we've been seeing each other for a while now." She went on to tell him that Trevor was Trevor Beckman, the only son of Rudolph Beckman. Rudolph Beckman not only owned the two Estate Agents that Bob had been sharing properties with but four other South London branches as well.

They didn't speak much more after that and soon arrived back at the shop. Lucy gave him a peck on the cheek and Bob gently squeezed her arms and offered as warm a smile as he could but he knew it didn't quite work.

He went back to sorting out his appointments for the next couple of days, but his mind was on the possibility of Lucy marrying Trevor Beckman. The thought crossed his mind that she would again be married to the only son of an Estate Agent. He laughed inwardly; he should keep that thought to himself.

For the next few weeks life and work continued as normal for Bob, except for Lucy's visits which had stopped completely. House sales had slowed considerably but Bob put this down to the unsettled times.

The labour government led by Ramsay MacDonald was desperately trying, and failing, to 'balance the books' and economy was just going from bad to worse. With the depression showing no signs of easing; it was good that they were still selling any houses at all.

Eventually, in the second week in December Lucy did come to the shop and they went off for a walk and a chat. "I'm glad you have carried on buying clothes" she said "The modern style suits you well and with the overcoat we chose you cut quite a figure." This was not her normal way of talking and Bob knew that Lucy had something to say, and it wasn't about his dress sense.

"I have agreed to marry Trevor, we think it will be in the New Year." She paused, "I do hope you will come," you will like Trevor if you get to know him better." Lucy was babbling and he couldn't understand why she was so nervous after all, in spite of pressure from others, there had never really been anything but friendship between them.

Lucy stopped and drew breath, "Trevor's going to come and talk to you" she said. "Why would he want to do that?" "He doesn't need my blessing does he?" laughed Bob. "It's not that" she said. "He wants to talk to you about the business." "Does he think I need some guidance?" Said Bob. He was now starting to feel a bit irritated.

He'd made the business a lot of money over the last year or so when other businesses were really struggling. Some other independent Estate Agents had closed but *C.R.Brathwaite Estate Agent* had gone from strength to strength. Lucy went on "He said he will come and see you after Christmas."

They had returned to the shop but Lucy didn't go in, she fished in her bag and pulled out a small box which she handed to him. "Happy birthday for tomorrow" she said. "I hope you like it." he watched her as she walked away; he had strange feeling of foreboding which stayed with him as he went back into the shop.

Bob took the decision to close the shop for four days over Christmas. He felt ok about doing this after all, apart from Lucy's one visit; nobody had been near the shop for a long time so would they even notice?

As he was driving back from what would be his last viewing before Christmas, in fact the only promising viewing for two weeks, the car had started making a loud knocking noise and blue smoke poured from the exhaust pipe. He had limped the car slowly to the garage where, after a listen to the engine and following a sharp intake of breath, the mechanic announced that it was most likely that a new engine that was needed. He told Bob that even if they could repair the engine it would be a number of weeks before the car would be back on the road.

Bob had been invited to spend Christmas with Dick and Brenda and he was looking forward to it. He had got used to driving everywhere but he really didn't mind using the bus to get to Dick's flat. He was enjoying the opportunity to look around and was noticing for the first time just how many businesses had closed down. More than a few shops had their windows boarded up and many of them had two or three men hanging about in the doorways sheltering from the icy wind and with, he assumed, no jobs to go to.

He spent a second nice Christmas with Dick and Brenda. They ate well and were together for all the usual Christmas things with the exception of Mass which of course Bob opted out of. There had been nothing but happy chatter and quite a bit of laughter. It had gone by quickly and it seemed that in no time he was on his way back to his rooms. During the journey he reflected on his lack of contact with his own family and wished it were different but couldn't see anything changing at the moment.

When he got back he found a letter waiting for him on the hall stand and recognising Jim's writing he went straight to his rooms, dumped his case on the bed and ripped open the letter. It was a long letter by Jim's standard and although Jim had said that he and Winnie and the children were all well it left Bob with some concern. Jim had written that he might not be working in the Business for much longer, although he didn't say why. He had also said that they were planning to move to London and had found a place in Wandsworth.

The following morning Beryl was waiting for him to open the shop and as they went in they exchanged news about their break. Beryl had used her wages, and the Christmas bonus that Bob had surprised her with, to give her parents a much better Christmas than they would have otherwise had. She had also managed to acquire from somewhere a new boyfriend!

The next few days came and went with nothing happening at all at the shop and New Years Eve arrived with Bob having no plans on how he would spend it. Last New Year had been spent with Lucy and apart from a very brief visit to the Braithwaites most of it had been spent in his rooms. He had bought some Champagne and they had seen in the New Year in a happily drunken state.

He went for a walk and after no more than fifteen minutes he passed a pub with the sound of some lively music coming for inside. He went in. It was only nine o clock in the evening but already people seemed to have had plenty to drink and some of them were haranguing the poor man playing the fiddle who was obviously trying to stop for a rest.

There was a piano in the bar, it stood with lid open and sheet music on the stand as though someone had just got up from it. Once Bob had got his pint of beer he asked the Barman where the pianist was. "He just up and walked out" said the

Barman. "Was that just now?" asked Bob, the barman was already serving the next customer and he turned to Bob and said "Nah, about two months ago." Bob went and sat down at the piano and almost immediately he was surrounded by people saying "Come on, give us a tune."

It was gone nine the next morning when Bob woke up. He had a splitting headache. He remembered playing for hours with a full pub singing along. He had worked his way through all the sheet music left on the piano and then played most of it again. All this time pints of beer just kept appearing on the top of the piano. He had little or no memory of how he got back to his rooms but nevertheless that's where he woke up.

He had enjoyed playing the piano; he hadn't played at all since leaving Manchester where he had occasionally played in the Church Hall. One of the few benefits of growing up in a wealthy family, in his view anyway, had been the piano lessons. He was taught piano by an ex pupil of Rachmaninoff. She had returned from working in America and was obviously horrendously expensive to hire as a tutor. He and all his siblings were given lessons in one art form or another and all by the best available.

Much of New Years day was spent recovering from the hangover. He really didn't do well with alcohol and promised himself that it wouldn't happen again, although there was the point that he had only actually paid for one pint.

Back at the shop early the next day, Beryl had only just arrived at eight thirty when the phone rang. She answered in her best secretary voice and then told Bob that a Mr Beckman was 'on the line for him', (Bob thought that she must have heard that in a film) he couldn't place the name for a moment but as he was taking the phone he remembered.

"Hello is that Trevor?" said Bob. "Yes, this is Trevor Beckman" was the reply. "Lucy told me that you wanted a chat." "I wouldn't say a chat was quite what I wanted, what else did Lucy tell you?" Trevor was sounding very haughty, "About the marriage plans?" asked Bob. "I didn't mean about my personal life," said Trevor, "I meant about the business."

Bob told him that Lucy had not spoken about the business at all to which Trevor had simply said that he would be along to see Bob that afternoon at 3pm. As he put the phone down Bob was pretty sure that he was not going to enjoy the coming visit.

How right he was! Trevor Beckman arrived at precisely 3pm. Bob was thinking that his favourite time for appointments had just lost its appeal. Trevor didn't waste any time getting to the point, "My father has bought Braithwaite's business" he said.

"Does Braithwaite actually know?" said Bob facetiously. Ignoring that, Trevor went on "From Monday I will be managing this branch until it reaches the standard that we expect," turning to Beryl he said "Beckman Estate Agents don't actually employ staff to do what you have been doing so....." he didn't finish just flapped his arm in the direction of the door.

He was feeling very much like punching Trevor on the nose but his non-violent beliefs coupled with his genteel upbringing were just about winning.

Bob was aware that he could appear somewhat autocratic in his manner and often tried to moderate it. He had used this in a nice way and to good effect with preaching and in selling houses. When it came to railway or hotel porters and the like however, he would say things like "My good man" and "Quickly if you please!" crooking his finger at them and fully expecting them to comply.

This autocratic side of Bob's nature was now fully in control and he said to Trevor "And what have you and daddy decided my role will be?" Trevor was stung by this and replied some-what testily "*I* have decided on your future here." He was going to continue but Bob cut him off, "*I* will tell *you* what is going to happen." He gestured to Beryl to join him, "We are leaving right now, I wish you luck in raising the standard here, though I suspect it will just be a coat of paint because I doubt you will improve sales one bit!" His speech over, he ushered a very wor-ried looking Beryl out of the door.

"Come on" said Bob, "Let's go and talk to Braithwaite."

He showed no outward signs of concern as had become his way these days; he didn't want Beryl any more worried than she already was.

But to himself he thought, *"For crying out loud, what next!"*

Chapter 7

Bob and Beryl arrived at the Braithwaite's house just as Mr and Mrs Braithwaite were leaving. "What on earth are you both doing here?" said Braithwaite, "We are just on our way to the office to see you...um, both."

"And you really expected to find us there after Trevor Beckman's visit, did you?" said Bob coldly. "I know getting Lucy to tell you what was happening was cowardly off me" said Braithwaite, "I just couldn't face it all." "He really isn't well" said Mrs Braithwaite, moving closer to him defensively. Bob's anger towards Braithwaite was subsiding very rapidly as it was becoming clear that Lucy had been trusted to tell him what was going and hadn't done so and also that Braithwaite himself was not at all the man that he had once been.

"Maybe we could go inside and talk about things?" Asked Bob. Once they were all inside and settled Mrs Braithwaite asked if they would like a cup tea and without waiting for an answer went off to put the kettle on. Bob told Braithwaite what had happened at the office, he was still inwardly fuming but being aware of Braithwaite's condition he spoke as calmly as he could.

It soon became clear that Trevor Beckman had overstepped the mark and things were not quite as he had described. Braithwaite had agreed with Rudolph Beckman that although Beryl would not be needed from the following week onwards she would be paid one month's wages while both he and Mrs Braithwaite used their local connections to try to get her another position.

Mrs Braithwaite came in with the tea tray. Without a word she removed the whisky that Braithwaite had poured himself and replaced it with a cup of tea. When they all had a cup in their hands Bob asked if his future had been discussed with the Beckmans? Braithwaite told Bob that all his dealings had been with Rudoph Beckman alone who seemed a kindly man and that he had, in fact, never met the son.

Rudolph Beckman had agreed that Bob should be offered the position of manager and that his son Trevor would take care of the transition of the office into their group. He had checked up on what Bob had been doing and liked what he found out. Apparently, he also liked very much Bob's idea of having house details displayed in the window and was planning to use it in all his branches.

As far as Bob was concerned there were two negatives to the offer. One, was that apparently there would be no more commission just a basic wage, and the other was that he had decided that he could not work with, for, or even near to Trevor Beckman under any circumstances.

It seemed that Braithwaite must have anticipated this reaction, and *he hadn't even met Trevor!* Thought Bob. An agreement had been reached that if Bob wanted to leave then he would be paid three months money at his average earning rate during the previous twelve months. Rudolph had accepted this, saying "Well, if it happens that way I will consider it part of the price of the sale and then Trevor may have to earn his money for a change by actually running a branch on his own."

Rudolph Beckman was not happy about Bob leaving in the way he had but he must have had some idea about his son's behaviour because he hadn't made an issue of it. Bob received, via Braithwaite, what he considered a very generous amount as severance.

A week or so later he was invited to join the Braithwaite's for a meal at their favoured restaurant. There was *some* good news; they had managed to find something for Beryl. It was fairly low pay but at least she had a job and Bob was relieved, he felt responsible even though none of what happened was his fault. His farewell was a good deal more emotional than he expected, with promises to keep in touch and a plea from Mrs Braithwaite for him not think too badly of Lucy. Bob realised that he hadn't actually thought about her at all but kept that to himself.

Just as he was leaving, he remembered something that had been on his mind to mention. "Do you know where the Hillman is?" he asked. "Come to think of it, no, I don't" said Braithwaite. Bob explained where it was and also what the mechanic had said. Braithwaite laughed and said that it was sold as part of the business, he'd let Rudolph know where it was.

Bob returned to his rooms that evening feeling a bit low, somehow the rooms didn't seem the same any more. They had only been a base from which he went to and fro to the office and also where he had occasionally enjoyed Lucy's company, although that had not happened for some months now. Neverthe-less, for some reason they had always felt a little like home, but not anymore.

He knew that he needed to be thinking about his future but not this evening. He went out and headed for the pub where he had played the piano. When he arrived, the pub was empty ex-cept for one old chap who was asleep with his head on the bar. He ordered a pint and as he paid for it the barman recognised him saying what a great night New Years Eve had turned out to be.

Bob asked if he could play the piano and the barman said yes, of course he could. He played for an hour using the sheet music that was still on the piano. The old chap woke up twice and then dropped off again. Two middle aged ladies came in and once they had their drinks, they asked him if he would play a song for them. He had never heard of the song they requested and told them that, after which they sat with their backs to him and talked very loudly. *It was amazing* thought Bob, it seemed quite normal now for women to come into a pub on their own, how things had changed in just a few years. As he was about to leave the Landlord appeared and came over to speak to him. He told Bob how pleased they were with what happened on New Year's Eve and said that Bob could come back as often as he wished. Bob thanked him and said he would definitely come back and play again. He left the pub and went off for a walk, which was something he always enjoyed.

He ended up back at his rooms and was soon in bed where he laid thinking about things for a while. He decided that to-morrow he would go to visit Jim and Winnie in their new place and try to get himself into a more positive frame of mind.

It was 11 o clock before Bob was ready to go out. He'd had a long soak in the bath and shaved very thoroughly. He'd put on a clean shirt and bundled up his laundry ready to drop off on his way to the bus stop. He had no work to go to but saw no reason not to keep his appearance up to scratch.

Bob had almost boarded the wrong bus, remembering just in time that Jim and Winnie were in Wandsworth. They had found lodgings there and had use of three rooms and a kitchen and was quite cheap to rent.

They were all really pleased to see each other and Jim and Winnie pressed Bob to bring them up to date with what he was doing. He told Jim and Winnie what had happened at Braithwaites and not surprisingly, while they thought it was disgraceful and that Bob should 'do something' about it, they were very concerned with their own pressing problem.

Jim's earlier concerns about his work had not been un-founded. The business had folded and all the employees were 'laid off' without warning or notice, receiving only the pay that was due to them for that week. Jim had felt strongly that re-turning to London would give him a better chance of finding some income. He hadn't said finding a job just *finding some income* but Bob didn't question him on it.

Jim had been earning a good wage but by no means a sub-stantial amount and he and Winnie had very little money put by. With the newspapers reporting an all time high for unem-ployment and virtually no jobs being advertised the situation was looking pretty grim. Unemployment benefit was minimal, and it was rumoured that the government would be reducing it. It would barely cover their rent and buy a bit of food as it was!

Bob was very sympathetic but it reminded him that he also was unemployed, albeit with more than three months pay in the bank. This money added to what he had in the bank already meant that, provided he was careful, he could survive for six months without income if he had to.

The journey back to his rooms was not a happy one. In the past he had always enjoyed the ride back whether by car or by bus, thinking about what the next day would bring and what new thing he had planned for the business. All he thought about this time was Jim's problem and, to a lesser degree, his own.

For the next few days Bob occupied himself with cleaning his rooms, picking up his laundry and even trying, unsuccessfully to cook something on the gas ring in his room. The cooking attempt told him that he was already getting bored.

Bob became aware that not only was he bored, he was also feeling a little lonely. In spite of Braithwaite's bluff and sometimes aggressive manner Bob had come to like him and also Mrs Braithwaite.

He hadn't seen much of them, particularly in the last year, but they had been there in the background and seeing Lucy regularly had somehow kept him feeling connected. He missed Lucy as well; at least he missed the old Lucy. He wasn't too sure about the one she seemed to have become. His family had made no attempt to contact him and he was certainly not going to change his belief, or lack of it, just to please them!

Something had to change and he set off for a brisk walk to think about it properly. It was a cold, grey Monday morning but he was determined to maintain a cheerful and positive outlook. His walk took him past the shop/office that had so recently been his. The facia had already been painted over in a bright blue colour and the sign writer was leaning on his ladder enjoying a smoke having completed the 'B'. There was no one in the office.

He planned to call in on the Braithwaites for a quick visit, to see them, of course but also to drop off the still unopened birthday present that Lucy had given him. Knowing Lucy as he did, it was certain to contain something very expensive but he had no wish to find out, and whatever it was he had no wish to keep it.

The Braithwaite's were not at home and so Bob walked back the way he had come and as he passed the shop again he had an idea. He would leave the box on one of the desks and Trevor could unwittingly return it. He would obviously show Lucy something that he had found on the office desk, wouldn't he? And Lucy would recognise what it was. The office was still unoccupied so he nipped in and left the box in the middle of the desk.

Bob walked on in the direction of his rooms intending to continue on for a few hours and see where he ended up but as he approached the house he could see, what he was pretty certain was the Hillman parked outside.

He wasn't too sure what to do; he had no wish, or need, to speak to Trevor Beckman who was in the driver's seat. "Just a moment if you please" called Trevor through the open window. Bob turned and looked at him without saying a word. Trevor quickly got out of the car and opened the rear door, almost as though he were a chauffeur, and then stepped back to allow a very elegant looking man to get out.

This has got to be Rudolph Beckman thought Bob. The man had neatly combed silver hair with a perfectly trimmed beard and moustache and he wore an immaculate dark suit. "This is the chap who helped Clive Braithwaite for a bit while he wasn't well," said Trevor. "Please get back in the car and wait for me Trevor" said the man quite sharply. Trevor did as he was told and the man turned to Bob "I'm Rudolph Beckman" he said, "Please excuse my son's rudeness."

He was a small man, barely five foot six inches tall but with an engaging presence and, as Bob discovered, a very strong handshake. "I know that Clive valued your work very much and I also know that you built the business back up from near failure." He spoke very precisely and Bob thought he detected a slightly foreign accent.

"I do not want to delay you from your business, I only wanted to find out where you obtained the holders that were in the shop window?" Bob reacted quickly, "I had them specially made" he said. "If you would tell me where from then I would like to order some" said Rudolph. "They are my design so you can order them from me." Bob was thinking this through as he was speaking; he needed to come up with a price.

"What is the cost?" said Rudolph, right on cue. Knowing how much the materials had cost, Bob thought that maybe doubling it might be about right, so he trebled it and gave the price. "Mmm...not so cheap are they, will I get a discount for thirty" said Rudolph.

He agreed a 10% discount and promised to deliver them a week later. They shook hands and Rudolph was driven off by a very sulky Trevor. Bob was a bit cross with himself, technically

the holders that were left in the shop window had actually be-
longed to him and Jim not Braithwaite. He had paid for the
materials and Jim had paid for them to be delivered to the local
Post Office, which wasn't cheap. It was too late to worry about
that now and Bob was wondering why on earth he had offered
to deliver thirty more of them in just a week! He would have to
go and talk to Jim as soon as he could get there.

He also had some plans to discuss with Jim and Winnie.

Chapter 8

Bob arrived at Jim and Winnie's lodgings that evening all ready to put his plans to them. He was a bit surprised to hear from Jim that he had already had the idea that he was going to try to start a business making and selling shop signs. No need to worry about the first part of his plan then thought Bob.

When Bob told him what had happened with Rudolph Beckman regarding the holders Jim was really excited and said that he had improved the design since making the first lot and couldn't wait to get started. Jim was suddenly looking concerned and said to Bob that the materials would cost quite a bit for that many holders and he had very little, if any money to spare. "Well I have my money from Braithwaite" said Bob, "let's work together. You are so good at making things and I seem to have some skill with selling, what do you think?"

Both Jim and Winnie thought that this was a great idea and while they were both still so animated Bob thought it was a good time to tell them about the time scale for delivery. "Good Lord, were all going to have some late nights!" said Jim.

The second part of his plan was to tell Jim and Winnie that he had lost his rooms in Norwood and needed somewhere to live. He knew that they would not have accepted any offer of money from him but if he was 'paying his way' while living with them then they would all benefit from it.

He hadn't actually lost his rooms but thought that a little white lie was justified. When he told them they immediately suggested that he come and live with them, with Winnie adding that "it made sense if they were to be working together." He did feel more than a twinge of guilt but he'd had the best of intentions so he just decided to forget it.

Bob had told himself that his ruse to move back was just about getting some money to Jim which he otherwise wouldn't take. That was true but he now realised how much he would enjoy being back with his brother and sister in-law so it was as much for him as for them.

The next day he travelled to his rooms in Norwood to collect his things and, unknown to Jim of course, to give notice that he was leaving and pay the rent due. It was late afternoon by the time he got back to Jim's and as he went in he found that everything needed to make the holders had been bought and was in the kitchen. Jim had commandeered the kitchen table and had started the 'manufacturing process'. Already the smell of sawdust and wood glue was quite strong.

Jim tried to give back some change from the money that Bob had left for the materials, "I had to buy some tools as well, I hope you don't mind?" he said. Bob refused telling Jim that the money was for them to start their business with whatever was needed.

The next five days were spent with Jim frantically working to make the thirty holders in time with he and Winnie pitching in to help in any way they could. Some of the time they argued about the best way to do things, almost every time ending up sticking to Jim's original plan. At other times they would all be in fits of laughter at something one of them had done wrong, usually Bob.

The grocery shop near their lodgings was owned and run by an elderly man. He was very friendly and cheerful, albeit a bit nosey. The first time Bob had gone in to buy some bread and sugar he had been questioned closely, the grocer wanted to know if he had moved into the area, and what he did for a living. He didn't mind and told him what he wanted to know, adding that if he needed a sign for the shop, he now knew the person to speak to.

The weekend arrived and the holders were all but finished with only three or four left to make; they would have to count them again to make sure. They were taking up quite a bit of space and that had prompted a discussion about how they were going to get them to Beckmans in Norwood. They had already abandoned the plan for all three of them to take the boxes on the bus.

Bob had noticed that 'Nosey Grocer' did deliveries and had a van outside his shop. He was wondering whether he would consider delivering the holders for them and if so, how much he would want for doing it.

He thought he would pop down quickly before the shop closed for the day. Rushing to get into the shop he only just managed not to bang his head on the door as his momentum carried him into the locked door with a crash, luckily not breaking the glass. He could see the man moving about inside and so he knocked on the door and after a few moments it was opened. "I'm open all day so that people can shop, and then at the end of the day I close" said the grocer sarcastically. Bob apologised and said that he only wanted to ask something and didn't want any shopping.

A bit later back at their lodgings Bob announced that he had solved the delivery problem and that he would be delivering the holders in the morning. He told them what had happened at the grocer's shop. The man had been very reluctant to consider driving to Norwood to make the delivery and they had not even talked about how much it would cost.

The man said that he only used the van once a week for deliveries and that was enough as it used a lot of petrol and, in his words, was a bugger to start. Bob was disappointed and was leaving as the man said "Have you got a driving licence?" Bob said that he had and the man went on "If you think you can drive that thing *and* you put petrol in for what you use then I suppose you could use it in the morning."

"That is so good of you and I'm sure I can drive it" said Bob. "Is there anything I can do for you in return" asked Bob. "Yes, you said you make signs, didn't you?" "We certainly do" said Bob. "Then make me an 'open and closed' sign for the door, people keep walking into it."

The next morning they loaded the holders into the back of the van. They'd scrounged four boxes from the grocer who was wandering about grumbling that *they would want him to make the bloody things soon!* The van was a Star, not very aptly named as turned out but they were yet to find that out. The grocer went through the starting routine with them, setting a lever on the steering wheel and showing them where the choke and throttle were. "Don't forget to put that lever back where it was once it's started" he said and disappeared back into the shop.

Jim had wanted to join Bob for the delivery and it was just as well that he had as it took the two of them quite some time to get the van started and Bob was glad to have someone along with him in this strange contraption. They went off very slowly, bouncing around a lot and with the noise level well above comfortable. 'Nosey Grocer' had told them to take care of the 'old girl' saying, "She was made at the start of the war you know."

"I wasn't even ten years old when this was made!" shouted Bob. "No, I didn't think we'd get them made either!" shouted Jim.

They finally made it to Beckman's in Norwood and were relieved to shut the thing down. They sat for a while with their ears gradually returning to normal before going into the shop to ask where they should put the holders. As far as Bob was concerned the very worst thing that could happen today was to run into Trevor Beckman and so, of course, that is what happened.

As they went back into the shop carrying two boxes each Trevor appeared from somewhere in the rear, "Make sure you put them in the corner tidily" he said. Before Bob could respond Jim said "Ah, you must be the lad that Bob told me about, it's nice that your father finds a few jobs for you to do, speaking of which, he is the person we need to see" Trevor didn't quite know how to respond, it was obvious to him that Jim was not much older than he was if at all, but had spoken to him as he would to a child and it had left him bewildered.

The other man in the shop, who was now trying to hide a smile, told them that Rudolph Beckman was at the new branch. He said he was soon to be the manager there and offered to walk with them. Bob thanked him but said he knew where it was and they would be happy to find Rudolph on their own. As they walked to the other shop Bob remembered to tell Jim about his promise of an 'open and closed' sign for the grocer's door.

Rudolph was sat at a large desk, now the only desk, in the middle of the shop. It looked to Bob as though the place was ready to open, there must be some more to be done but he just couldn't see what. Bob introduced Jim and they all chatted for a while, mostly about their new venture. Jim glanced at Bob as he mentioned that there would soon be a new line of 'open and closed' signs which he thought might be useful for the Beckman shops.

After a while Rudolph said he needed to get on and asked who he should make the cheque payable to. Jim straight away said that the discount they had offered was based on a cash sale. Bob was a bit surprised at how direct Jim was and also because the method of payment had not been discussed at all.

It didn't seem to bother Rudolph one bit and he explained that there was no cash at the shop and he certainly didn't carry that much on him. What he could do, he said was to make out a cheque 'to cash' and they could present it at the bank and receive the money straight away if that was acceptable to them. They walked back to the van passing the cheque backward and forward between them and laughing.

The laughter stopped as they tried and tried to start the van, it simply didn't want to start. They had almost worn themselves out turning the starting handle with it seeming to get stiffer all the time when Bob suddenly remembered the lever on the steering wheel. With the lever in the right place and few more turns of the handle it finally started, making a big cloud of smoke and with a few pops and bangs they got under way. "I wonder why it took so long to start" said Bob.

They decided that one of them would stay in the van and keep the engine running while the other went into the bank and cashed the cheque. By the time Jim came out with the money there was steam rising from somewhere at the front of the van but they chose to ignore it and didn't see it again as they drove back to Wandsworth and parked outside the grocery shop.

The man had watched them park from inside his shop and then came out; he seemed surprised that they had made it and asked if they had had any problems with the van. They assured him that all had been well and that using the van had been so much help.

As they gave him back the key and left, he remained standing there on the pavement looking at the van and shaking his head. He called to them as they walked away, "Don't forget my sign for the door!"

Chapter 9

Bob used the grocer's van for a delivery just once more to save him making two trips on the bus. This time he remembered to stop at a garage and have some petrol put in. The garage man put in two gallons and then offered to check the oil. He lifted the bonnet and from somewhere under there he produced a metal rod and, waving it in Bob's direction, he said "There's not a bloody drop in there!" He went off and filled a quart jug with oil and poured it into the engine.

Bob told him that would be enough and paid him the eight shillings he asked for. The man grumbled to Bob, "Mark my words, if it goes up to three and six a gallon there'll be no cars left on the road." For once the van started straight away and was so much quieter as he got back in and drove off, *much better* thought Bob even if it was now trailing a cloud of blue smoke!

For the next few months Bob and Jim settled into a kind of routine, as much as possible anyway. The unpredictability of sales and adding more products as they went along meant that never really knew what was ahead. Bob was out every day selling things and Jim was busy making whatever was needed so there was a kind of rhythm to it.

Bob was finding more Estate Agents to sell the holders to and he and Jim had thought that a smaller version would be good as menu holders for Cafes and Restaurants and some had already been sold.

Jim had made a nice wooden 'Open and Closed' sign for the 'Nosey Grocer' and a few more of them had since been sold. They were increasing the range of products all the time and Jim was also working on an illuminated sign that could be easily changed to suit a particular purpose.

Although he was working hard, the way things were going now gave Bob the opportunity to indulge in a couple of his interests, namely betting on the horses and playing Snooker. He had soon found a 'Bookie' and was using the 'runner' to place his bets. He studied racing form in the daily papers and had quite a bit of success. He would have to find another 'Bookie' soon, they didn't like paying out quite so often!

He found his way into the local Billiard hall two or three times a week and made some money winning frames of both Billiards and Snooker until all of the other members had found out that he really wasn't someone they should play for money!

As far as Bob was concerned things were going along very nicely, so when Jim and Winnie broached the subject of moving out of London to the coast he was not immediately overjoyed.

Jim was very persuasive and extolled the virtues of fresh sea air and lots of new customers. Bob had been travelling further and further out each day as he looked for more shops and businesses to call on, so he was attracted to the idea of a fresh area, not so concerned about the quality of the air though. They all eventually agreed on a move and that they would try to find somewhere on the Sussex coast.

Bognor Regis was chosen for two main reasons, the first being that Winnie thought "It was a nice little seaside town." Secondly it was placed within easy reach of Worthing one way, Littlehampton the other and not too far from Brighton which would give Bob plenty of potential customers. The other good thing was that Jim had found a furnished bungalow for virtually the same rent as they had been paying for their lodgings in Wandsworth!

Jim, Winnie and the children moved first, leaving Bob to deliver the last few signs and collect the money before following on a couple of weeks later. When the time came for him to leave he decided to go to Victoria station and get the fast train to Brighton, just for the experience. He only had a small suitcase containing his clothes and he was a little self conscious about carrying his heavy overcoat on what was actually quite a warm day, but he was definitely not leaving it behind!

He couldn't believe how quickly he had arrived at Brighton station; the train had reached some exhilarating speeds on the way. The station was bustling, mostly with holiday makers. Lots of families arriving with the children full of excitement at the coming week or two. Other families obviously starting the journey home with the parents looking a little fed up, a lot sunburnt and with the children dragging along behind, some of them still clutching buckets and spades.

Bob wandered out of the Station; he already liked the more relaxed atmosphere of a holiday town and made his way past the clock tower and down the hill to the sea front. He took off his suit jacket and his tie and sat on the edge of the promenade watching the people enjoying themselves on the crowded beach. After a while he began to feel hungry so he went and joined the queue for some fish and chips at a place near to one of the piers.

He trudged back up the hill to Brighton station and then had quite a wait for the train to West Worthing where he could change for Bognor Regis. The last leg of the journey to Bognor was very short and as he got off the train he was met by a cheerful and chatty young porter.

"Alright guvnor, you gonna need a taxi?" he had taken Bob's case and overcoat and was marching toward the gate where another man was taking a ticket from the only other passenger to get off the train. "You ere' on business then?" he didn't wait for an answer, "Mostly holiday people we get here, should have seen the last train, packed on like sardines they was." "We can't call it Bognor any more you know, oh no, has to be Bognor *Regis* now since his nibs came to see us." "That will be King George to you lad" said the man taking Bob's ticket and touching his cap, "Thank you sir" he said.

Outside the station Bob went up to the first person he saw and, fishing out the piece of paper with the address on it he asked for directions. He was about to have his first experience of dealing with a born and bred Sussex person.

Looking at the address the old chap took off his cap and scratched his head then thought for a while, "You got a car?" Bob said that he hadn't, "Well it's same the distance if you're walking" said the man, still not giving any directions. "Know someone there do you?" "No" said Bob, "Well yes we're just moving there." "Lot of people moving here these days, can't say as I like it much," muttered the old chap.

Bob was now beginning to get impatient, "Can you tell me how to get there please?" "In a rush are you?" said the man.

"Not particularly" said Bob. "That's the thing with newcomers, always in rush" He had put his cap back on and was looking at the paper again. "You turn right at the end of this road and just keep going; you'll see the bungalows on the right." "Is it far?" asked Bob. "You said you was driving?" said the man, "No, I'm walking!" said Bob, now really finding it hard to stay calm. "When you go round that corner" said the man, pointing just over the road, "it's two or three minutes down there, maybe ten if you're walking"

The bungalow was really nice, although built as a holiday home it was nicely furnished and well equipped and had a nice garden. Apparently the owner had not got it ready in time to advertise for holidays and so it was available through the summer, and possibly round to next spring. When he arrived Winnie had just got the children asleep and Jim was working on a sign of some sort with everything spread out on the kitchen table.

They had eaten earlier and Winnie was concerned about Bob but he told her that he had eaten fish and chips on Brighton sea front. A bit later on they sat down with some sandwiches and a cup of tea and chatted about their plans.

Bob was keen to get out and start selling. They'd agreed that it made sense for Bob to start close to where they were and work outwards as needed, so the next day he headed for the town centre carrying his box of samples. Jim had made some small versions of their products so that Bob was able to show their range to people without lugging round a huge box.

He soon discovered that this was not like London! The first few places that he called on would not even talk to him, one of them even threatening to call the police if he didn't leave immediately!

Bob found his way to the sea front and sat down to think. It was going to be a problem if the local shopkeepers were so wary of strangers, how would he make any sales. After his chat with Jim and Winnie he was aware that he needed to get some money coming in pretty quickly!

After a while Bob was ready to start again only this time with a plan. He went back to the Tobacconist that he had called on earlier. This time he left his box of samples by the window and went forward to the counter to be served. When his turn came, he asked for ten Players and a box of matches and as he was paying casually asked if the man knew the owner of the toy shop further down the parade. "That'll be Mr Hooley" he said, "Why do you ask?" Bob said he was delivering something and had forgotten the name.

Just as he was leaving the shop Bob turned to the man and said "I wonder if I could leave this box with you for a moment while I deliver one of our signs to Mr Hooley?" "I suppose so, leave it there by the window" said the man. "Thank you so much Mr...?" "Lewis" said the man, "Stan Lewis."

Carrying just the one sample Bob went into the toy shop and waited while the young women shouted to the owner that there was someone to see him. Eventually he was told to go through to the back and he found the owner had just finished unpacking boxes onto shelves and was still puffing from the effort.

"Hello Mr Hooley, I've just come from Mr Lewis the tobacconist, he's got some of our signs in his shop and I thought maybe you could benefit from some signage as well." Bob waited for Mr Hooley to reply, he'd learnt how effective silence could be. Finally, Mr Hooley spoke, "So what's old Stan bought then?" "I hope you don't think that I would discuss other people's business" said Bob looking suitably hurt.

"You had better show me what you've got then." Handing over the one sample Bob said he would be back in a tick and went to collect his box. Mr Hooley was impressed with the signs and ordered two for his window plus an 'open and closed' sign for the door. They would all be delivered next week said Bob, shaking hands with Bill, as he was now allowed to call him.

An hour after buying his cigarettes Bob was back in the Tobacconist. "Hello again Mr Lewis," he said. "Mr Hooley is pleased with the signs he bought and I thought you might like to look at some too"

Thirty minutes later Bob had an order for two more signs and was just hoping that the two shopkeepers didn't speak to each other for a while, he'd get the signs delivered as quickly as he could! Bob was thinking that far from being easier out of London it looked like being hard work.

Selling to businesses in Sussex needed a very different approach, and Bob was adapting quickly. In London he had been able to just walk into shops, offices or cafes and talk to the owners or managers without making appointments or even knowing their names. Not so in Bognor or Worthing. He needed to find out owners names before calling on them.

Often with the larger businesses he would have to telephone first which wasn't easy as there was only one telephone box anywhere near and that was outside the station. It was pretty much guaranteed that, however quiet it was as he dialled the number, the moment he pressed button A to be connected at least one train would arrive with all the associated noise making it nearly impossible to hear anything.

In spite of all the difficulties they did well with the business and with the range of products being settled on it became more profitable as they were able to buy the materials in bigger quantities.

Although Bob had now started calling on businesses in Brighton, he still had many people to call back on that were closer to 'home.' With all that in mind it came as a surprise to Bob when, returning one evening with a nice order for menu holders from a Brighton cafe, he was asked what he thought about moving on.

He didn't know then that this was to be a something that would happen fairly regularly over the next couple of years. They all moved to Torquay, Worcester and Cardiff, spending no more than eight months in any of them before finally arriving in Birmingham.

He did admit that he enjoyed the challenge of new places but rather hoped that having arrived in Birmingham they might stay for a bit longer. It was huge compared to the other places they had been so there was plenty of scope for the business. Winnie particularly would enjoy being in one place for a while, thought Bob. She had coped so well looking after two young children through all the moving from place to place but it had to be tiring.

Chapter 10

They found a nice three bedroom furnished flat in the outskirts of Birmingham and took a few days to get settled in. They also needed to get materials so that Jim could start making things again. This was a routine that they had become used to over the last couple of years and went about it without much fuss or discussion.

Soon Bob was making sales at a steady rate and although the business wasn't setting the world alight it was going along quite nicely. They never took this for granted because all around them were the signs of people struggling to get by. Unemployment was much higher here than in the South of England and getting worse.

Ramsay MacDonald's National Government was losing support to the Conservative Party and in spite of what some in government were saying the economy was still not recovering, at least not for the working people as far as Bob could see. He still read the Daily papers avidly and kept up with the political situation as best he could.

One day as he was walking past the open door of what appeared to be a church hall what he heard was *definitely not* a sermon, at least not one like he'd ever heard before. There was stamping of feet followed by cheering and chanting but he couldn't make out what was going on so he went in to find out.

Things quietened down as the speaker left the small stage at the back of the hall and before the next speaker started Bob asked the man next to him what was going on. It was a meeting of the SPGB said the man and seeing Bob's blank expression he went on, it's the Socialist Party of Great Britain. Bob had heard of this party but thought that they were only active in London, he was obviously mistaken.

He stayed until the last speaker had finished and he had been impressed by the way they had made a case for the government to be more supportive of the working people and less of those who held all the wealth. Bob thought that some of it was bordering on revolutionary but told himself there was nothing wrong with a bit of passion if anything was to get done!

As he was leaving the man who had been next to him appeared again and introduced another man who he described as 'our leader.' The man shook hands with Bob and asked him if he had enjoyed the meeting and Bob said that he had. "Right" said the man "If you want to show some support you can give sixpence and your name and address to Alfie here, and thank you very much" and then he marched off to catch up with the others.

Bob did what he was asked and was given a small card in return with SPGB on one side. On the other side was a hand written number 1486 with a box underneath in which had been written his name. He pocketed the card and went off to continue his day without giving it another thought.

Things carried on without any real incident for the next few months. Bob would occasionally help Jim with the manufacturing if a few orders were taken close together and Jim would help with deliveries when needed. Winnie was busy with the children, Keith had started at the local school and had settled in well.

Bob was always conscious of the fact that they were a home based business especially when calling on the larger companies who generally wouldn't deal with anyone who, at the very least, didn't have business cards with an office address. The cards were no problem to have made but would only have served to highlight the lack of an office.

He had encountered this more lately as he started to call on some of the businesses with multiple branches. This was still on his mind when he went into a rather strange shop that seemed to stock just about everything. After his best efforts he had resigned himself to only making a small sale of an 'Open and Closed' sign. It was then that he noticed an advert lying on the counter which said OFFICE TO RENT. LOW RENT. AVAILABLE NOW. Once he had finished writing the order in his book he pointed to the advert and asked the shop proprietor where the office was.

The office was above the shop and Bob went up for a look. It was just one large room with a chimney breast and fireplace with cupboards in the alcoves on both sides. It had a large desk in the middle of the room and a faded red rug on the floorboards.

The shop owner told Bob that the previous person had left one day without giving any notice and without paying the rent that was due. Apparently a rather unsavoury looking character had called on the man, stayed for around ten minutes and left, slamming the door on his way out. Less than an hour later the man had gone, never to be seen again.

"I don't know what he did up there but he was on the phone a lot. It's still connected by the way, and I've got the chairs down here which you can have if you take the office." He told Bob what the rent was and Bob promised to get back to him the next day.

When he got back to the flat that evening he told Jim and Winnie all about the office and how low the rent was. They weren't too keen at first but Bob listed all the benefits. All the manufacturing could be done there so no more mess in the flat. A business address and phone number for customers. Jim could work regular hours without interruption. They could store all the materials there. Bob was trying to think of some other things to say but Jim said "Stop, I'm convinced, what about you Winnie?" "Well it's certainly cheap enough" said Winnie "And with another baby on the way we could certainly use the space".

The next day they all went to see the office. The shop owner was pleased to see them and Bob introduced Jim and Winnie as his business partners getting a smirk from Winnie. They went up for a look and Jim said straight away that it was fine for what they needed. Winnie went over to the cupboards and opened one of them, "There are some old books in here" she said. The man said that he would throw them out but Bob told him not to worry, they would deal with it once they had moved in. He was thinking that they might be used in the fire place if it got really cold up there. They arranged to start renting from the coming Monday and then went off to Lyons Corner House for a cup of tea and some cake.

On Monday morning Bob and Jim took all the materials that were stored at the flat to the office. The shop owner had put two chairs back up there and they sat at the desk chatting for a while until Bob said he really ought to go and sell something. He went downstairs planning to pay the first weeks rent on his way through.

The shop keeper was leaning on the counter enjoying a smoke and immediately offered one to Bob, once Bob had lit up the shop keeper said "I'm William, I suppose I should know who I am renting the office to." Bob realised that he had sold the man a sign for the shop *and* rented an office from him without once giving him his name and he had only introduced Jim as his partner.

Bob gave William, "I don't like to be called Bill," their names and also told him what they planned to do in the office. William said "I don't care what you do up there as long as it's legal and you pay the rent." They shook hands and Bob went on his way.

He hadn't got very far, not even to the end of the road when he became aware of a man keeping pace with him on the other side of the road. He noticed the man partly because he was wearing a belted Mac and a trilby even though it was actually quite warm, but also because the man was openly staring at him as they walked along. There was something disturbing about the man and Bob increased his pace as he turned the corner and walked very quickly, making several more turns before taking a look back.

As Bob turned back to walk on, he nearly jumped out of his skin, the man was standing right in front of him. He seemed to have come out of nowhere! "Trying to lose me were you?" said the man, looking down at Bob. At six feet one inch Bob was not short but this man was at least six inches taller. He had a large hook nose and deep-set eyes that looked black in the shadow of his hat.

Bob stepped back so that he was not looking up at the man, at least not too much anyway, "Is this something to do with the office?" Bob asked. "You tell me, is it?" said the man. Bob was now getting a bit irritated, he could feel his temper rising, "I think you need to tell me what you want right now!" "Are you planning to use the premises for meetings?" said the man. Now Bob was really puzzled, "I have no idea what you are talking about" he said. The man reached into his pocket and produced a small leather wallet which he flipped open to show a card. Bob just had time to notice that there was a crown printed on the top before it was snapped shut and pocketed.

"Come on now sir" said the man, emphasising the word sir just a bit too much. "We know that you are a member of the SPGB so you can't be surprised that you are being watched."

Bob started to say that he wasn't a member of anything but then he remembered the meeting he had gone into all those months ago and the card he was given. Did that mean that he was a member? And if so was that so bad?

He explained to the man exactly what had happened that day and producing a wodge of papers from his top pocket he searched for, and found, the card that he had been given that day. The man listened without interrupting until Bob had finished and then asked Bob if he intended to go to any more meetings.

When Bob said "Probably not" the man said "I need you to say definitely not, and because I believe you are genuine, I'm going to tell you why you shouldn't." He told Bob that the SPGB had aligned themselves with the Communist Party and that meant that they were now a subject of interest to MI5.

He went on to say that 'we' view this as seriously here as 'we' view Oswald Mosley's Fascists in London. "Two sides of the same coin if you want my opinion" he said. Bob wondered briefly about saying that he didn't but thought better of it. "Stay away from them, you're on a list now so we'll be keeping an eye." As he said this it looked to Bob like he tried to tap the side of his nose with his finger but missed, which was odd thought Bob, *it was big enough*. He deftly took the SPGB card from between Bob's fingers and walked away.

Bob tried to continue his day as planned but just couldn't get his mind on off what had happened so he headed to the Snooker Hall for a few frames. The Bookies runner was often in there so he might be able to get a couple of bets on as well. That would take his mind of things for a while he thought, but he was wrong.

His thoughts kept returning to what happened earlier. He alternated between thinking on the one hand that it was just a bit absurd and on the other that it was very sinister. He remembered reading an article about Oswald Mosley holding a meeting of the Fascist Party in Birmingham at which there was reported to be more than 10,000 people, but that was probably a couple of years back.

More recently he had read in the newspaper about a new Act of Parliament called something like 'The Incitement to Disaffection Act.' The police and security services were using it to arrest the more extreme among both Fascist and Communist demonstrators. *Maybe this would soon be happening in Birmingham and not just in London* he thought.

His sympathies definitely lay with socialist ideals and he had deeply held views about the equality of all and the principle of sharing wealth in the community but he would never agree with the use of violence which seemed to be getting more common of late.

Thinking back to his meeting with the 'Mac and hat' man he wondered what it was about the man that had discouraged him from his normal response. He was aware that if challenged in any way then he could become instantly overbearing and arrogant, there were plenty of examples for him to remember.

He would use his 'upper class' voice and eloquence and a wagged finger to demand that the person should do as he said, warning them that they would be severely dealt with if they chose not to do whatever it was that he was demanding. Very few people had ever actually asked "By whom?" He would often laugh at himself after these incidents realising that his behaviour was so much at odds with what he really believed.

He decided not to say anything to Jim and Winnie about his brush with the Secret Service. Thinking of it like that made him smile. He decided that it was all nonsense and resolved not to worry about it anymore and he was certainly not going to give Jim and Winnie any cause to worry.

It was about six o clock when he arrived back at the flat, Jim had arrived a few minutes before and was showing Winnie what looked like a book. "I'm not too sure what this is" he said," holding it out to Bob, "Whatever it is there's a lot more of them in the cupboards at the office." Winnie said that she had told them there were old books in the cupboard and they should have let the man dispose of them.

As soon as he opened it and recognised the contents Bob was immediately engrossed, only putting it down when Winnie called him for their meal. After the meal he took the 'book' and settled down for the evening, his mind now fully occupied with the contents.

Making notes on a piece of paper as he went through it, he became so absorbed that it was after midnight before he finally went off to bed. He couldn't wait to get to the office in the morning to see what more there was in the cupboards!

Chapter 11

It was only just getting light as Bob got to the office, he had to knock on the door as the shop keeper was doing something in the back room and quite a nice sign on the door said **CLOSED**. Finally the man heard the knocking and came to let Bob in, "Blimey you're early" he said. Bob rushed up the stairs calling out "Morning!" as he went.

In each of the alcoves there was a very large cupboard with another tall cupboard on top, filling the alcoves from floor to ceiling. They were all completely full of books. As he opened them and took a book from each one Bob grew even more excited if that were possible! He had a quick look and then replaced each book exactly where it had come from, realising now that there was a method in the way they had been stored.

What the cupboards were filled with were Racing Form books, actually more like folders than books. They had been meticulously put together with what seemed to be information on horses and results from all over the country.

Two hours later when Jim arrived at the office Bob had worked out the filing system and was now pretty certain that his earlier thoughts were right. The folders contained the horse's names, the weights they carried, the jockeys that rode them and where they were placed in every race at what appeared to be every major race course in the Country. There were also details of the weather at the time of each race meeting and details on whether the track was soft, firm or hard at the time. A huge amount of information had been put together and all of it really important if you were a serious gambler.

Jim worked all day putting together shop signs for delivery the following week. It was Friday and he liked to have the next week's orders ready by Friday evenings if he could. All that day Bob sat in the corner near the cupboards studying the contents of the folders and scribbling away in a note book which he'd bought from downstairs.

Apart from going down to buy the notebook and a couple of trips to the toilet Bob had not moved all day and he'd hardly said a word. As Jim prepared to leave at the end of the day Bob finally looked up and said to Jim, "This could be like printing money you know." Although Jim enjoyed the odd bet now and then he was far from being as knowledgeable on the subject as Bob and so he didn't really understand what Bob was saying.

As they walked back to the flat Bob tried to explain to Jim about race handicapping and how it was worked out. The information he now had would allow him to go through the upcoming races and work out where the handicap was either not right or at least very generous to a particular horse. This meant, said Bob, that the chances of placing winning bets were increased to a level that would make betting a profitable occupation.

They talked about the person that had left the office and exchanged a few ideas as to what had happened to make him disappear the way he had. They wondered if he would suddenly turn up again demanding his form books but decided it was unlikely and anyway, as Bob pointed out, possession was nine points of the law. Or something like that.

What Bob had been doing all through that Friday was to work out, using the form books which horses he would bet on at Wolverhampton races the next day. He invited Jim to go with him so that he could see how things worked and once Jim had made a deal promising Winnie a 'children free' day on Sunday he agreed to go. He was quite intrigued by everything that Bob was saying but still didn't really understand it that well.

They arrived at the course early the next day and already it was a hive of activity with horses being walked around and the Bookmakers setting up their stands. Plenty of people had already arrived and the little cafe was already doing good business. Bob told Jim that he already knew which horses he was betting on so he would go and place his bets now, explaining that he would get better odds by placing early bets. By the time Jim had queued for the teas and then found somewhere to sit Bob was back having spread all his bets among five Bookmakers. They don't like it if you keep winning, he told Jim, better to use as many different Bookies as possible he said.

They had agreed that Bob would only bet with five pounds so that at the end of the day Jim could see if there really was something to justify Bob's excitement. Jim had a piece of paper listing all the horses that Bob had chosen and the amount wagered. He had asked Bob what an 'each way' bet was and was told that even if the horse came in second or third some money would be paid out, except for the first race where there wasn't enough runners.

The first race was over and the chosen horse had finished second so there was nothing to come from the ten shillings that Bob had put on, Bob seemed unconcerned and said to Jim "No problem, six more races to go!" The second race was already under way and again at the finish Bob's horse was narrowly beaten into second place but this time the bet was 'each way'. After some swift calculations Bob had worked out that the winnings had simply replaced the loss on the first race.

The next two selections both won and seemingly very easily, the first winner had odds of three to one which meant that bob now had two pounds. The second winner had much better odds of twelve to one giving Bob a total now of eight pounds and ten shillings. His selections were both 'placed' in the remaining two races with a second and a third place giving winnings together of two pounds and fifteen shillings. The grand total for the day was eleven pounds and five shillings, more than double what they had started with and Bob was delighted!

Jim was more cautious about the success and asked Bob if he had chosen the horses purely on the basis of what he had studied or whether there was some element of instinct about it, "After all" he said to Bob "You have always been *quite* successful with your betting." Bob replied honestly that he had chosen the horses first and then checked his selection against what the form books told him. He had made four changes to his selections and so it was the form books that had given him the success today.

Over the next two weeks Bob had spent much more time studying the form books than he had selling. He had placed numerous bets with the local bookie through his runner and had also been to Uttoxeter races for a day. This had been even more successful than the Wolverhamton day and now Jim was beginning to believe that there really was money to be made.

Over the next six months or so they devoted all their time to the betting with Bob studying the form books and working out the horses and races on which they would bet and Jim placing many of the bets with Bookies runners. They had to constantly keep finding different Bookies with each one soon reaching the point at which they would no longer take the bets. Jim was out and about quite a lot placing bets, even travelling to neighbouring towns to find Bookies that didn't know them. He still made things when he was in the office and had some time, mainly the little menu holders because they still had some materials left and they were easy to make and store.

Bob was travelling to race courses all over the Midlands and the North of England. He'd even been to the Boxing Day racing at Wolverhamton and had an extremely successful day. They were making more money at this than they had ever made with their sign business but Bob knew that it couldn't last.

Things were gradually changing and Bob could feel that this 'little gold mine' was drying up. Other things were happening too. The shop owner came up to see him and said that he was really sorry but his rent on the shop had nearly doubled in the last year and he had no choice but to put the office rent up. It was by no means expensive now but where it had been irresistibly cheap, that was no longer the case.

Bob was thinking that it was almost as if someone above had decided that life would now be harder. Within a week of the office rent going up they received a note to say that the rent on their flat would be going up, and quite substantially at that. Unemployment in the arca was rising dramatically and it seemed to be that the worse off people got, the more prices went up on the essentials of life.

The income from betting was gradually getting lower, the information in the form books was becoming less useful as it was getting out of date. It would have been very expensive to keep the information up to date so Bob had never considered it. Eventually, after seven months of living entirely on the proceeds of betting, they decided that it was time to get back to their business of sign making.

Life did get harder for them with sales getting more and more difficult to make. The price of the materials had risen like everything else but Bob had to sell their products ever cheaper just to keep some money coming in. There was little choice but to carry on and that was what they did, but it was hard. Sometimes they sold personal possessions to raise money just to buy some food. Bob sold his Art Deco lamp for a lot more than he expected but was sad to see it go.

Occasionally Bob would have a flurry of sales and they would catch up with paying the rent and other bills. They would live 'normally' for a while but it would always go back to being a struggle.

Baby Ruth had arrived and Jim and Winnie were so happy with the new addition to the family but they knew that before long something needed to change. Bob knew this as well but none of them quite knew how they could change anything with so little money coming in and the prospect of any improvement looking bleak.

The months went by and of course, little changed. Sales were hard to come by and they had to be really careful with money, making sure that they spent enough on replacing materials while trying to survive on what was left. There were no more visits to the Snooker hall for Bob and definitely no bets being placed.

They saw in the New Year of 1936 more in hope than expectation that things would improve. All around there was the evidence of extreme poverty and although the Newspapers were regularly carrying news of the economic recovery, there were no signs of it that anyone here could see.

Somehow, they had got through the spring and summer and were now facing what was predicted to be a very cold winter. Bob was sitting in a small cafe where he had been for the last hour nursing the remains of a cup of tea while he waited for the owner to arrive. He was hoping to sell some menu holders but looking at state of the decor and the tables didn't fill him with hope.

He was thinking back over the previous months. This year so far had been the most difficult time he had ever known. Aside from the recent arrival of David, Jim and Winnie's fourth child, the rest of the year had been horrible. Winnie's parents had both passed away and not long after that Bob and Jim had lost their father. Bob had not gone to London for the funeral, he just couldn't face it and quite apart from that he didn't have the money. He wrote to his mother expressing his sympathy but she had not replied.

The owner of the cafe arrived and walked straight through into the kitchen, he heard the woman in the kitchen say "There's a bloke out there wanting to sell you something." *Oh dear* thought Bob, that's the end of that then. The owner poked his head out of the kitchen door and spotting Bob with his box of samples he said "No thank you whatever it is." Sometimes it just wasn't worth trying thought Bob, and he just left.

Bob didn't normally dwell on the past and his determined and unfailing level of cheerful optimism kept him going in the face of setbacks that would have the majority of people giving up. He was aware of this trait and sometimes wondered what it would be like just to give in and let someone help him, or at the least tell him what to do next. He knew that he was never really going to let that happen.

Lately he had become even more determined not to show any form of emotion when faced with a problem, even when faced with an emergency in fact. It was probably something which came down through the family he thought. His father had never been one to show his feelings, seeing it as a form of weakness. So for Bob to show that he was upset, panicked or even embarrassed in any way simply wasn't allowed.

He decided that he would go to the station where he could buy a newspaper and sit and read for a while before marching on to make at least two sales! The news paper was full of reports about some trouble in the East End of London.

They were calling it 'The Battle of Cable Street'. The police had been trying to stop a pitched battle between Oswald Mosley's Fascists and numbers of Anarchist, Communist and Socialist groups that had travelled there to join with the Jewish residents to disrupt the Fascist march.

Further on in the paper there was a report that Stanley Baldwin was planning to confront King Edward about his relationship with Wallis Simpson, Bob thought that she sounded like a lot of fun to be with and good luck to him! He went on to the racing page and marked his selection of horses, he might risk a shilling later he thought, when he had made some sales.

He watched the comings and goings of the people using the station and had a brief moment thinking that he would like to be boarding a train to somewhere but he didn't know where. He couldn't shake off the feeling that something was going to happen, he'd had this feeling a lot lately but had no idea why and put it to the back of his mind. It was getting late in the morning so he picked up his box of samples and walked off briskly to find his next customer.

Chapter 12

Christmas arrived and they made the best of it with presents for the children and the three adults spending ages making paper chains and hanging them up. Restrictions on the importing of Christmas trees had been brought in by the government a couple of years earlier and that meant as most of the trees were now grown in Britain, there were now fewer available and, of course, they were more expensive. They were very surprised when Bob arrived at the flat on Christmas Eve carrying a four foot tree and even more surprised when he produced a box of tree decorations!

Bob had got chatting to a man on one of the Christmas stalls in the town centre and after a while the man had asked him if he would mind looking after the stall. The man said it would only be for an hour or so while he "took care of a bit of business," winking at Bob and tapping his nose, which he didn't miss.

When he returned over two hours later and just as Bob was thinking of leaving, he had a very worried look about him. Without speaking to Bob at all and constantly looking around, he started to quickly pack the things on the stall, mainly small Christmas decorations, into a cardboard box.

Bob was just saying "Goodbye, don't mention it, my pleasure," when the man just picked up his box and ran off. Within seconds two Constables came past, looking around them and puffing hard; they glanced briefly at Bob and the empty stall and rushed on. The stall wasn't completely cleared though because leaning against one end was a four foot tree and next to it was a box of tree decorations.

Two weeks later the local paper had the headline XMAS EVE THIEF FOILED BY POLICE. The story was of a man snatching the money bag from a rent collector who was walking near the town centre. While laying in wait he had failed to notice that there were two police officers nearby and as soon as he had made his move they had given chase.

He had dropped the bag and run off in the direction of the Christmas Market. He was also believed to have been involved in the earlier theft of a van carrying Christmas trees and decorations. *The Police would like to hear from anyone with information about either of the incidents to contact them.*

Bob was reluctant to go to the police station but Winnie persuaded him. She pointed out that anyone who had seen him looking after the stall might give his description to the police. If he didn't tell the police about what happened first, it could look suspicious.

The next day Bob headed off to the police station, rehearsing in his head as he walked there the best way to describe his involvement to the absolute minimum. As he was nearing the steps leading up the police station door he couldn't believe who was just coming out of the door. It was 'Hat and Mac' man! Bob looked away and started to walk past but he had been recognised. "Hello, I thought it was you, not been hanging around with any of them commies have you?" Bob shook his head, not wanting to get into a conversation. "Of course you haven't" said the man, "I'd know if you had." Bob just wanted to go but 'Hat and Mac' went on, "I thought for a moment you were coming in here, did you have something to tell us?" he asked. Bob was already walking away and saying, "No, nothing at all."

It was a long time since any of them had had any spare money to spend on clothes or shoes, apart from on the children of course, and it was beginning to show. Bob took good care of his two suits but they were both inevitably showing signs of wear. It was a bitterly cold January and so, wearing his overcoat which was still looking ok, he felt respectable enough to be calling on business people.

It was no surprise really when one of his shoes gave out with what was left of the sole parting company with the top of the shoe. Bob was doing an enormous amount of walking, he did enjoy walking but now it was mainly about saving money on bus fares. The sole was flapping about as he walked and he was unable to hide it, the only solution was to rip it off altogether so that, unless he lifted his foot up, it was not obvious to anyone unless they looked closely at his feet.

By the time he got back that evening his foot was aching and he could hardly feel his toes. He realised that he would not be able to carry on that way the next day. Of course, he would have to buy a new pair of shoes but there was not going to be money for that for a little while yet. He thought about ways in which he could make a repair but nothing seemed remotely possible, he would need to do something though.

A possible solution came to him and he decided to carry on with his calls as planned tomorrow and find out if it would work. He asked Winnie if he could have a white cot sheet from the bundle that she had picked up at the church jumble sale. There were two in the bundle that were quite badly marked and she gave him those but had no idea what he was going to do with them.

The next morning Bob cut one of the sheets into strips and bandaged his foot with several layers before forcing on his shoe, he had cut the toe cap off so that now his 'bandaged' foot was visible to all. He practiced limping but soon found that he didn't need to, it was so difficult to walk properly that he had a natural limp.

He made it to the first of his planned calls and 'limped' in, he explained to the lady owner that he had injured his foot and had needed to cut his shoe to get it on. She was very sympathetic and Bob had a suspicion that it had helped him to make the sale but he gladly took her order for two signs and went on to the next shop.

He finished the day having made three more sales and apart from a couple of people who had not been impressed by his 'carrying on in spite of injury' he had had a very successful day! By the time he made it back to the flat his foot and leg ached from the unnatural way he was walking, he wouldn't be able to do this for too long.

Bob and Jim had finally decided that they had to give up renting the office. They knew that the shop owner would find it difficult to let again but they just couldn't afford to keep paying for it. It wouldn't be easy for Jim to be making things at the flat which was already quite cramped, but he would make the best of it.

Things got a little better over the next two weeks with some orders delivered and the money collected. This, combined with not paying out for the office, meant that there was a little more money for them and Bob had bought some shoes and had one of his suits repaired and cleaned.

He was up early and actually looking forward to going out to make some sales, of course he didn't make a sale every time he went out, but he always thought of it that way.

In the flat a kind of unofficial rota regarding the use of the bathroom in the mornings had evolved and worked well considering the number of them using it. It was his turn but he waited ten minutes just to make sure that it was clear.

Whistling a tune he went into the bathroom and then, standing in front of the small mirror above the sink, he lathered his face and began to shave. It was then that he had the feeling that he was not alone and a quick glance to his left confirmed it. Winnie was in the bath!

How could he have not noticed?! Bob quickly reasoned that to make a fuss now would be embarrassing for Winnie and certainly his rushing out with lather all over his face would only serve to alert everybody to what had happened. His reaction was to offer a cheery "good morning!" to Winnie and simply carry on with his shave. Once finished he left, making sure that he didn't look in the direction of the bath and saying "See you later" as he closed the door.

What he hadn't seen was that Winnie, in her effort to turn toward the wall, had inadvertently pulled the bath plug out with her foot. Instead of being able to stay under the water and bubbles until Bob had finished shaving, she had been desperately trying to replace the plug as well as trying to cover herself as the water slowly drained from the bath.

Winnie was upset, but not terribly, by what had happened. After all she said "you can't have four children and still be too worried about things like that" but she did tell Jim that she thought Bob really should have just left the room rather than carry on shaving.

Even though Winnie had said that she wasn't too upset, Jim most certainly was. Maybe it was caused by the strain of the months of struggling or possibly by the cramped conditions but whatever it was his furious reaction was out of character. He went well beyond anything that Winnie or Bob would have expected, Bob particularly, still thinking he had done the right thing. Shouting that Bob had just been ogling Winnie and that he knew full well that it was her turn to be in the bathroom so he must have gone in on purpose!

Bob left the flat and went off to find some customers. He was very hurt by what Jim had said and had left without saying anything at all. What had started as a happier day than most of late had been soured and he felt that an injustice had been done, his only motive had been to avoid any embarrassment for Winnie and, of course, not to show any on his part.

The atmosphere was a bit frosty when he returned that evening. It appeared that Winnie was cross with both of them. She thought that Bob had handled it all wrong but she also thought that Jim was way over the top with his reaction to it so they were all annoyed with each other.

Over the next few weeks the 'Winnie in the bath' incident faded in importance and things had improved to the point of

114

being almost back to normal. What hadn't improved and had in fact worsened considerably were the sales. Apart from the fact that Bob was running out of new places to sell to, those that he did find were struggling themselves, to the point where the last thing they wanted to do was to spend money on anything not absolutely essential.

Things were fast becoming desperate and thinking back to his 'injured foot sales' he decided he would have to try something else along those lines. He didn't like it but they had to get some money somehow. They hadn't had enough money to buy any more materials and apart from two unfinished menu holders everything had now gone.

He found some paper that they had planned to use for printed menus but had abandoned the idea. There was mostly white paper but they had a little black as well and Bob and Jim spent an evening folding the paper so that it would stand up on its own and drawing and cutting out small black letters to stick on the paper that said MENU.

It was slow work and by eleven o clock they ran out of paper having only made six. Jim had almost thrown them in the bin but Bob insisted that he would try to sell them to someone, somehow and anyway, he said, they had nothing to lose.

The next morning he went off as usual. He walked for a mile or so until he came to a cafe that he had visited, unsuccessfully, when they had first arrived in Birmingham. He didn't think that they would remember his earlier visit but it didn't really matter for what he had in mind.

He took a deep breath and prepared himself and went into the cafe. Approaching the counter, he started talking to the lady who was stood there waiting to take orders. He was stuttering and mumbling about seeing the owner. Once she had understood that he wanted the owner she called to someone in the kitchen and another lady came out asked Bob what he wanted.

"I am r-r-recovering from a b-b-breakdown" he said, shaking a bit just to add to the seriousness of his breakdown. "I c-cut these out myself, it says m-menu and look you can write on here what you have on the menu and it stands up on its own." He had produced one of the paper things which looked even worse in the light of day. The women were now looking at each other not quite knowing what to do while he sat there doing a bit of shaking to keep things going.

"Right" said the owner, obviously coming to a decision, "How much are they duck?" Bob couldn't recall ever before being called 'duck' but this was no time to think about that. He gave a price that he thought might just be ok for one and said "It would be g-good if you bought one" while trying to look pathetic.

"How many of those have you got in there?" she asked. He pretended to count them, making it four the first time and seven the next. "Give it here my duck" she said pulling the box towards her. *Blimey, I'm her duck now!* Thought Bob. "There's five in here and one on the table so that's six, I'm going to buy them from you but I don't want you coming in with anything else now." She went to the till behind the counter and took out the money. For some reason she went and found an envelope to put the money in before passing it to Bob.

Bob was embarrassed by the generosity of the woman because he recognised it as just that. He promised himself that in future if he couldn't sell something properly, he wouldn't sell it at all. But for now, he had some much needed money to take back to the flat and set out to walk back.

Chapter 13

Bob had thought things couldn't get any worse but he was wrong. They most definitely could. 1936 had not been good year by any standards. Apart from the family losses, with Bob and Jim's father dying and Winnie losing both parents, it had been horribly tough just to keep their heads above water.

The newspapers had been depressing with news of Crystal Palace burning down. The Jarrow March, as it became known, with miners marching to London protesting about the poverty and unemployment. The abdication of King Edward the eighth, not that Bob had found that bit of news particularly depressing, his thoughts at the time were more along the lines of *Good luck to you! Enjoy!* There had been news of Germany building up their army and weapons but nobody seemed particularly concerned. Nothing was being reported on the front three or four pages anyway.

Bob, Jim and Winnie were in the flat totting up their combined wealth. The result was that they had enough for the rent, the gas meter and food for the week if they were careful, or more accurately if Winnie was careful. There was nothing left for buying materials to make anything or paying bus fares for

Bob's selling trips which, by necessity, were getting further and further away.

Up to now Bob had worked to a system, fairly flexible, but a system nonetheless. Once he had taken orders for an amount that he could deliver in one trip, hopefully by bus, he would stop calling on businesses in that area and move on. The idea was that when, a week or so later, he delivered the orders he would then stay in the area using that to hopefully gain introductions to their close business neighbours.

The problem that he had now was that sales were so few and far between and usually for just one or maybe two things at best. This was difficult because not only because Bob was walking long distances but also that he was having to carry enough stock (mostly menu holders) to sell directly rather than take orders and deliver later.

This meant that he needed to leave his box of stock outside when calling into shops or cafes, which were his main targets now. This was not ideal and Bob was convinced that sooner or later he would come out of a call and find that his box had disappeared!

Going back to the meeting, Jim suggested that, as he had nothing to make, he could go out and try to sell some things as well. It was obvious that he was not too keen on being a salesman and it was not as though there were hundreds of businesses just waiting to be called on.

Eventually it was agreed that Bob and Jim would go together and that way they could carry more stock and also the boxes would be safe while Bob went into places to sell to them, or try to. The next morning they set off at a brisk pace carrying three boxes between them, taking turns at carrying two as after a while they did feel quite heavy.

One thing that they had not thought about the day before was the fact that Bob was the only one with an overcoat. He still had the coat that Lucy had bought him all those years ago. It was very cold and so every time they stopped to change the boxes over the one that would be then carrying just one box took over the coat, their theory being that carrying two boxes would keep that person warmer.

After walking for more than an hour they reached the area that Bob had chosen. He had spotted it one day the week before and because it was getting late, he had kept it in mind for another time. It was a long road on a main bus route with a number of shops and there were also two small groups of factories nearby.

The reason why Bob was interested was that this was cafe territory. There was a large corner cafe close to where they were now and there were four other smaller ones within a mile or so before the end of the road.

The sky was grey and heavy dark clouds had been building up as they had walked and now as they arrived, a few snowflakes had started to drift down. Bob said to Jim that he would need to look reasonably smart when he was going in to try and sell to people and that meant wearing the overcoat to cover up his worn and shiny suit.

He promised to be as quick as he could and left Jim standing round the corner out of sight with the three boxes while he took just one menu holder as a sample and went into the cafe. At first Jim was pleased to see Bob coming back around the corner. He had been very quick, but then he realised that all that meant was that there had been no sale. Bob told him that the cafe was closing in two weeks as it had been losing money and the owner had given up trying to sell it.

Bob kept up his cheerful optimism, saying to Jim, "Come on, we'll make a sale at the next one, after all they'll be doing more business with this one closing down." Jim was glad to be back in the coat and they picked up the boxes and walked on to the next cafe.

It seemed a bit perverse to Jim that Bob would put the coat on to go inside a warm cafe but he agreed that Bob needed to look reasonably smart in order to talk to business owners. They reached the next cafe which was much smaller than the first one and was in the middle of a terrace of shops, most of which were closed and boarded up.

There was an alley between the cafe and the shop next door and Jim sheltered there with the boxes, it was marginally warmer and no snow, which had now got a little heavier, was getting in there.

Jim waited much longer this time and so in spite of being really cold he kept his spirits up hoping that this was a good sign and that soon Bob would be coming to get some menu holders to deliver.

No sale at this one either, Bob had tried his best and had even offered the menu holders at a silly price. The cafe owner had said that there was just no money to buy anything other than the food they needed to carry on the business. Bob had known things were getting worse for some time but what these people were saying was particularly worrying.

"Right, onwards and upwards" he said to Jim, "If I sold to every business I called on we would be rich men by now." Bob was relentlessly cheerful but it was having the opposite effect on Jim who just put the coat on, pulled the collar up and followed Bob up the road.

The next cafe was a bit further along the road and as they walked to it there were subtle signs that this area was faring a little better. They had both noticed it and were encouraged, a few more shops were open and looked generally a bit more cheerful.

There was a little shelter just to the side of the cafe and Jim, having given up the coat again, put the boxes in there and went in himself. He couldn't work out what the purpose of the shelter was but it did smell a bit unpleasant. It turned out not to matter though, before he had time to worry about the smell Bob was back. The owner only visits the cafe on a Saturday he told Jim, "So it's another no sale I'm afraid."

As far as Bob could remember there were only two more cafes along this road. They were about half a mile further along and quite close together near to the where the road ended in a T junction. He was now very concerned. If he didn't sell to at least one of these cafes's, where were they going next? They kept on walking. At least it had stopped snowing for now.

He was used to battling on in these situations but Jim hadn't experienced much of this. There were times when it would be late in the day and he hadn't made a sale but he would just keep going, becoming even more determined and often this would get him a result. Today would be different, he couldn't expect Jim to keep going in the way he had up to now and anyway the bitter cold was affecting both of them.

"We'll try these next two places as we are almost there" said Bob, trying to sound positive, "Let's head for home after that shall we?" Jim agreed and when, shortly afterwards, they reached the cafe he put down his boxes, took off the coat and passed it to Bob.

As he put on the coat and started for the door of the cafe Bob was wondering what on earth he would do if he didn't sell at one of these last two calls. They would be going home with no money and why would tomorrow be any different? Though he couldn't show it to Jim he was very worried that he was going to let them all down, after all he was the salesman wasn't he?

He had taken six menu holders from one of the boxes and holding these in both hands he tried to open the door but it didn't open easily and he dropped some on the floor just inside with the door trying to close itself with him on the outside. A woman who was just serving some mugs of tea at a table close by held the door open, smiling at him as he came in and picked up the holders.

He headed for the counter at the back of the room and when the lady who was serving came back he asked for the owner. There was no plan and he had not even known that he was going to do it, not consciously anyway, not until the very second that he did it. He had promised himself that he would never do this again but he had started now and so he had to continue.

"I w-w-would like to sh-show you these" he said, holding out the holders as best he could without dropping them again. The lady said that she was the owner and smiling at him again she suggested that he put them down on a nearby empty table.

Bob had always suffered with poor circulation in his fingers and with the cold today they were very white. As he put the holders down on the table the lady noticed his fingers,

"Good heavens" she said, "Look at your fingers, "You must be frozen!" "Not *too* bad" said Bob 'bravely'. "I must t-tell you about w-what I'm selling" he said, now getting into the role in spite of himself.

Apart for an interruption while she served a customer the lady had sat and listened as Bob stuttered and twitched his way through the story of recovering from a breakdown and trying, unsuccessfully to make a living selling the holders. He ended by telling her the price which was somewhat lower than normal but he just needed to sell them.

Once he had finished she looked at him for a while and then said that she was going to buy one for each table in the cafe, there was six tables. She told Bob that they could sort that out in a while and then said, "Have you eaten today?" Without really thinking Bob replied that he hadn't, at which point she called to someone in the rear to ask what cooked food was ready.

It wasn't quite lunchtime but they had some sausages and potatoes ready and before he knew what was happening, he was sat in front of a cup of tea and a plate full of hot food. Looking out of the window he saw that it had started to snow again. He also saw Jim who was waiting on the other side of the road.

There was nowhere to shelter and Jim was stamping his feet to try to keep them warm and then putting the boxes down so that he could brush off the snow which was building up on his head and shoulders before going through the whole routine again. The only variation to the routine was when he waved his arms about and then tucked his hands under his arms for a moment.

Bob tried his best to hurry things along, he'd eaten the meal in what was probably a record time but this didn't help because, mistaking his speed for hunger he was immediately given some more! Finally, he succeeded in getting paid for the holders and was able to put his coat on and, after promising to come back and see them, he made his escape.

Jim was in a sorry state. Snow had melted on his jacket which was now very wet and his shoes were obviously soaked. He took the coat and put it on quickly as Bob held all the boxes to keep them off the snow which was now about two inches deep.

They walked up the road until they found a doorway big enough to shelter in and then Bob told Jim what had happened. He left out the bit about him pretending to have had a break-down just saying that he'd had to reduce the price to make a sale.

Jim had seen him sitting down and eating and asked, a lit-tle testily, what that was all about. Bob explained that the lady had just ordered it put it in front of him and it would have been rude to refuse it as well as endangering the sale by upsetting her. Jim seemed to accept this but it was a bit hard to tell now as he turned away to stop the snow hitting his face.

Before they left the little bit of shelter in the doorway Bob said that he wanted to go to the last cafe before they finished for the day. He convinced Jim that the best time to make a call was immediately following a successful one and so they headed off toward the end of the road.

This time the door opened easily and Bob, with six more holders, made a more dignified entrance which in fact didn't help his cause. His haphazard entrance into the last place, although not intentional, had helped set the scene for what had followed. At the counter he asked to speak to the owner and the young woman shouted loudly into the back room for her father to come out. The volume of the call had attracted the interest of all six customers who now seemed overly interested in what Bob was doing.

The man came out of the back room, drying his hands and it was obvious that he was irritated at the interruption. Bob went into his routine. Although he was addressing the man he was aware of that he had the attention of seven other sets of eyes and ears. Far from putting him off this actually motivated Bob to give, in his opinion anyway, an even better performance.

It was noticeable that the owner who had looked at Bob fairly sternly as he started, was now looking a little bit more sympathetic. Bob finished talking, tailing off quietly, which he thought was a good touch to the performance.

"I would like to put one of those on every table" said the man, "But I just can't afford to spend that much." Bob's heart sank. The daughter was frowning at her father and six other people suddenly became less interested in their food and were now openly looking at him. "I'll tell you what, how about I just take three and throw in a free meal?"

Bob thought quickly, "I c-can't eat when I'm out, t-t-too nervous, g-gives me t-terrible indigestion." "Oh right" said the man, "At least sit down and have a cup of tea before you go." The young woman brought the money for the holders and a cup of tea to the table by the window where she had put Bob.

The money from the first sale was safely stored in the inside pocket of the overcoat and Bob made sure that this money went in there as well. He reached for the tea and tried to drink it quickly but it was too hot and he started blowing on it to cool it down.

The window was steamed up and, using his sleeve, he cleared a small area and peered out to see that Jim was right outside staring in at him! It was snowing steadily, Jim and the boxes, now on the ground, were covered. Bob just left what remained of his tea and rushed outside.

He immediately held out the coat but Jim didn't take it, "I've had enough of this" said Jim, angrily brushing snow from his head and shoulders. "You're treating me like some kind of servant" he said. Bob started to explain what he had been doing but Jim was not interested, "Don't start giving me all your sales spiel, I'm not listening."

Bob dropped the remaining three holders and the coat on top of the boxes and they stood looking at each other for a moment. Almost at the same time they turned from each other and walked away in opposite directions. Neither of them looked back and the *stock, the coat and the money* remained where it was outside the cafe.

Chapter 14

ob was angry. He'd done his best to get some money for them all hadn't he? He knew that he should have told Jim what he was doing with his 'breakdown' routine but he hated having to use it and, as he now realised, he had been embarrassed to talk about it.

He walked quickly back to the flat and went straight to his room. He took his old suitcase down from on top of the wardrobe and his threw his few clothes and possessions in it and was heading for the door before Winnie even realised that he was back.

"What's going on?" asked Winnie. "You've not been arguing about the silly bath thing again surely" she said. "No" said Bob, "We've not argued about that." You had best ask Jim when he gets back." Then, giving Winnie a quick hug and a peck on the cheek, he left.

Bob walked to the station with a vague feeling of wanting to get back to London. For some reason he had always felt different there, more comfortable maybe, even when things had been really bad he had not felt as low as he did at the moment.

At the station he made straight for the Station Masters office. Luckily it was 2.0pm and the Station Master had just returned from his lunch. Lunch must have involved some alcohol because he was a little unsteady as he went round to sit at his desk. He was a large man with a very ruddy complexion and his uniform waistcoat was just about holding together as he sat down.

"Well young sir, what can we be doing for you?" he said. Bob detected a slight slurring of the words and hoped that the alcohol intake would help, not hinder his cause. Making it up as he went along Bob started his story, "I have been working on some business here and my company in London have sent a cheque to cover my journey back but unfortunately it has not arrived yet and I must get back urgently due to a family problem."

"Did you want me to lay on a special train then?" said the Station Master laughing loudly at his own joke for several minutes. Bob tried to pretend that he found it funny but it didn't matter anyway, the man was oblivious.

Finally, Bob was able to carry on and said "I need a ticket to Euston now and I can pay for it tomorrow when I have some funds." His story was so full of holes, why couldn't he just go to a bank that his company could contact for instance? Would the station Master want to telephone his 'Company' for confirmation? There were so many reasons that this was not going to work that Bob almost got up and left without waiting for an answer.

What actually happened was that the Station Master reached into a drawer took out a small white pad and asked Bob for his full name and address which he wrote down. Bob had given him the address of his old rooms in Norwood. It was the only one he could think of and he wasn't sure that it was right anyway.

He took the signed hand written ticket from the man, thanked him and left the office. As he walked away the Station Master called after him, "Don't forget to pay for that tomorrow!" Bob thought to himself *I won't forget but I don't know how.*

He just managed to get on the 2.15pm train and settled down in the carriage. His suit was drying out but now had lost what little shape it had kept and his shoes were dull and showing some white lines where they were drying. Bob was normally very concerned with his appearance. There was no vanity in it he just felt that he should always be as clean and smart as possible, but at the moment he had other things to concern him.

He gradually warmed up and was beginning to feel drowsy but he didn't want to go to sleep. He had to work out what he was going to do when he got to London, more to the point when he got off the train. It felt a little surreal. This morning everything had been normal, at least as normal as it ever got living with his brother and sister-in-law and their four children. Now he was heading for London with no idea of even where he would sleep tonight and not a penny in his pocket!

By the time the train pulled in to Euston station he still had no plan except a vague idea about heading towards his old rooms. Although it was about five years since he had left his rooms he thought that they might have somewhere for him, or know somewhere even. If they remembered him as he hoped, maybe they would let him stay while he figured out how to earn some money. That was about as far as he had got with any kind of a plan. He had fleetingly considered contacting his mother but immediately dismissed it.

It was four thirty by the time he left the station. He'd had to take the piece of paper to the ticket office and give his name and address again. There was no snow but it was extremely cold and already very dark. Bob pulled his jacket tight round him, turned up the collar and walked off toward Norwood.

He kept up a good pace as much to try to keep warm as anything else. He was fairly familiar with the route so for much of the way he was deep in thought, worrying about Jim and Winnie and what they would do next as well as his own dilemma. He had no reason to think that anything good was about to happen but he would not let any negative thoughts take hold and remained determinedly optimistic. Something would turn up!

As it happened, the route he had chosen took him past the pub where he had played piano all that time ago. He still had a bit further to go before reaching the house where he had rented the rooms but on impulse he went in thinking that, at the very least, he could warm up a little.

It had started to drizzle, turning to sleet, a little while before Bob reached the pub and as he went in and walked up to the bar he was shivering as well as looking a bit bedraggled. The barman served his next customer and then came towards Bob, "Blimey mate! You look arf frozen, should 'ave a coat on this weather." He looked at Bob more closely and then said, "I don't believe it, you're the bloke that played the old joanna New Years eve a few years back" he went, "Don't tell me, its Roger.. no Robert." Bob was amazed, he hadn't recognised the barman at all, and he was still working here all these years later. "Bob" he said, "My name is Bob."

The landlord appeared at the bar and the barman called out "You'll never guess who's here Reg." It turned out that the landlord couldn't guess even when he was in front of Bob. The barman told him and he made a pretence of remembering and then said "We could do with a bit of music to cheer the place up.

Bob was still shivering and now and then some water from his hair was dripping down the back of his neck. Realising that Bob still didn't have a drink the barman asked him what he wanted and not wanting to be in, or cause, any trouble told him that he had no money. Giving Bob a wink, the barman went and got a glass of whiskey and gave it to him. He came back to Bob in between serving others and Bob started to tell him a little of how he had arrived at the pub.

The pub was getting a little busier and the barman was not getting back to Bob so much now. He said to the landlord, "Ere' Reg, you want to 'ear what this blokes done today." Reg had been joined by a woman who Bob took to be his wife, and they both came over to him. "What's got our man so interested then" said the woman. Bob told them everything that had happened that day and also a little of what had led up to it.

When he finished telling them the woman said that he was still looking frozen and went and put more whisky in his glass. I'm guessing the first one was free she said, looking at the bar-man, he looked a bit worried but she smiled and said "Don't worry, I've done the same."

"Do you know, I remember that New Years Eve. It was the most money we've ever taken in one night" said the woman,

"And that was really you playing the piano?" Bob said yes it really was. The whiskey was doing its job now and Bob was beginning to warm up. It had also stopped him worrying so much about where he was going to sleep that night even though he still had no idea.

Reg and Edna, who had turned out to be his wife, had been talking at the other end of the bar. Edna came back to him, "Do you feel up to giving us a couple of tunes now?" she asked. "Yes, of course" said Bob, he wasn't sure if it was him or the Whisky talking but he had agreed.

The piano had been pushed up against a wall and they had to push it round so that there was enough room for him to sit down to play, but there was no piano stool. Edna said that she had forgotten what had happened to it but a man who had been sitting on a stool at the bar came over and told Bob what had happened.

A few months ago after the fiddle player had finally agreed to stop playing, Reg had found a pianist who would play three times a week on Wednesdays, Fridays and Saturdays. He bought his own music saying that he was a *professional* and did not want to play any of the music that was stacked on top of the piano, dumping it on a shelf behind the bar.

His choice of music was bad enough, more suited to funeral parlour they thought, but he seemed incapable of hitting six right notes in a row, and worse still seemed completely oblivious to it.

Bob could see that he was enjoying telling the story and he went on. Because Reg had not acted on their complaints a few regulars had decided to take matters into their own hands, and hatched a plan to get rid of the so called pianist.

Just as he had started on one of his dirges, and at a prearranged signal, three of them picked up the piano stool with him still sat on it and carried it outside and dumped it, and the pianist, on the pavement. Bob asked if he came back in and was told that they never saw him again. "So where is the stool," asked Bob, "Well that's the thing" said the man, "We never saw the stool again either."

I'd better play something cheerful thought Bob. He found the sheet music on the shelf and moved it to the top of the piano and then took a chair from one of the tables. As far as he could remember the music seemed to be exactly the same as when he played there last with maybe a couple of additions. He selected a few that were always popular and started to play.

Before long three or four people were standing by the piano singing along and a drink for Bob had appeared on top. In the end he played six or seven songs and when he stopped quite a number of people were calling for him to play more.

Reg and Edna were beckoning him through to the rear of the bar while telling the customers that they might well hear Bob play again. As Bob got up he staggered a little. The alcohol coupled with the warming up after being so cold was having an effect. Edna came straight over to offer some help but Bob refused saying he was just a little tired.

Once they were all in the room behind the bar Reg and Edna told him that they had an idea which might suit him. The idea was that Bob could play for three evenings a week as the previous *pianist* would have done and that they would pay him at the same rate as they had offered the so called 'professional.'

Bob was about to reply when Edna carried on talking, if he didn't mind 'roughing it' tonight she said, he could sleep in the back room on a camp bed. He was so grateful to them and was thanking them when Reg interrupted, "Don't thank us" he said, "I'm sure our takings will improve once you're playing regularly."

"There is something else" said Edna, "I have taken the liberty of talking to a friend of mine who has a boarding house." She paused, "I hope you don't mind my doing this but she has agreed to let you have a room with breakfast and an evening meal for roughly what we will pay you to play the piano here."

Of course, Bob accepted that and, having sat at one of the tables in the bar dozing off for an hour or so he was now under a pile of blankets on the camp bed in the back room. His still damp jacket, trousers and shirt were hanging on a chair by the door. Was it only this morning that he had been *selling* the menu holders in Birmingham? Now here he was in bed, of sorts, in a room behind the bar in a London pub. He drifted off, helped by the whisky, wondering what tomorrow would bring.

Chapter 15

There was a delivery taking place and Bob could hear the sounds of crates being stacked and Reg laughing and joking with the Drayman. For a few seconds he just couldn't think where he was and sat up quickly almost falling out of the rather flimsy camp bed. "I've given this a quick iron" said Edna, holding his shirt. He quickly covered himself up, it was all coming back to him now.

"Come and join us for a bit of breakfast, Reg is nearly finished." After that she said, they could go and meet Violet and get him into his room. "You will be able to unpack that case before it falls apart, well I hope it's yours" she said, "I found it under the table when we locked up." She was still standing there, smiling and holding his shirt out to him but he was not about to get out of bed until she had left.

"What are you doing in there?" called Reg, "Oops, I'd better go" She said, laughing.

Over breakfast they chatted about his piano playing and how much they would pay him for it which was, *coincidently*, exactly the same as the cost of his room and board. They assured him that there would be no pressure for payment from Violet until he was 'sorted out' as they put it. Maybe he was imagining it but whenever one of them mentioned Violet there was just something.., he dismissed it.

He picked up his case and followed Edna out of the pub, he felt so much better this morning. A boiled egg and a cup of tea coupled with dry clothes was having a positive effect and even though he was still very cold as they walked to Violet's house, he was not the shivering wreck of last night.

Edna told him that Violet had three other lodgers and luckily for him the only other room had become vacant last week. The house was only two streets away and ten minutes later they were stood at the door waiting for it to open.

Violet was a middle-aged woman of what Bob thought of as ample proportions. She wore a lot of make-up even though it was early in the day and her hair was styled in a fashion much favoured by the 'flappers.' He thought it looked rather ridiculous but well, if it made her happy.

Violet introduced them, "This is Violet Lovely" she said, and then, "This is Bob" realising as she said it that she didn't actually know his name. "My name is Chaloner" he said and "Should I call you Mrs Lovely?" She took his hand and pulled him inside, "That's so sweet" she said "But Violet is fine." Edna followed them down the narrow hallway and up the stairs to what would be Bob's room.

Violet went through her 'house rules' which were very few but she liked people to be there for meals and told him the times that they were served. "I hope you're not going to be a naughty boy" she said, tapping him on the chest in a rather coquettish way. Bob felt a little uncomfortable but was rescued by Edna saying, "Thank you Violet, we've got to dash, if you give Bob his key he can drop his case off and come back later to unpack and then he will be here for the evening meal."

As they walked back towards the pub Edna spoke about Violet. She told him that they had been friends for years. Violet had never been quite the same since Mr Ludley had walked out some years ago.

Excuse me said Bob "What was his name? She thought for a moment and then told Bob he was called Stuart. "No" he said "His surname." She told him it was Ludley, as she had said before. "Oh dear" he said, "I called her Mrs Lovely. "I know, she really liked it didn't she" said Edna, laughing and walking on.

It turned out that after paying Violet for his board and lodgings he had a little left over and he wondered who had made that small but important change. He was now able to buy a daily paper and the odd packet of Players cigarettes. He was never short of a drink when playing and some of the regulars just left money with the barman for future drinks because he already had pints lined up.

After a couple of weeks he began to notice that on the evenings that he played piano the pub was getting a lot busier and the 'sing songs' were getting longer and louder. One evening he mentioned this to Reg who said that yes, they were taking more money on those nights than they ever had before.

The next time he went to the pub Reg told him that they were going to pay him more. It was only fair he said as they were doing so much better with the takings. Bob was amazed. The next time he was paid it was almost half as much again as previously.

After two weeks of this extra pay Bob had been able to improve his wardrobe somewhat and get a haircut. He had even felt able to put a couple of bets on and one of them had paid out very well. The Barman, who he now knew as TJ but without knowing why, had asked him to put the same bets on for him and so he was enjoying a nice win as well.

Bob had written a short letter to his brother Jim just to say he was alright and that he hoped that they were. That had been two weeks ago and he still had not heard anything. He knew that both he and Jim had been a bit silly and he really did want to know if they were all ok, but for now all he could do was to wait and hope for a reply.

Although he never viewed his current situation as being permanent, at the moment he was happy to just go along with it. He had a little money and somewhere to live, being so popular with the pub patrons was quite a nice feeling as well.

He only had one small problem although it felt to him a little unkind to think of it in that way. Violet seemed to have a sixth sense, or some other method, to know exactly when he was entering the house. Almost every time he came in she would catch him halfway down the narrow hallway and then *have* to squeeze past, saying "We must stop meeting like this," pinning him to the wall with her ample bosom and not hurrying at all to release him.

If that had been the only thing then it wouldn't have been too bad but Violet had wheedled out of him what his favourite meals were and was now serving them up regularly to the disgust of the other boarders. She was constantly touching his shoulders and chest and saying, "There's nothing of you, we must get you fattened up." Bob was wondering what for!

Rather than spend too much time at his lodgings Bob had taken to sitting in the pub on the evenings he wasn't playing.

He often sat with a particular group who were mostly business types and he enjoyed their banter about how badly one or the other was doing. One evening the man sitting next to him, who the others called Benjy, said to Bob that he didn't strike him as someone who just played piano. He didn't go on but just looked at Bob inviting him to answer.

Bob told him a bit about what he had been doing before arriving at the pub and Benjy was more than a little interested. "Listen Bob" he said "I've got something that you might be interested in." Bob asked what it was but Benjy said that he should come and see him tomorrow. He produced a business card from his inside pocket and handed it to Bob.

Printed on the card was, **Benjamin Wiley. Wholesale Goods. Telephone NORwood 1893** There was no address but Benjy had scrawled it on the back. "I'll take the card back when you've found the place" he said.

The next morning he planned to get out as soon as possible after breakfast and, having only suffered a short shoulder massage as Violet 'squeezed' past through a gap of a mere six feet, he managed to escape. One of the other boarders had given him rough directions and he headed off to find Benjy's place.

He found the place without too much trouble as he was walking but, he thought, if you were driving it would be very hard to spot. The entrance was in the middle of a terrace of houses and was just a gap with two large wooden gates hanging open. Above the gates the houses were joined by what must have been an extra bedroom for one of them.

Bob walked through the 'tunnel like' entrance and found himself in a cobbled courtyard which fronted a large single storey warehouse. The building had a loading dock over which there were two padlocked doors. The paint was peeling off the doors, on the left-hand door the word WILEY could just be made out while on the right hand door only a W remained. There was an old van parked to one side and behind that he found a door with OFFICE painted on it.

The door was opened as soon as he knocked and Benjy ushered him in. Benjy was almost completely bald but with a large moustache drooping down at the ends before finishing in little curls. He was about the same height as Bob and also wore a suit, but there was no comparison with Bob's. His suit was light brown in colour with a 'loud' check and had a matching waistcoat. He wore a pocket watch and chain and was constantly checking it but Bob soon realised that it was just a habit.

There was no office just an old desk with a chair in front. The desk was partly covered with papers and a telephone was placed in the middle. Looking around, he could see that full shelves covered the walls right round the warehouse. On the floor in the middle were stacked three rows of boxes with some reaching shoulder height.

Benjy showed him round and as they walked, he could see that there was an extraordinary range of things stored here. There were tins and packets of food on one side, clothes and small household items along the back and on the other wall there was stationery and toys.

On the floor there were unmarked boxes which contained many different types of bottled beer and spirits. He recognised some of those boxes from the back room at the pub.

"Well, what do you think?" asked Benjy. "You certainly have a lot of stock here" said Bob, wondering what he was here for. "You've got right on to it Bob, I knew you were smart." Bob

hadn't a clue what he'd 'got right on to' but he smiled and nodded and Benjy carried on. "What I need to do is get some of this
sold" he said.

Over the next hour Benjy spoke about his business and how
he thought Bob could help both of them to make some more
money. He explained that his suppliers, he put some emphasis
on the word suppliers, were pressing him to take more stock.
There were two problems with this, firstly, the lack of space
until he sold more of his existing stock and secondly, he needed
more money in order to pay for it.

Benjy had quite a large number of regulars who he could
just call on and take orders. He would deliver their orders and
collect the money. This was going along nicely but since his
'mate' had gone he was not getting any new customers and not
selling many of the 'one off specials', as he called them. Apart
from not having much time it was just not his 'thing' he said.

Bob agreed to start selling for Benjy and left the warehouse
with a list of products with prices. Benjy had known that he
would not have the money to buy stock to sell on and had said
that to start off with he would pay Bob a percentage on what
he sold. Once Bob had enough money to start buying and selling he would, according to Benjy anyway, make a great deal
more money.

That evening, having successfully negotiated the mine field
that was Violet before, during and after meal times, he was
now safely in his room. He looked at Benjy's product list and
wondered how he was going to approach this very different
selling job.

Benjy had laid out some 'rules.' He was not to call on any
businesses in Norwood in order to avoid Benjy's regulars and

if, outside that area, he came across any existing customers he was to leave them alone. Apparently, there were not many of those. None of this was a problem as there was a huge area left to cover. He just had to work out how to do it.

Chapter 16

The next morning Bob was up, breakfasted and out in record time. Either he was becoming more skilled at avoiding Violet's advances or she was finally easing up.

He had some idea of how he was going to start selling the range of products on the list by targeting particular types of shops. Today was going to be grocers and he would get familiar with the products as he went along.

After a couple of unsuccessful visits, he began to develop a line of patter that would get him at least to the point of looking through the list with the shopkeepers. He soon came to see which of the products were of more interest than others and by lunchtime he had taken his first order.

He treated himself to a cup of tea and a sandwich in a small cafe and then called on two more shops. Both of the shopkeepers had promised to order from him in the future at the prices he was offering but said they had enough of everything for now. He jotted down the addresses for future reference and then decided to head back to Norwood.

He got back in plenty of time for the evening meal and for once he made it to his room without 'bumping into' Violet. Washed and changed into his 'piano playing clothes' he made it all the way down to the dining table without any sign of Violet. This had never happened before. All four boarders were now sitting at the table with no idea what do and in the next ten minutes they spoke to each other more than they ever had, certainly since Bob had been there.

Just as they had decided to go and investigate Violet appeared at the dining room door. Her hair was sticking out in all directions and her make-up looked as if she had put it on without looking. Most of the lipstick had not actually made it to her lips. She had got quite close to her top lip and it now looked like she had very thick top lip above some very red teeth.

She staggered over and dumped two dinner plates on the table. "Sorrry isslate" she said. "Bester lay n never, I always lay, ooh did I lay say." One of the plates had four uncooked potatoes arranged in a circle with an unopened tin of peas perfectly placed in the middle, the other was completely empty. She staggered out of the room and didn't return.

Two of the boarders were obviously friends and one said to the other that they could share his biscuits up in his room and off they went. The third man just got up and left without a word, shortly afterwards Bob heard the outer door slam shut. Left alone in the dining room he really couldn't decide what to do, just leaving seemed wrong but then he didn't want to intrude on Violets privacy.

He decided to go quietly through and see if he could help or least make sure that Violet was ok. She was not in the kitchen and he went on through the other door which led to her private rooms. As soon as he entered what was obviously her living room, the smell of alcohol was overpowering.

Violet was laying half on and half off a large couch snoring gently. A photo in a frame was on the floor beside her. Bob turned it over and saw that it was a holiday snap of a tall good looking man, standing on the beach with his arm around Violet. They were both smiling at the camera.

He carefully moved her so that she was completely on the couch. Looking around and spotting a coat hanging on the door, he used it to cover her and quietly left.

Later at the pub when he was taking a break from playing, he told Edna what had happened with Violet and about the picture. She wasn't certain but thought that it might be the wedding anniversary or maybe the anniversary of her husband leaving. Edna told Bob that she thought he was very kind to have checked on Violet and to have made her comfortable before he left.

Returning to his lodgings he saw that it was all in darkness. Previously there had always been a light showing in the left-hand ground floor window and more often than not Violet would have found a reason to be in the hallway. Tonight, all was quiet and strangely he missed the 'getting past Violet game' that so often took place.

The next morning Bob and the other three men were seated at the breakfast table as normal. They could hear noises coming from the kitchen and the cups and saucers, tea pot and milk were on the table as usual.

One the 'biscuit friends' said "Shall I be mother?" and poured the tea. He had just finished the pouring when Violet appeared carrying four plates, her normal trick, with one in each hand and one balanced on each arm. She distributed the plates with each of the men getting their preferred breakfast.

Violet looked to Bob to be completely recovered, her make-up was heavy but perfectly applied as usual and her hair was back in its normal 'flapper' style.

"Well, if there's nothing else I'll leave you gentlemen to get on," she said quite cheerfully and left the room.

No one spoke, Violet was still in the kitchen within earshot so they all ate their breakfasts and left. Life at the lodgings appeared to have returned to normal thought Bob, apart from not being pinned to the wall or massaged that day but he was sure that it was only a temporary respite.

For the next couple of months he worked hard, out selling in the day time and still playing piano on three evenings a week. His sales method had changed since his early efforts and now he just concentrated on selling Benjy's so called 'one off specials.'

The point at which he could start buying from Benjy rather than working on commission had arrived much sooner than either of them expected. He was now earning very nearly twice as much from each sale as he had before. He was working hard and also had the benefit of Benjy's very low prices.

Soon after his first meeting with Benjy he had made a conscious decision not to ask where the stock came from.

Sometimes things just seemed to work out and this was one of those times. The man with a van who Benjy occasionally used as back-up had lost his main customer and Bob needed someone to deliver for him. The timing was perfect. His delivery problem was solved before it had even started.

Spring arrived and everyone seemed so much happier. London had definitely not suffered as much as elsewhere with the economic depression. There was much more money around and selling to people, whatever product it happened to be, was so much easier. Bob was taking full advantage of this and was selling more and more all the time. He was aware that he was getting very tired, playing piano in the evenings was taking its toll and he knew that before long he would have to give it up.

Reg and Edna had been so kind to him when he really needed it and so, apart from the fact that he enjoyed it, he was reluctant to stop playing there until they had a replacement. They in turn had always known that Bob would not stay for long and were resigned to looking for another pianist.

A letter from Jim arrived addressed to him care of the pub. It was very short, simply saying that they were all well and hoped he was too. It wasn't mentioned in the letter but he noticed that Jim and Winnie's return address on the letter was in Darlington. They had moved again. Bob was glad to hear that they were ok, it had been at the back of his mind all the time.

Reg had found another pianist, actually a pianist and a fiddle player, they came as a pair. Reg confided to Bob that he was a bit concerned about their playing but considering that there were two of them they were quite cheap. He hoped that the normal raucous singing would cover it and maybe playing three nights a week would give them the practice they needed.

TJ had left the previous week without telling them why or giving notice. Reg said he was fed up with this happening and now they were going to manage on their own.

The freedom from playing piano brought about another change for Bob. Knowing that he now didn't have to return to the pub he was travelling further away all the time finding customers for the 'job lots.' He couldn't always get back to his lodgings and had no way to let Violet know in advance.

He spoke to Violet about this and she was really upset at the prospect of him leaving. She told him that she didn't mind if he just couldn't make it back sometimes, she would understand. When he said that this was not fair on her she even suggested that she could have a telephone installed so that he could ring her.

Finally, it was agreed that he would come back on Saturdays and leave on Monday mornings but, Bob insisted, if she was able to let the room full time then she must do so and he would leave.

Violet had become quite tearful during their talk and when Bob got up to leave, she gave him a hug and said "See you on Saturday night then, take care." He hugged her back for the first time ever and said that he wouldn't be too late on Saturday. He had become quite fond of Violet.

Carrying more and more money on him was beginning to worry Bob and in spite of Benjy telling him it was the best thing to do he had decided to have a bank account. He popped into the National Provincial in Norwood where years ago on Braithwaite's recommendation, he had opened an account.

This time he wasn't met by the manager and stood in front of a newly installed counter with glass separating him from the clerk. He gave his details and was amazed to discover that he still had an account open and that the balance was five shillings and eleven pence.

"Do you have any cheques left" asked the clerk, as if he had been in just the week before. Bob told the clerk that he would need another cheque book, he didn't say that he had no idea what had happened to the last one.

He felt a little better having banked £100 pounds but still had a lot of money on him. There was no way round that, Benjy only wanted cash payments and likewise the delivery driver. Bob was travelling by buses and trains and, more and more these days, by taxi so he needed to carry cash.

He really didn't like it when people paid for things by ostentatiously peeling some notes off a large roll, often held together with a rubber band. Benjy did this and it was probably the only thing about him that Bob didn't like.

He needed to carry cash but was determined not to be drawn into the big roll of notes thing and he solved the problem by spreading his money around in various pockets, only ever keeping a few notes in his wallet.

The weather was particularly good and the temperature was higher than average for May. Bob wondered if it was this that was making people so happy. It seemed to him that people were almost unnaturally cheerful.

The newspapers had been reporting some terrible things happening in Spain. Only a week ago there had been a report that a large number of German planes known as the Condor Legion had bombed Guernica the Capital of the Basque region. It was reported that the town was almost completely destroyed with many hundreds of people killed.

Reports were that elsewhere in Spain there were casualties among the British men who had gone to join the International Brigade fighting against General Franco's forces. There were also numerous reports on the sinister happenings in Germany but as far as Bob could work out people were either not reading them or maybe reading them and not believing them.

Of course, there was the Coronation of George VI in a few days time and there was evidence of the preparations everywhere. Bob was convinced that a lot of people were using the news of this event as a reason to be cheerful while keeping the bad news, of which there had been a lot, to the back of their minds. He also thought that he should stop presuming to analyse his fellow beings.

Whether it was the cheerful atmosphere or just that he was getting better at selling he didn't know but whatever it was Bob was now doing a lot of business. His delivery man was virtually working full time for him and as he was being paid a generous rate he was a very happy man.

His life had been transformed over the last few months. He was mostly staying at decent hotels during the week and paying Violet enough that she didn't need to let his room to anyone else. The advantage of this was that he could leave his things there and had somewhere to stay if he happened to be close by.

Shopping for clothes was not his favourite pastime but with some help and advice from Edna he had now improved his wardrobe to the point of looking pretty smart.

He was using taxis a great deal and he had got to know two of the drivers quite well. They were now happy to wait outside shops for him if he needed them to, knowing that at the end of the journey they would be well paid. On a couple of occasions when he had been overrun with orders one of the drivers had even agreed to do some deliveries for him.

Bob's social life had improved considerably. From being a little aimless when he first arrived back in London, he had now become very busy. He played Snooker with Benjy at the local hall at least one evening a week and went to see Reg and Edna at the pub regularly.

He often made his visit to the pub on a Monday or Tuesday when the double act was not there and there was time for them to chat. Sometimes he would play the piano for an hour or so, just for the enjoyment.

He was also about to become a theatregoer.

His first ever trip to the theatre had come about through an invitation from one of his customers. They had been the first to order one of his 'job lots' and had continued ordering from him since, making them one of his regular calls. As with many of his customers he was now on first name terms with the couple who owned and ran the shop and he thought of Anne and Michael more as friends than customers.

On his last visit to their shop Anne had asked him if he was free to join her and Michael on the following Saturday night to see a show. A friend of theirs had offered them three tickets at half price and being keen theatre goers they had bought the three without hesitation.

Anne said to Bob that she wouldn't mind if he said no, they didn't even know if he liked the theatre. Bob told to her that he had never been before and then she insisted that he join them, telling him that he would be 'hooked' just as they were. Bob said that he would get a taxi and pick them up in plenty of time to get there. They argued with him for a while but he was adamant. He would be paying for the taxi.

He was back at Violet's house earlier than usual on the Saturday and although she had not been expecting him until much later violet insisted on preparing something for him to eat. She seemed to have adopted a more motherly role with him now and he was happy to let her fuss over him. After all he wasn't spending that much time there and it was preferable to being 'hunted.'

Wearing his best suit and freshly polished shoes he used the mirror on the hall stand to give his hair a quick comb. Violet was watching from the other end of the hallway and gave him a wolf whistle. He waved goodbye and went out to the taxi.

It was a great evening! The show was Ivor Novello's The Dancing Years at Drury Lane Theatre. From the moment he walked into the foyer Bob was captivated. The theatre itself, the people, the glamour, this was a different world.

He didn't recall much of what the show was actually about, for most of the first half he was just letting it all wash over him. They were seated in the stalls and had a good view of the stage. He was transfixed. Even the 'theatre smell' was a new and heady experience.

After the intermission and being more used his surroundings, he focused more on the show and particularly the individual cast members. He was so impressed, everything was so professional.

After a while he noticed one of the dancers in particular, they were all pretty but this one just seemed to grab his attention. He didn't take his eyes off her the whole time she was performing and the odd thing was that every time she looked out from the stage she was looking straight at him and smiling!

The taxi driver had promised Bob that he would be there to pick them up after the show and was as good as his word. Five minutes after they came out of the theatre, he was there to pick them up. There were still plenty of people trying to hail taxis and several were turned away from *theirs* as they approached it.

Anne said that she felt like royalty as the driver came around and opened the door for them. "Evening Bob" said the driver, giving Bob a wink. "How was the show?" Bob said that he thought it was wonderful. Anne and Michael were both laughing and told him how stunned he had looked, especially in the second half. He didn't tell them why.

They dropped off Anne and Michael at their shop which they lived above, and then went on to Bob's lodgings. He was very surprised when trying to pay the fare because the driver refused, saying that it was his treat for all the business that Bob had bought his way. "So will you be going to the theatre again?" asked the driver.

"I most definitely will" said Bob.

Chapter 17

Bob did go to the theatre again, the following Tuesday. He worked towards the City pretending to himself that this was a good idea in spite of not having passed a likely customer for at least the last half an hour. The theatre box office happily sold him a ticket for that evening and he went off to find something to eat before the show started.

The first thing he noticed was that with only ten minutes to the start of the show the foyer was not crowded as it had been on Saturday evening. Dress standards were not as high with many people seemingly not dressed up at all. The theatre was only two thirds full and he was seated very close to where he had been on Saturday. There were three empty seats on each side of him. Things were very different compared to his first visit.

This was all forgotten about very soon as the show started and the dancers came on stage. He quickly spotted 'his' dancer and watched her avidly, feeling disappointed each time she left the stage. She was looking at him again and smiling, he resisted the temptation to wave.

During the intermission he noticed a young lad carrying something up the steps at the side of the stage. He moved over to where he could intercept the lad if he came back down and after a few minutes the lad did indeed come back down.

Bob asked him if he worked in the theatre and the lad said that he didn't *actually* work there but all the people in the cast knew him well. They paid him to bring them cigarettes or drinks or whatever else they needed. "I know them all" he said to Bob, with obvious pride in that knowledge.

Bob questioned the lad about the dancers, describing where 'his' dancer had been positioned on the stage and giving a very accurate description of what she was wearing. With no hesitation he told Bob that it was definitely Trixie. She was one of his favourites he told Bob, because she never spoke down to him and always said please and thank you, as well as being very pretty he added.

So he now knew that she was well mannered as well as pretty and he had her name. He had no idea what to do next but he had the whole of the second half to ponder that.

By the time the curtain came down for the last time he had a plan, pretty flimsy he had to admit and there were a dozen things that could go wrong but it was a plan.

As he was leaving he asked the uniformed man in the foyer where he could find the stage door. The man gave him what Bob thought was a sympathetic smile and told him to turn right outside the theatre and then take the first right into Russell street where he would find it about a hundred yards up.

There weren't too many people outside the theatre but several were trying to flag down taxis as they approached. Bob walked briskly away from the theatre toward to the corner of the street and then was almost run down as he stood in the road and with his arm up.

"Blimey mate, you trying to get yourself killed!" yelled the taxi driver. Bob was in the cab in a flash, "would you mind waiting here on the corner for a while?" "I have to collect someone from the stage door" said Bob. "Nah mate, there's people up there ready to go now and I've got a living to make."

Bob broke one of his own rules and produced roll of notes from his pocket. He made sure that it could be seen and then peeled off a ten-shilling note and passed it to the driver, telling him that it would be worth his while. The taxi driver had a change of heart and agreed to wait on the corner.

Now waiting outside the stage door, he was having doubts about his plan and kept changing his mind about what he was going to do when Trixie came out. When she finally did come out, she was chatting and laughing with two other girls. The first of the many things which could go wrong had just gone wrong.

With nothing to lose now Bob carried on with his 'plan', "Taxi for Trixie" he called out, looking in the general direction of the girls. They stopped chatting and Trixie took a step towards him, "I haven't ordered a taxi," she said.

Close up Bob was seeing that she was even prettier without her stage make up, with very large blue eyes and a mass of blonde curls and he was finding it difficult to speak.

"It's been ordered for you" he managed to say.

"I see, and by who?" she was looking at him suspiciously now.

This was all going wrong.

"I don't know, it was just ordered to get you home" he said, "It's waiting on the corner there if you would follow me?"

She turned to the other girls and said, "Come on, we've got
a ride home," and to Bob she said, "We all live in the same place
so you have three passengers." She had assumed that he was
the driver.

The girls piled into the taxi and then, as Bob got in as well
they realised that the driver was already there. One of the girls
was looking very worried and asked Bob what was going on.
He told them there was nothing to worry about, they were in a
licenced taxi and there were three of them after all. He told
them to give the driver their address and that he would explain
on the way.

They gave the driver an address in Wandsworth and Bob
told him that he would want to go on to Norwood after that.
The driver said that he would need another one of these, holding up the ten-shilling note, and once Bob had obliged they
were finally under way.

Bob had decided that the only thing he could do now was to
come clean and tell Trixie everything. Trixie and her friends
listened to him without interruption while he told them the
whole story, starting with his first visit on Saturday.

As he reached the end of the explanation, he added that if
Trixie hadn't kept looking at him and smiling, he would never
have had the nerve to try to meet her.

They had all started to smile as he told his story but when
he added the bit about Trixie looking at him, they looked at
each other and roared with laughter. This went on for a while
and Bob was beginning to get annoyed. He had bared his soul
and was paying for their ride home and all they were doing was
laughing at him!

Trixie was first to notice that he was becoming upset and quietened the others down.

"I'm sorry" she said, "I'm not laughing at you." She explained that with the footlights on they could not see the audience at all and were told to just find a spot to look at and smile. That way with all of them finding a different spot it was hoped that everybody would feel favoured with a smile. She added that anyway to see that far she needed to wear her glasses.

Bob was embarrassed, saying that he had been stupid and was sorry. He added "Well at least you all got a free ride home," For the rest of the journey they sat in silence, with Trixie's friends obviously trying hard not to laugh any more.

They arrived at the house which turned out to be quite close to where he had stayed with Jim and Winnnie. They got out saying thank you for the ride and started down the short path to the door, except Trixie who stood by the open car door and said to Bob, "Do you know Berman's cafe here in the High street?" He didn't, but said that he did.

"Meet me there at twelve tomorrow?" she asked.

 "Ok" said Bob.

"What's your name?" she asked, laughing again.

"It's Bob" he said.

"See you tomorrow then Bob and by the way, I'm Angela."

Chapter 18

Bob found the cafe without too much trouble and was there by eleven thirty. Sitting at a window table with a cup of tea and hoping that Angela would actually turn up. He didn't have to wait long because ten minutes later she was there.

"I didn't think you would be here yet" she said, and before he could reply "I'm glad you are though, I don't believe in all this fashionably late stuff, what a waste of time"

She sat opposite him and they shook hands across the table. He leaned over and gave her a peck on the cheek which made her giggle. They chatted for more than two hours, ordering and finishing sandwiches and more tea.

Angela was from Birmingham and had worked hard to lose the accent but as she became more relaxed it became more noticeable. Bob was amazed to discover that her parent's home was only a mile or so from where he had lived with Jim and Winnie, so that was twice their paths could have crossed. She told him that she was very lucky to have a place in a West End show. Her friend had got her an audition after someone dropped out and she succeeded in getting in.

They arranged to meet again a few days later and Bob said he would think of something that they could do, "Maybe the Cinema?" "Whatever you choose" she said, and giving him a peck on the cheek she was off.

As he was going to be staying in Norwood that night he decided to pop in and see Benjy. By the time the taxi dropped him off it was late afternoon. He expected to find Benjy loading his van as usual ready for his next morning's deliveries but that was not the case. Benjy was not loading stock he was sat at his desk looking very glum. He greeted Bob and waved him to sit down on a stack of three boxes placed by the desk.

He pushed an old cup towards Bob and half filled it with whiskey before topping up his own. "I've got a bit of a problem" he said and took a big swig at his drink. "The people that sell me this stuff are getting a bit nasty" He was pointing at the whiskey bottle. "They want me to take a hundred and fifty cases." "I told them I couldn't take that many but they sent their man round with a message."

The message was that the delivery was arriving tomorrow and if he didn't take it, and pay for it, there would be no more stock coming his way, ever. The man had hinted at other repercussions but didn't elaborate.

Bob said that if money was a problem he would help out but Benjy said that payment was not the issue. His problem was where to put the hundred and fifty cases and how was he supposed to move them on quickly enough? He and Bob together were selling around five or six cases a week at present and at that rate it would take until Christmas to get rid of it all!

Benjy topped his cup up again and Bob thought if his plan was to drink enough to make some space then he had a long way to go! He left Benjy with not much remaining in the bottle and with a promise that he would think of something by the morning. Why did he feel responsible for solving Benjy's problem? It wasn't just about helping his friend; he actually felt that it was down to him to solve it.

He walked off towards Violet's house, hoping that she would have enough food to include him for dinner. He had tried to creep in quietly last night but Violet was still up and was pleased to see him. There were only three of them for breakfast this morning, he must remember to ask her about it.

Of course Violet had enough food to include him and in fact served him one of his favourite meals. He had meat pie with peas and potatoes with a nice thick gravy. He always felt so much better after one of Violet's meals.

That night he laid in bed thinking about the whiskey problem. He could concentrate on selling it and not worry about any other products for a while. The best he could hope for would be orders of ten, maybe fifteen cases and those types of customers would not be easy to find. It would still take a long time and where to keep them in the meanwhile?

His last thoughts before dropping off were about finding somewhere else to store the whiskey rather than trying to sell it quickly.

In the morning his first thought was of Reg and Edna or more accurately their back room. As soon after breakfast as he could he walked as fast as he could to the pub. He caught Reg and Edna as they were getting ready to go out. Apologising for holding them up he said he would like to talk to them for a few minutes about something. They all went and sat at a table near the bar.

They listened to Bob as he told them all about the problem. Reg was nodding and tutting in what Bob hoped was a sympathetic way. When he finished Edna was the first to speak saying that surely this was Benjy's problem and not his. He hadn't answered that when Reg asked him why he was telling them about it.

Bob asked them how many bottles of whiskey they sold in a week. Reg, thinking that Bob wanted to sell them some, told him that on an average week it would only be about six bottles. We're more of a beer type of pub he said but he could take maybe, ten cases if the price was right.

Bob told Reg what he had in mind, and that was that they could store all one hundred and fifty cases in the back room where he slept that first night. In return for having it there Reg could take whatever he needed for the pub without any charge for however long it was stored there.

There would be no record of any purchase and he would not have to lay out any money at all. Edna was not as keen on this as Reg but nevertheless they agreed to store it and also that Bob and Benjy could bring it over that afternoon.

Later that morning when he arrived at the warehouse the delivery had already been made and the whiskey was outside in two stacks. Benjy was inside moving some boxes in a hopeless attempt at making some space. It was never going to work.

When Bob explained to him what he had arranged with Reg his first reaction was to explode, angrily asking Bob if he had gone mad! "Give a pub landlord a chance of free stock, he'll clean us out in no time!" he said.

Bob stayed calm and explained his thinking to a still fuming Benjy. "He is an honest man and they only sell about six bottles a week, he won't take any more than they normally sell." Benjy was starting to calm down and Bob continued, "If it takes six months for us to get rid of it he will have only taken about twelve cases and that's not even ten percent." Benjy was beginning to see this as a great solution. "They might have forced me to take this delivery but the price was amazingly low, we could be alright after all," he smiled at Bob, "I knew you were smart. When can we take it round there?"

It took them four trips in the van and they had to stack the cases up quite high to get them all in the room. It was a warm day and they were sweating profusely by the time they finished. They sat in the closed bar with Reg and enjoyed a few beers to cool off. For once Benjy refused a whiskey.

As usual lately their talk turned to Germany and in particular Adolf Hitler. Benjy was convinced that there would be a war starting before Christmas and Bob was tending to agree. Last year Hitler had sent troops to occupy Austria and was continuing a massive build up of troops and arms in Germany.

The papers were now full of news about the growing threat of war with Germany. In April younger men around twenty years old had been required to register for six months training in the armed forces. The plan was that once they had finished the six months training then they would return to civilian life and be on call if needed.

Journalists were predicting that these 'Militia Men' as they were called would not be returning to 'Civvie Street.' The feeling everywhere was that war was coming and it was now the subject of almost every conversation.

Benjy insisted that Bob brought them up to date on how his meeting with 'Trixie' had gone. He told them how well it turned out and reminded Benjy that her name was Angela but he said he just preferred Trixie. At least their conversation had ended on a more cheerful note.

They thanked Reg for the use of his room and left the pub. Benjy drove back to the warehouse and Bob walked round to Violet's house. Tomorrow he planned to start selling some of the whiskey, the price was still really low even after the addition of Benjy's profit.

The next morning Bob had a delivery going to Coulsdon and he planned to go with his driver as far as Croydon. There were two likely customers there for what he hoped might be a decent amount of the whiskey.

He walked round to the warehouse and as he approached he could see that there was something different about the entrance, it looked darker than usual and he soon found out why.

The second of two police cars was almost filling the entrance. It must have been hard getting out of it because there was only just enough room for Bob to squeeze past. The first car had stopped in the middle of the yard and a young constable was standing next to it.

"What's going on?" asked Bob. "We've had a tip-off" said the constable, and was just about to go on when an extremely large man in uniform came out of the 'office' door. "That's enough PC Morris, the police ask the questions and the public answer them." "Yes sarge, sorry sarge," the young PC studied his feet. Bob couldn't resist, "What's going on?" he asked the sergeant.

This may not have been the best thing that Bob could have done as Sergeant Brook turned out to be a very nasty individual. Benjy came out of the door stood behind Sergeant Brook making signals at Bob who had no idea what any of them meant.

"Do you know this man Mr Wiles?" said the sergeant, pointing at Bob.

Benjy said "Wiley."

"So he's a relative of yours then?"

"No, I'm Wiley" said Benjy.

"And this man is called Wiley but is not related?" The sergeant was puzzled.

"No, he is not called Wiley and he is not related to me!"

"So why did you tell me his name was Wiley, are you taking the Mickey?" Sergeant Brook was beginning to look a bit threatening.

"Excuse me, can I speak?" said Bob.

The sergeant turned to Bob, fixing him with a malevolent stare, and said "That's two questions now out of an allowance of exactly none"

"My name is Chaloner, Bob Chaloner"

It was then that two more policemen came out of the main doors and one of them called out "It's not in there sarge, not a sign of it"

Sergeant Brook was obviously annoyed and snapped at PC Morris to take statements from Mr Willis and Mr Chandler and meet him back at the station double quick! He marched off towards the car in the entrance and then realised that there was no way he could possibly get through to open the door. He must have arrived in the first car.

Bob and Benjy went inside leaving Sergeant Brook waving his arms and yelling at one of the other constables to "Move the damn thing now!"

PC Morris took their statements, basically that they knew nothing about a delivery of whiskey. He got their names right, after getting Bob to spell Chaloner, and they signed at the bottom. As he was leaving, he stopped at the door and said, "It's alright for you two, I have to work with him all the time!"

Benjy filled Bob in on what it was all about. Apparently, the police were investigating a major robbery of wines and spirits and there had been a tip-off that part of the haul had been delivered to a ware house in the Norwood area. There were only two likely warehouses in the area and the other one had been searched the previous evening.

The police detectives had been very busy with special 'war preparation exercises' and so it had fallen to the uniformed branch to follow up. Sergeant Brook was not a happy policeman.

Bob suddenly realised that he had not seen his driver at all and asked Benjy if he had been there. Benjy said that he had told Al that Bob wanted to go with him and Al had said that he would wait at the end of the street. He had obviously driven off as soon as he saw the police arrive and would no doubt be back later when he was sure that the coast was clear.

They decided that it would not serve any useful purpose to tell Reg what had happened. It would only worry him and particularly Edna. The less they knew the better. It was also agreed that they shouldn't try to sell any of the whiskey for a while, just in case it raised suspicion with anyone.

Benjy was looking quite pale and was constantly mopping his brow. He said that he needed a day off to recover from the strain after his lucky escape from, at the very least, being arrested for receiving stolen goods. Bob asked him if he was sure that their whiskey was part of that robbery and Benjy just gave him a look.

They decided to finish for the day and that tomorrow they would have a day at the races for some light relief. Brighton races were chosen and they arranged to meet at the warehouse in the morning. Bob would arrange a taxi to pick them up and get them to Victoria station in time for the early train.

When he arrived at the warehouse the following morning there was an envelope with a note inside pinned to the office door. It was from Benjy saying that he wasn't feeling too good and that he had helped Al load up Bob's deliveries for the day and gone back home to bed. He wished Bob a great day and asked him to choose a horse and put a pound on it for him, the pound was folded inside the envelope.

The taxi arrived and Bob went off to Victoria station to catch the Brighton train. He found a seat away from others and put Benjy's pound with his own cash making sure it was secure in his inside pocket. Race courses were attractive places for pick pockets and other rogues so he had only taken five pounds for betting with plus a few pounds for food and travel. The rest of his cash was safely in his room hidden under the mattress.

It was a long walk from Brighton station uphill through Whitehawk to the course on Race Hill but he made good time and was there in plenty of time before the first race of the day.

As usual he had studied the race card the night before and made selections for every race but there were always changes when he got to the course. It was very different actually being there, much more exciting. There were Bookies shouting out odds on the horses in the first race. The 'tic tac' men were signalling odds from one Bookie to another. Approaching the betting ring he took in the smell of grass, beer and horses mixed with cigar smoke. He loved the atmosphere.

There were seven races for the day and Bob decided to stick with his choices from the previous evening to use as an 'accumulator' on which he would place a five shilling bet. The accumulator meant that that if the first horse won its race then the winnings would automatically be put on the chosen horse in the next race and so on for each race. As soon as one horse did not win the bet was lost. It was rare for a bet like this to win, in this case it required the correct selection of the winner of seven races.

He thoroughly enjoyed his day, putting different bets on all the races as they were run. There were some wins and losses but overall he was doing ok and with one race to go he was about ten pounds up. The bet for Benjy had won four pounds and Bob stuck it in his back pocket for tomorrow.

As he went to place his last bet of the day, he realised that he hadn't checked on the results of his accumulator. He was staggered to discover that so far all six horses had won and he quickly worked out that he had around twenty pounds going on to the horse in the last race.

He went to the Bookmaker that he placed the bet with to see what the odds were on the last horse. The newspaper had shown the odds at 12/1 the night before but the odds showing on the board now were 7/1, they had dropped to almost half. The bookmaker recognised Bob and told him that his bet alone was responsible for the 'shortening of the odds' on that horse. The more money that was bet on a horse the lower the odds would get to protect the Bookies profit.

The last horse won its race! It was just one of those days. The payout was huge and although the Bookmaker had spread his risk around with other bookmakers it had cost him a lot of money. After tax his winnings came to just under one hundred and twenty pounds.

Bob made his way down to the station feeling good after what was probably his best ever day of betting. Entering the station and then waiting for his train Bob was remembering arriving here on his way to join Jim and Winnie in Bognor. It was only a few years earlier but it seemed so long ago.

The train was not that crowded and he was seated on his own opposite a group of men who were getting playing cards out and preparing for a game. The train had not even left the station and already there was a pile of coins in the middle of their table.

As the train finally pulled out of the station the first game ended and one of the men scooped up all the money. The winner of that game noticed that Bob was looking on and invited him to join them.

By the time the train had reached its first stop Bob had won two games and was already two pounds up. They all agreed to increase the stakes and were now putting in pound notes rather than coins. Slowly at first and then more rapidly Bob was losing money and so when they suggested putting the bets up to five pounds it seemed like a chance to get some money back.

As the train slowed down on the approach to Victoria Bob was gambling his last five pounds, needing to use his last few coins to make the total. He lost again.

The following evening he joined Benjy with his friends at the pub and as business was slow Reg joined them as well. Bob told the story of his day at the races. Nobody at the table believed him until he produced the betting slip that he had retrieved from the Bookie.

Benjy couldn't believe that Bob was so cheerful about what had happened on the train and asked him if he had been upset at the time. Bob told them that he thought the men were a pretty decent bunch. After all they had given him back enough for a cup of tea on the station and his fare home.

He suddenly remembered that he had Benjy's winnings in his back pocket. He took out the four pounds and gave them to him and told him which horse he had chosen for him.

Reg started telling Bob that he had been a victim of a gang of card sharks and the others were agreeing. Bob held his hands up to stop them and said "Look sometimes we pay to learn and any way I had a great day, I left in the morning with five pounds and that's what my day out cost me." Benjy said "And it doesn't bother you at all?" "No" said Bob, "It's all just part of life's rich tapestry." "Blimey" said one of the friends, "You should have been a preacher."

"Funny you should say that" said Bob.

Chapter 19

am speaking to you from the Cabinet Room at 10 Downing Street

This morning the British Ambassador in Berlin handed the German Government a final note stating that unless we heard from them by 11 o'clock, that they were prepared at once to withdraw their troops from Poland, a state of war would exist between us.

I have to tell you now that no such undertaking has been received, and that consequently this country is at war with Germany."

Reg had brought the radio downstairs to the bar and they had gathered round to listen. There was Edna of course, and Al had driven Benjy over in the van. Bob had arrived with Angela and several of the pub regulars had been let in.

Neville Chamberlain's speech came to an end and for a minute or so there was silence in the bar. Al was the first to speak saying, "I can't believe that we are at war again, it doesn't seem very long ago that I survived the last one!" That broke the silence and they all started to talk about it. None of them realised at that moment just how much and for how long it would affect their lives.

Over the next three months things changed very quickly for almost everybody. Rationing was coming in and petrol sales were being controlled with essential services taking priority. Clothing, household items and toys were very quickly in short supply and therefore more expensive. Many items of food were now in short supply due to the shipping casualties in the Atlantic and rationing was planned to include almost everything with the exception of vegetables and bread.

Conscription to the armed forces had started in September with 20 and 21 year old single men being 'called up' first. Being thirty-three Bob knew that as things stood he was unlikely to be conscripted for some time as they worked their way up the age range.

There were several things which affected Bob personally in the first three months of the war and they weren't all bad.

The first thing to happen was that Ivor Novello decided to close his show, The Dancing Years, very soon after Chamberlain's declaration of war. This was not what Angela wanted at all but from Bob's point of view it meant that he could see her a great deal more often. In spite of the general gloom they managed to have a lot of fun together.

The shortages of almost everything meant that Benjy's stock was suddenly a great deal more valuable. It was no longer a case of *selling* the stock but more a case of allocating amounts that customers could have and setting the prices. Bob never questioned Benjy about his 'suppliers' but he was aware that often the scarcer that certain items became the more they appeared in the warehouse.

There were more than a few heated discussions between Bob and Benjy with regard to prices. Benjy had a simple view about supply and demand being that the more the demand the higher the price. The way things were going, with shortages of almost everything, his prices were rocketing. Bob was paying Benjy more for everything but he was trying not to pass too much of the increase to his regular customers. In the end he had to put prices up considerably but contented himself with the fact that at least they were getting things that many others were not.

Although he was not likely to be 'called up' for some while yet Bob had thought a great deal about enlisting and had almost made up his mind to do so straight after Christmas. Angela was worried about her parents and planned to go back to Birmingham in the New Year before it became even more difficult to travel. Benjy was having no difficulty in moving his stock and no longer really needed Bob's extra business. There was also the need for Benjy to be keeping a much lower profile when dealing with things in what was now becoming known as the 'black market'

What finally convinced Bob to enlist was the letter from Jim saying that he and the family had moved to Weymouth in Dorset and that he was soon to enlist in the army.

Not knowing what was ahead Bob was determined to have as good a Christmas as he possibly could manage and that meant for all his friends as well.

He got Edna and Angela to work together to decorate the pub. Benjy actually managed to overcome his horror of giving *anything* away and supplied all the decorations free. They had paper chains to glue together and some chains that simply opened up like long concertinas. There were several large col-ourful paper bells that when opened up could be hung from the ceiling.

Bob had succeeded in getting a decent Christmas tree and convinced a grumbling Benjy that 'decorations' included things for the tree. Violet had agreed to be in charge of the food pro-vided that her other two boarders could join them in the pub.

On Christmas Eve morning Bob and Al went off in the van with Violet's shopping list. The tinned and packet things were mostly available from the warehouse and Bob had to pay Benjy who said that as it was Christmas, he was only charging whole-sale prices.

Vegetables were no problem to get at the market but there was noticeably less fruit for sale. Bob managed to get a decent turkey in exchange for some bottles of wine and spirits.

That afternoon he went shopping for presents leaving An-gela with Violet, who was trying to teach her how to pluck the turkey, it was not going well. Reg and Al had become good friends since discovering that they had served in similar roles during the Great War. Together with several invited regulars they were now well into a pre-Christmas drink session as they were calling it.

It was all very strange with the 'black out' making even familiar places hard to recognise. Bob didn't waste any time, getting his gift shopping done as quickly as he could and luck-ily grabbing a taxi to take him back to his lodgings.

Back at Violet's house he wrapped and labelled his pre-sents as best he could. He packed them in his old suitcase and set off to walk back to the pub. It was still only five-thirty but had been dark since he had left Oxford Street an hour or so earlier. In the narrow streets and with no lights on it was even darker as he arrived at the pub.

He knocked on the door in the 'special way' and waited to be let in. He had been aware of someone keeping pace with him on the other side of the street and whoever it was had stopped and was now just standing still looking across at him. Reg opened the door after a few moments and Bob went in quickly. He was about to tell Reg about the person watching him when there was a shout, "Oi you!" Bob looked back. "Get that bloody light out!" Reg closed the door quickly and said, "That's the second time this week, one of our windows wasn't blacked out properly and he shouted at me about that." He went on, "Anybody would think the Germans are going to bomb London!"

Bob took his case through to the back room and put it on top of the cases of whiskey ready to retrieve the next day. Everybody was in the bar and by the looks of them they had all had a bit to drink already.

They had gone overboard with the paper chains and they almost covered the ceiling completely. The tree was decorated tastefully according to Angela. Violet and Edna had put together some food and laid it out buffet style on a side table, the fire had been lit and was burning well. Bob stopped in the doorway and looked at the scene, these were good friends and he was going to miss them all.

Angela came over to him and pulled him into the room. "Come on we've been waiting for you" she said. They had moved the piano further out into the room and it stood there waiting for Bob. He played and they sang and there was plenty to eat and drink. Every so often Bob would take a break from playing and tell them stories about his selling days with Jim which had them all laughing.

Eventually they were all running out of steam, it had been a long day. Reg produced some new sheet music that he had got hold of and gave it to Bob. He played 'We'll Meet Again' and Angela stood by the piano and sang very well. Finally, he played 'There'll Always Be an England' which they all sang at the top of their voices. Violet was shedding some tears now and Bob noticed that Benjy was comforting her.

Bob and Angela left before Violet, Benjy had told them not to worry and he would see her home safely. Angela asked him if Benjy was married and he realised then that, apart from the business, he knew almost nothing about Benjy's life. All the others left and staggered off down the street still singing loudly except for Al who was in no condition to go anywhere. Reg had told them that he would be fine staying there for the night if he needed to.

The next morning Bob and Angela got up quite late and, finding themselves alone in the house, they left and strolled arm in arm to the pub. They were surprised to find that almost all of those from last night were already back sitting in the bar chatting. The smell of the turkey cooking was drifting through the pub and making Bob feel quite hungry.

Violet came down and said good morning to them and asked them if they had slept well and had they eaten anything? She seemed to have extended her maternal concern to include Angela. They assured her that they could hold out until Christmas dinner was ready.

"Has anybody seen Benjy this morning?" asked Bob.

"He's upstairs helping Violet with the vegetables, that's why I'm down here, I've been ousted from my own kitchen" said Edna, smiling at Violet who was off upstairs again.

Benjy peeling vegetables! Thought Bob, well it just goes to show, you think you know someone but you really don't.

Violet shouted that the meal would be ready in ten minutes and they all got busy putting tables together and laying out the settings. Reg and Edna didn't have enough plates or cutlery and apparently Benjy and Violet had bought some with them this morning.

Bob was surprised and mouthed at Angela, "Violet and Benjy arrived together" She laughed and said quietly, "Well they are grown-ups."

They all sat down to eat. There was eleven of them and once the frenzy of making sure everybody had everything it went quiet as they all enjoyed the food. As far as Bob was concerned Violet had worked a miracle. How she had produced a full Christmas dinner, well cooked and served hot for that many people was beyond him.

When they had finished eating Bob proposed a toast to Violet for a wonderful meal and they all raised their glasses to her. She was very embarrassed and said they shouldn't forget that Benjy had helped. She couldn't have done it without him she said, while resting her hand on his shoulder.

Angela said that she and Bob would wash up and they went upstairs to the kitchen, only then seeing the enormity of the task ahead. They had just about finished and were stacking Violet's plates and cutlery separately when Reg called up the stairs, "The king is about to start his speech."

Reg had set the radio up on the bar as usual when there was anything important on. They all gathered round to listen.

Taking a few deep breaths, he began to speak, slowly yet solidly. Measuring his words carefully, King George VI began his speech.

"A new year is at hand. We cannot tell what it will bring. If it brings peace, how thankful we shall all be. If it brings us continued struggle we shall remain undaunted."

As he neared the end of his speech he said.

"I feel that we may all find a message of encouragement in the lines which, in my closing words, I would like to say to you:"

His 13-year-old daughter, Princess Elizabeth had given him a poem and he read it.

"I said to the man who stood at the Gate of the Year, 'Give me a light that I may tread safely into the unknown.' And he replied, 'Go out into the darkness, and put your hand into the Hand of God. That shall be better than light, and safer than a known way.'"

He paused and then said

"May that Almighty Hand guide and uphold us all."

Even Bob, not a royalist and with strongly held atheist views, was moved by the speech and they all raised their glasses again.

Later on they exchanged presents, Bob had bought Angela a bracelet in the form of dancers joined together and she had bought him a silver tie pin in the shape of a piano. Before long Bob was on the piano again and the singing started. The pub was not open as such but Reg was not turning away the few people that came in and everybody sang and drank until after midnight.

Although it had not been planned everybody seemed to have decided to go their separate ways on Boxing Day. Benjy was going to show Violet the warehouse and then on to his house. Reg and Edna were going to visit Reg's sister in the East End and had invited Al to go with them.

Bob and Angela decided to spend the morning in his room then go and find something to eat followed by the rest of the day in his room. Angela was leaving for Birmingham the next day so they were going to spend as much time together as they could.

Later that night he put Angela in a taxi to go back to her lodgings. She didn't want him to see her off in the morning, saying that it would be easier to say goodbye now. They promised to keep in touch but they knew really that this was most probably the end.

The next day Bob walked to the shop for a newspaper. He had lost all sense of the days and was surprised to find that it was Wednesday. He was constantly surprised at how he, and almost everyone else, had just got used to carrying their gas masks everywhere. Air raid sirens had become commonplace and people were beginning to just ignore them.

Everything seemed a bit flat after the last few days which he had enjoyed so much but, never one to dwell on things, Bob started to organise things in readiness for his enlistment. He knew where the recruitment place was but beyond that he had no idea where he would be going or what he would be doing.

He spent the rest of the day making sure that he had said goodbye to everyone. Back at his lodgings he wrote a brief letter to Jim letting him know what he was up to.

Violet had not been around at all. He was a bit concerned and went off to see if she had turned up at the pub. Apparently she had popped in for a quick drink with Benjy earlier and they were both going on to the warehouse.

At the warehouse he found Violet sitting at the desk. She was on the phone and obviously taking an order from someone. Benjy was loading boxes into his van and whistling cheerfully out of tune while doing it. Bob had never heard him whistle before and for anyone who knew Benjy, *cheerful* was not the first word that came to mind.

Violet finished taking the order and put the phone down as Benjy came over and joined her. It was then that Bob understood that in just the last few days they had become a couple. *Perhaps this is what happened in wartime* he thought. He was also quite pleased to think that he was the one that had brought them together, albeit unwittingly.

He said goodbye to Benjy who said "It won't be long before we are back in the old routine, and anyway you'll be back here on leave before you know it" he paused and then, "You will come back here won't you?" Bob said "Of course, where else?"

Violet said she ought to get back to the house and start getting a meal ready. She still had her two boarders and, taking Bob's arm she said, "You will need feeding as well."

As they walked back together, she told Bob that Benjy was going to move in with her in a couple of days. She explained to Bob that she had an Anderson air raid shelter in her back garden and there wasn't enough room for Benjy to have one put in at his house so it was best if he stayed at her house. Bob was laughing and said "Absolutely, that's a good reason to move in with somebody." Violet laughed with him and punched him on the arm saying, "You are a cheeky boy."

In all the time he had been in Norwood he had, for some reason, avoided going anywhere near what had been Braithwaite's Estate Agency shop. Now, as he was soon to leave for what was an uncertain future, he decided to at least have a walk past the shop.

He walked past quickly, glancing in the window as he went by. There was a woman sat at the desk and he caught a glimpse of two boys sitting to one side.

Walking on for a short way he told himself that he was being stupid and turned around to go back. He would go into the shop and ask the woman about Lucy and, of course, Trevor and his father Rudolph.

He was almost inside the shop when he realised that the woman was Lucy. It had been around eight years since Bob had seen her last and was shocked at how she appeared to have aged. Her hair was darker than he recalled and hung straight down to her shoulders and her faced was lined with worry. The only things that hadn't changed at all were her eyes, dark brown with the sort of distant look that had so appealed to him when he first met her.

She came round the desk to meet him and said, "Did you just walk by going the other way?" Bob told her he had. "Plucking up the courage to come in and see me eh?" she was smiling at him now. He didn't say that he hadn't recognised her and just said "Yes, you're right."

One of the boys had stood up while they were talking and Lucy said to him, "You remember Bob don't you?" "I think so" said the boy, who Bob now realised was Thomas. They shook hands rather formally and Thomas said "I'm thirteen and I take care of mum now".

The other younger boy was still sitting down and was engrossed in a book. Lucy said "That's George, he's very studious" Bob said hello but there was no response.

Over the next hour or so they swapped their stories. Lucy was surprised at how far he had travelled only to end up back in Norwood and so close to where he had been when they were 'together' as she put it.

Lucy told Bob a very sad story. Almost four years ago Rudolph had received a letter from his sister in Germany asking him if he could help her and her husband to leave. He wrote back straight away saying he would help and asking what he should do but heard nothing in reply. After three months without any news he decided to go to their home town in Germany himself and bring them back.

In spite of all Trevor's efforts and those of the British Embassy in Berlin nothing had been heard of Rudolph since his departure and there was no trace of any of his family.

Lucy had persuaded Trevor not to go to Germany but he continued to try everything possible to locate his father but without success. He enlisted as soon as war was declared and apart from a short delay caused by his German descent, he was posted to somewhere, the whereabouts of which Lucy had no idea.

"So here I am running the business, such as it is now. We've already sold four of the other branches for what we could get and this one will have to go soon." Lucy spread her hands on the desk, "So there you are, all up to date." Bob would have liked to have stayed and talked longer but he had to go.

He stood up to leave and Lucy came to stand next to him, "I wonder if we could have ever..." she trailed off not finishing. "It was a pity that you didn't come to the wedding but I know it was very quick after we...." she trailed off again. "Rudolph insisted that we get married before the bump showed too much," she looked fondly at George. "Bad enough with Trevor marrying a gentile without my condition adding to it," she said.

Lucy gave Bob a hug and Thomas shook his hand. As Bob was halfway through the door George finally stood up to say goodbye. He was a slim boy and rather tall for his eight years. As he turned to go back to his seat he shook his thick black hair away from his eyes.

Chapter 20

One week later he was on a train with about thirty other men heading north to a place he had never heard of for what the recruiting officer had described as 'knocking into shape.'

He couldn't believe how quickly it had all happened. Only a day after he had walked into the recruiting office, he found himself standing naked in a curtained cubicle waiting for his medical.

As he waited he had noticed that the eye test chart was on the wall just outside the cubicle and he started to memorise the last two lines of letters and the maker's name which was in very small print along the bottom. After a time, he could close his eyes and visualise the letters and maker's name. He had no idea why he had done that and certainly no idea that he was going to use it on his eye test, but that's what happened.

He was called and went across to the Doctor who looked into his mouth, held a stethoscope to his chest for about two seconds, tapped his knees with a little hammer and finally grunted "Reasonably healthy."

The last thing was the eye test and Bob stood on the line and was told to read down as far as he could. By this time the

Doctor was sitting at his desk writing, presumably that he had passed the examination and appearing to pay no attention to what Bob was reading. He read down as far as he could and then, seeing that the Doctor was still not paying attention, continued with the memorised letters ending up by 'reading' the maker's name.

There was a pause and the Doctor looked up from writing. He looked at the chart then looked at Bob. "Just read the bottom line again would you" he asked. Bob was going to own up at that point but looking at the Doctors serious face he decided not to. He reeled off the row of letters and innocently asked the Doctor if that was correct?

The Doctor went to the chart and pointing to various letters he asked Bob what they were and Bob answered correctly. Finally, he pointed to the chart makers name and Bob 'read' it for him. "Remarkable" said the Doctor, "Never seen anything like it!" He went back to his desk and wrote for a minute or two more before telling Bob that his was 'fit to serve' and calling the next man.

Bob chuckled to himself at the memory of the Doctor's face but soon forgot that as, having arrived on the station platform they were soon formed up and marched off two miles to the camp.

They were split into groups and allocated their huts. Inside the huts there were three bunk beds down each side and very little else. Bob made for a bunk in the middle of the hut and threw his case on the top one. Over the next few minutes there were a few scuffles and heated words as some of the men argued over which bunk they wanted.

No sooner had they dropped their stuff on the bunks than they were called outside and given knives forks and spoons and sent off to get some food. They queued up with a lot of others and eventually got to the point where food was thrown onto their plates.

There was no hanging around as others were coming in and they quickly went and found a table, actually three planks of wood resting on two trestles. Without discussion the new arrivals had obviously decided to stick together and the twelve of them managed to get round the table. The re-constituted potato was tasteless and the unidentified meat needed a fair bit of chewing, Bob was already missing Violet's meals.

Some introductions were managed and it seemed that they all came from roughly the same part of London. There was a lot questioning amongst them about who knew which road or shop or business but Bob kept quiet. He would keep knowledge of Benjy's place to himself.

On his right there was a smallish man called Charlie who nudged him every time he spoke, Bob made a mental note not to sit next to Charlie again. To his left there was a smartly dressed man who introduced himself as Edward, the man on his other side said "Hi Eddie." The reply was "I didn't say my name was Eddie, I said Edward." *I suppose we'll all sort ourselves out soon* thought Bob.

They had hardly finished eating when a large, red faced man in uniform came to their 'table' and shouted "Come on you lot, time to get you measured up!" As they filed out Bob turned to the man and said "I've got my measurements all written down if that helps at all?" The man looked at him as if he was speaking a foreign language.

"What's your name son?"

"Bob"

"No its not" said the man, the others had stopped to listen.

"Yes it's definitely Bob" The man had now moved very close to Bob and said quietly,

"I'm not going to have trouble with you am I, now what is your name?"

"Chaloner?" said Bob. "You asking me or telling me?" said the man.

Bob was thinking this was all madness but said "It's Chaloner." Turning theatrically to the others, the man said loudly "I think he's got it!" and pointing at Charlie he said "What's your name lad?" "Wilkins" said Charlie. "See it's easy; now get yourselves over there to be kitted out."

The store was housed in what looked like a giant version of the camp huts. They filed past a counter where the man behind the counter just looked each of them up and down and called a size to another man.

The second man piled everything up on the end of the counter for each of them to pick up. It was quite a pile and included two battle dress uniforms, an overcoat, two pairs of boots and a rifle and bayonet plus all the other bits they would need as soldiers. On top of the pile was their working uniform which they were told to put on in the morning, Reveille was at six.

As soon as they had got to their hut the man from earlier was back. "Right" he bellowed, "It's my misfortune to have been given the job of turning you lot into soldiers." He ordered them to stand up and pay attention as he introduced himself.

He was Sergeant Barkinshaw but he explained to them that they would just be calling him sergeant. He asked them to practice by saying it all together, yes sergeant, no sergeant. They were instructed in the rules of the camp, about 'lights out' and about the washing facilities. Once he had gone they all agreed it was like being back in school, or worse.

The 'shower block' was actually just a hut with water tanks above which would sometimes provide a trickle of cold water for showering and the same at the sinks. As with the rest of his section Bob became very adept at showering really quickly with the minimum of water.

He studied the way things were organised around washing and breakfasting and could see a much better way in which this could be done and couldn't wait to see what Sergeant Barkinshaw thought.

They next morning after the hut inspection, they had done rather well for a change, he took what he thought was the ideal opportunity to speak to the sergeant.

"Excuse me sergeant, I've had some thoughts on how things are done in the mornings."

Bob was about to continue when Sergeant Barkinshaw, who had been about to leave, turned and strode back to stand in front of Bob. Their noses were almost touching and the sergeant seemed to Bob as though he was shaking slightly.

"You can explain your ideas to me all day long today, the only thing is I might not be able to hear you. Do you know why that is?"

"No sergeant" said Bob.

"Well that's because I will be drilling the rest of this section but you will be cleaning the latrines."

The sergeant walked to door and then turned and said "Report there now private, and don't forget to share your ideas with the toilet bowls will you."

Ten minutes later Bob was equipped with a mop and bucket plus all the other things he would need in order to be a toilet cleaner.

After a day in the latrines Bob decided that he would have to curb his desire to discuss things with the sergeant. And for the next three days in spite of everything that the sergeant threw at him he managed to keep quiet.

As the weeks went by they were becoming hardened to the tough regime and were not even minding the cold as much as they had. Bob was actually feeling quite cheerful as he, along with the rest of the section, had mastered much of what was being drilled into them. This morning he was last to get back from the wash house and seeing a couple of his mates as he started up the steps to the hut he called out, "I wonder what Sergeant Barking mad has in store for us today?"

The two lads in the doorway parted to reveal Sergeant Barkinshaw standing there shaking his head.

For the whole of the next morning Bob peeled hundreds of potatoes and in the afternoon he cleaned pots and pans until they shone like mirrors.

Bob was thinking that this would have Hitler shivering in his boots!

It was nearing the end of their fourth week and they finally been given an easier day with a chance to relax for a few hours. Bob was enjoying a game of cards with three others when a corporal came in and shouted for him. He was given orders to report to the Colonel at seven in the morning with all his kit.

This was a bit worrying as he was convinced that it was something to do with his behaviour with the sergeant.

The next morning he reported to the colonel's office as ordered but was told to wait outside with the others and they would be collected shortly. There were five others waiting and none of them knew what was going on. They had all come from different sections, two of them from a different camp entirely!

Eventually an officer came for them and the six of them were marched off to a different area of the camp. They were shown their new quarters which were luxurious compared with where they had been. There were six beds, not bunks, and at the back of the hut was a stove. The officer told them to get settled in and someone would be along to talk to them soon.

Once they had made some introductions, they tried to figure out what they were all there for but they couldn't work it out at all. Later a sergeant came to see them and told them what they would be doing the next day. It turned out not to be a great deal more than going to the canteen to eat and coming back.

Around mid morning the sergeant came into their hut and ordered them to attention. The officer who had collected them the day before arrived shortly afterwards and told them to stand at ease. He explained why they were there and what they would be doing.

The officer told them that at their medical examination anything that was above the normal level such as physical stature or musculature or faculties would be noted by the doctor and included with their records. In their case it was exceptional eyesight and so they had been 'volunteered' to be trained for special duties. He didn't go into exactly what those 'special' duties would be except for the fact that they would require in-volve intensive rifle training.

Now Bob understood the effect of his nonsense with the eye test and was thinking that he really should come clean. He decided not to on the basis that so far everything he had said to Sergeant Barkinshaw other than yes or no had resulted in a punishment. Why would speaking to an officer be any different?

It didn't matter anyway because the officer had abruptly finished speaking and left. The sergeant stepped forward and informed them that he was their instructor and training would start in the morning and then he also left.

There was an air of excitement in the hut that evening with them all wondering what was in store for them after training, except for Bob who was wondering what was in store for him during the training!

The next day was a disappointment as they were all up and ready for action at seven but all that happened was that they were given lots of material to read. One part was all about an-gles of fire, wind deflection and many other things that they didn't understand. The second part was about the use and maintenance of a rifle which was not the one that they were issued with.

Apart from some enforced PT in the morning the next day was going along the same way until late in the afternoon when the sergeant arrived with two soldiers carrying a large crate and struggling to keep up with him. They were ordered to go inside their hut and stand by their beds with their rifles.

Their rifles were swapped for the ones that had been in the crate and the sergeant said, "Right you lucky boys, You now have in your hands the Lee-Enfield No 4 Rifle Mark one." He paused, looking from one to the other, presumably to make sure that they were pleased. "Nobody else in this camp has one of these, familiarise yourselves with it because you'll be using it tomorrow."

They did as they were ordered and spent time examining and handling their new rifles. The rifles were heavier and had a slightly longer barrel than the old ones but they all agreed that they seemed to be an improvement. They were actually brand new, which was an improvement in itself.

The next morning they were all instructed in the handling and maintenance of their new rifles. It was very repetitive and went on for hours. Finally, in the afternoon they were taken to the firing range and issued with live ammunition.

This was to be a little different to the normal sessions they were told by the sergeant. Firstly, they would be the only ones on the range and secondly, they would have markers to indicate where they had hit the targets. After each group of shots, the markers would move from the sides of the targets and indicate with what looked like small white table tennis bats.

They were called forward one at a time to their places on the line and shown how to correctly adopt the position for prone shooting. After some more advice from their instructor about the sights on their rifles they began to shoot at the targets.

After a while and with encouragement from the sergeant they were all starting to score very well, all that is except for Bob, who so far in spite of much coaching had yet to hit a target at all!

Bob was relieved when finally the sergeant called a halt to the practice and they returned to the camp. The others chatted excitedly about their success at the range, nobody seemed aware of how badly Bob had done and the sergeant had made no comment at all.

The next day they were back at the range and were told that today they would be shooting from prone, kneeling and standing positions. Bob was moved from his position at the end of the line to a place near the centre.

Having shown remarkable restraint up to now the sergeant finally called Bob away from the line and yelled at him, "Do you realise that so far you have only hit a target once and that wasn't yours!" he took a breath, "And that's not all, I moved you from the end of the line because yesterday you nearly shot one of the markers and now, even with you in the centre they are refusing to go anywhere near if you are even on the range!"

"Can you even see the targets?" he asked.

"Only just" said Bob.

"What!"

"I can only just make out where they are," Bob had decided that he needed to stop the farce.

The sergeant was more puzzled than annoyed now, "But you're here because you have exceptional eyesight" he said.

"I know that" said Bob. He was wondering where this would go next but was certainly not going to make any admissions to the sergeant.

"It seems that you may have developed a problem, I'm going to arrange for you to see the M.O in the morning for an examination"

"Thank you, sergeant" said Bob.

Chapter 21

After his second examination in as many months Bob was pronounced physically fit and all that remained was the eye test. He read confidently down to the fourth line of letters on the chart and then started to struggle. The Medical officer pointed to various letters nearer the bottom of the chart of which Bob identified none at all.

The M.O spoke seriously, "I have never witnessed such a rapid deterioration in eyesight, in only a few weeks you have gone from having exceptional eyesight to the point of almost needing spectacles." Bob tried to look suitably concerned, the M.O continued. "You must report it if your eyesight gets any worse, I have to say that I am most concerned. In all other respects you are fitter than you were at your last examination which makes it a real puzzle."

He was told to return to his quarters and await further orders. When the others returned from their exercises he told them what had happened at his 'medical' and they were very sympathetic. He was embarrassed but thought it wise not to tell them what had really happened.

The following day he was ordered back to his original section where he was greeted warmly by everyone, even 'call me

Edward' put an arm on his shoulder and seemed genuinely pleased to see him. He gave them the edited version of what had happened but any sympathy they might have shown was cut short by the arrival of Sergeant Barkinshaw.

"Private Chaloner!" yelled the sergeant. Bob did something then that surprised him, the rest of the section and, not least Sergeant Barking mad. He stood perfectly to attention and snapped off a smart salute, looking straight ahead he said loudly "sergeant!" There was complete silence for several seconds after which the sergeant simply turned and left the hut.

Charlie Wilkins was the first to start laughing, "Oh dear Edward, if Bob is going to act like that you might be keeping your position as the Sergeant's favourite victim." Now Bob understood why Edward had been so welcoming.

The last two weeks of basic training were very intense and several times Bob noticed Sergeant Barkinshaw staring at him suspiciously but they went by without incident. They were all given orders and travel documents to get to the next stage of training with their actual regiments. In Bob's case this was now the Royal Engineers. He had no idea why. He was happy enough as he had a few days leave before reporting for duty at a camp just south of London.

On the train heading back to London Bob enjoyed reading the newspaper and occasionally listening to the talk in the carriage, the subject was always the war or lack of it mostly. They hadn't been given much news in the training camp and newspapers had not been available very often.

According to the newspaper it seemed that nothing much was happening. British soldiers were being kept busy by digging defences on the border between France and Belgium. On the back page there were a few lines about some ships sunk by mines in the Atlantic. Bob was wondering if he might have been a bit hasty in enlisting when he had.

Arriving at Euston station he was struck by how quiet it was, the last time he had arrived there it had been bustling with all sorts of people. The vast majority of passengers getting off the train were soldiers carrying their kit bags as he was. There were only a few people waiting and the train that he had arrived on was the only one in the station.

Bob was pleased to find a taxi on the rank outside the station and throwing his kit bag in the back he climbed in after it. He couldn't decide who to see first so he said to the cabby "Norwood High Street please." The cabby looked back at him and said, "Sorry soldier, I can't go that far, I only have enough fuel left for a few more local runs today." Bob offered to pay for some more fuel but the cabby explained that he had used his allowance and that was that.

He climbed back out of the cab and set off to the bus stop. The first bus that came along was packed to the point that people were standing on the open platform with the conductor squashed in behind them, no one got off and it pulled away. The next one was pretty much the same but this time the conductor shouted "Come on ladies and gents make room for a soldier!" He got on, pushing his kit bag ahead of him and for the next few stops he hung precariously onto the rail just inches from the edge of the platform until finally a few people got off and there was more room. The conductor made no effort to collect his fare or give him a ticket.

Bob got off the bus in Norwood High Street and decided to go and see Benjy. As he walked towards the warehouse he passed several people, some of whom he knew vaguely, they all seemed relaxed and happy and most of them smiled and nodded at him, he assumed it was the uniform.

Bob had found out earlier in the day that fuel was a problem which explained why the roads were a bit quieter than usual. He already knew that food rationing, now including meat, was making life harder for everyone but as he looked around him on this sunny and quite warm March afternoon there was nothing really to show that the country was at war.

When he arrived at the warehouse it was almost as though time had stood still since he had left in January. Violet was on the telephone taking an order and Benjy was loading some boxes onto the van.

The moment that Violet noticed him she just put the phone receiver down on the desk and rushed through the door to give him a huge and prolonged hug. Once she had let go of him Benjy took over, giving him a hug and then holding him at arm's length with a big grin on his face. Bob was a little overcome with the warmth of their greeting and it made him realise how close they had all become since his arrival in the area.

They started to tell Bob their news but became aware of a tinny sounding voice saying "Hello, hello." Violet went to the desk and picked up the receiver and said "Something important has cropped up, you'll have to ring back later" and then just hung up. They all burst out laughing. Once they had stopped Benjy carried on with their news which was that he and Violet were to be married.

Bob congratulated them and was surprised to find out that the wedding was in a week's time. Violet said that there was no point in waiting, they already lived together and anyway who knew what would happen in the future with another war started?

It was getting late in the afternoon and Bob wanted to see Reg and Edna so Benjy locked up and they all walked round to the pub. On the way Bob asked about Al and Benjy told him that he only needed help on one or two days a week but Al was finding odd jobs here and there and was making out ok. Apparently Reg and Al had become firm friends since the Christmas get together and Al was helping out behind the bar when needed.

His arrival at the pub was similar to his arrival at the warehouse with both Reg and Edna giving him a hug. Edna suggested that they all stay for a meal before the pub opened and once they had established that there really was enough food, they all agreed. Violet and Edna went off upstairs to start cooking leaving Bob, Benjy and Reg to catch up with 'non wedding' news.

Benjy was concerned about the level of stock in his warehouse saying that even his 'suppliers' were finding it harder to get hold of some things and when they did the prices were double or more than even three months ago. Reg was finding that spirits were in short supply and getting expensive except of course what was still stacked up in the back room. Fortunately beer was plentiful and, so far anyway, was still a relatively cheap drink.

Bob had waited until they were all together again before he told them of his experiences in the army which had them laughing all through the meal, especially when he told them what had happened because of the eye test. Violet told him he was a "Very naughty boy" and made him promise to be careful what he got up to in the future. This was not the same Violet that had 'preyed' on him when he first arrived at her house and he was touched by her obvious and genuine concern for him.

The evening went by quickly and, as he had hoped, he was able to stay at Violet's house. His room was exactly as it had been when he left. What was very different was that there were no boarders now and when he went down to breakfast it was just him and Benjy. Violet served them and then finally joined them with her own breakfast.

They were disappointed that he was not able to be there for their wedding but they understood that he would not be able to get leave for it, "As they were not actually family" Violet said, sniffing and reaching for a handkerchief.

Bob decided to get a nice wedding present for them and leave it with Reg to give to them on the day.

He had to repack everything in his kit bag to make sure that the four bottles of whiskey were safely in the middle. He had asked Benjy if he could buy a bottle to take with him and then had *four* bottles forced on him with no charge, there would have been more but for the fact that he couldn't fit them in his bag!

He left Violet and Benjy at mid morning and seeing a taxi cab coming along he stuck his arm out. He was surprised when it pulled up and the cabby asked "Where to guv?" He took the taxi the short distance to the bank and asked the driver if he could wait and then take him on to the shops. "You forgotten me already?" asked the driver. Bob looked at him again and realised it was the driver who had driven him around so much last year, even helping him to deliver stock on a couple of occasions.

He chatted with the driver as they went to the bank, "I remember taking you to the theatre with that couple from the shop." He chatted on about things they had done and Bob realised that he hadn't thought about his customers and friends Anne and Michael at all. He felt a bit guilty about that as they had been responsible for starting what was a very happy time for him, albeit quite short. Perhaps he would look them up when he came back next time.

He was in and out of the bank as quickly as he could and off to the shops where he paid the cabby and said that he hoped to see him when he came back on leave. The cabby wished him luck. After a bit of indecision, he finally bought a rather expensive mantle clock and arranged for it to be packaged and delivered to Benjy and Violet on the day of their wedding, for which he paid quite a bit extra.

With the wedding present taken care of it was time for him to think about getting to the barracks. He wasn't actually due to report until the morning but thought it would be wise to get there the evening before. It proved to be surprisingly easy, getting another taxi to the station and boarding a train almost immediately.

The train was full of soldiers, all apparently heading for the same destination. He vaguely recognised some faces from the training camp but nobody seemed in the mood for talking and it was, thankfully, a fairly short journey to the station nearest the barracks.

There was a line of four Lorries waiting outside the station and a corporal was checking paperwork and pointing men to the one they should climb on to. By the time Bob got to the lorry the benches running down each side were full so he went back to the corporal to tell him but as he got there he noticed that men were getting on and standing between the full benches, he turned round to go back but too late. "Is there a problem private!?" yelled the corporal. *For crying out loud, not again,* thought Bob. "No corporal, no problem" he said and marched quickly away towards the lorry.

They reached the barracks and just like at the training camp they were split into groups, this time in groups of twelve, and allocated quarters in one of the many huts. Bob just went to the first available bed and put his kit bag down next to it and sat down, most of the others did the same. The huts were much more substantial than the ones at the training camp and there were beds not bunks so the comfort level had improved.

It was as Bob started to unpack his kitbag that he realised that he had a problem. He had four bottles of whiskey in his bag and nowhere to put them out of sight.

After giving it some thought, and being conscious of the rather despondent atmosphere in the hut, he decided that the best thing to do was to be open about the whiskey. Producing a bottle from his kitbag he held it up and said "Anyone for a drop of the hard stuff?" That broke the sombre mood and tin cups were soon clinking together and lots of introductions followed by "Cheers."

Bob noticed that not everybody had come over for a whiskey, two of their group were sat together on the end bed deep in conversation and had not joined in the introductions at all. Initially he was a bit concerned but then thought well, it was up to them wasn't it? He gave it no more thought.

That evening the group split up with five playing a noisy game of cards and the rest chatting about where they had come from and what they thought might be ahead. Fred and Ginger as they had already been christened, one of them did in fact have very red hair, kept apart from the others and appeared to be reading a book together.

The next day they were pretty much left to their own devices and found out where the shower block was and importantly where the food was served, or as one of the lads said, where it was thrown at their plates. Towards the end of the day a corporal came to see them and introduced himself as Tony Lewis, he was a tall thin man with sharp, rather hawkish features and his uniform seemed to be hung on him rather than him wearing it. He told them that he would be in charge of them as a section and then explained that today had been all about lots of new recruits arriving and settling in but tomorrow, they would begin training again in earnest.

Before he left, he signalled Bob to follow him outside. They moved a short distance from the hut and then the corporal said "It's Bob isn't it?" "Yes corporal" replied Bob. "It's Tony when we are not in earshot of the sergeant" he continued, "Look, none of us really want to be doing this and if it wasn't for the war I would still be running my dad's shop in Bognor, just have to make the best of it though, don't you agree?" *'Small world'* thought Bob, wondering where this was going.

"It has been brought it to my attention that you have been sharing some whiskey around the section"

"You do know that bringing alcohol into the camp is an offence I suppose."

"I'm not sure" said Bob.

"Well let me tell you that it most definitely is," he carried on, "Worse than that though is bringing alcohol into the camp and not making sure that your corporal gets to enjoy some of it, that can bring some real trouble," he laughed.

"Ah, I see" said Bob. Something about the way the corporal was speaking was making him uncomfortable. On the surface Corporal Tony Lewis seemed friendly enough but Bob had the feeling he was being drawn into something.

He went and got one of his three remaining bottles of whiskey, took it outside and gave it to the corporal. "Thank you very much, most unexpected" said the corporal, "Nothing stays secret very long in an army camp you know, it's all about choosing your friends really. Sergeant Collins and I will enjoy this very much." "It's my pleasure" said Bob drily. Corporal Lewis looked him sternly and holding up the bottle he said, "I know that these days you don't just get bottles of whiskey like this without having some connections."He emphasised the last word. "Might be useful for us both in the future eh?"

Bob knew that Benjy had only meant well in giving him the whiskey but he was thinking now that it might be the cause of some problems for him. He would just have to see how it worked out.

As Bob went back into the hut he noticed the two non drinkers staring at him and then looking away quickly, getting back to their private conversation. He was now pretty sure who had been speaking to the corporal about the whiskey. There wasn't too much time for Bob to think about Fred and Ginger's sneaky behaviour as not ten minutes later a sergeant burst through the door and yelled at them to come to attention!

They didn't do too bad getting to the end of their beds and standing to attention. The sergeant strode up and down, he was short, rather overweight and had a rolling walk which had one or two of them leaning backwards as he passed. Seemingly satisfied he said "You horrible lot are part of my platoon and you will not let me down in any way. Do you all understand? "Yes sergeant" was the immediate response from all of them. Bob thought *we've all had the same indoctrination.* "At ease," they all breathed again.

"I'm making a small change in this section" said the sergeant. "Davies and Seymore where are you?" 'Fred' and 'Ginger' both stepped forward. "Right, get your kit together, you two are moving to 'B' section." They began to repack their kitbags, "At the double!" shouted the sergeant, "Corporal Lewis will show you to your new quarters." They went outside where the corporal was waiting. Bob was pretty sure that he and the rest of the section had just met Sergeant Collins.

A few minutes after 'Fred' and 'Ginger' had left the hut their replacements arrived. "Hello all, I'm Charlie and this 'ere streak of piss is Eddie." "My name is Edward" said the other man. They spotted Bob and the three of them were laughing and greeting each other like old friends. Somehow the arrival of Charlie and 'Call me Edward' seemed to have instantly cheered up the whole section.

The next day training started again and they were back to drilling, marching and daily physical training. The weather had worsened and it rained often making everything more unpleasant especially the assault course which they were struggling round every other day.

They all got on well together and that helped morale a lot. Bob had found himself the sort of 'father' of the section. He had no wish for any kind of position whether unofficial or otherwise but his avuncular manner, and apparent influence with Corporal Lewis (another bottle had changed hands), had made him the 'one.' They were now trying to make Bob's last bottle stretch as far as they could.

Chapter 22

It had begun a few weeks earlier but now the pain in Bob's toe joint was now excruciating. At first it would just be a bit painful after a march or some extended drilling but lately it had worsened to the point that he was losing sleep and the others had noticed him suffering. He really didn't want to report it but eventually he was persuaded by the lads to at least tell Corporal Lewis.

He was surprised by the corporal's reaction which was to immediately arrange for him to see the M.O and even more surprised to receive orders to report to the medical block on the following day at 3pm.

Early the next morning they were formed up with several other platoons and then they marched for fifteen minutes to a muddy field with what looked like an old farmhouse in the middle. A major exercise was being held with some platoons staging mock attacks on the old building and others defending it.

They were part of the 'attack' and Sergeant Collins was determined that they would perform well, yelling new instructions for Corporal Lewis to pass on every few seconds until in the end they all just ignored them completely just and plunged on, crossing a foot deep stream and 'fighting' their way through the mud towards the house.

This went on and on with them alternately 'attacking' and then 'defending' the farmhouse. It had passed lunchtime and Bob had tried several times to speak to Sergeant Collins about his appointment with the M.O but without success, Corporal Lewis seemed to have disappeared completely.

Eventually, with only thirty minutes before he was due to be at the medical block, he forced himself in front of the sergeant came to attention and said loudly "Permission to be excused Sergeant!" He produced his now very muddy piece of paper and showed it to the sergeant. The sergeant read what was on the paper and said to anyone that was listening "Stop the battle immediately! Private Chaloner has to see the M.O! Just a moment Mr Hitler one of my men isn't feeling well!" Bob just walked away.

He was covered in mud plus some other substances from the field and his feet were still soaked from wading the stream several times. With only twenty minutes or so to get cleaned up he raced back to camp as fast as he could. There was one benefit of his feet being so wet and cold, at least he wasn't feeling any pain from his toe joint.

Rushing into the hut he grabbed some clean socks and shoes and then, realising that he would not now have time to clean up properly, he decided to just wash his feet and put on the clean socks. This was tricky, standing on one foot with other foot in the sink and time was going fast. It was now two minutes to three and he had to get from the hut to the medical block yet. *I've got the foot clean* he thought, *that will have to do,* and so he put a clean sock on that foot and rushed off to see the M.O.

Having had the importance of obeying orders drummed into him for the last twelve weeks Bob had done everything he could to get to the M.O on time but now he was sat waiting and had been for some time.

He was inwardly fuming at being kept waiting, after the nonsense from Sergeant Collins and the effort he had made to get here as ordered it was just not right! As usual shortly after doing any exercise his foot was starting to become painful and it was then that it dawned on him that he had washed the wrong foot.

There was just no possibilty that Bob was going to show the M.O a dirty smelly foot, he would be too embarrassed. The Doctor was finally ready for him and after reading some notes asked Bob to remove his shoes and socks, Bob told him it was just the one foot and he impatiently said "Well just show me that one, I haven't got all day" He examined the foot, asking Bob to move his toes and questioning him about exactly where the pain was and when it came on.

He returned to the hut in time to meet the others coming back. They were very bedraggled and obviously worn out. Joining them as they all got cleaned up and changed he heard that they had all performed well and were having a day off from anything physical the next day.

They were keen to know how he had got on with the M.O and he told them what had happened. None of them could believe that he let the doctor examine the wrong foot. "He must have seen thousands of dirty feet before" said Charlie, "and smelly," said 'Call me Edward' turning his nose up as if he could smell them now. "Well not mine" said Bob. They wanted to know what the Doctor had said but apart from hearing something that sounded like *Halex Rigidus* Bob had no idea what was happening, if anything.

It wasn't long before he got the results of his visit to the medical block, not from the M.O though. The following morning he got the news which came via Captain Smith to Sergeant Collins, on to Corporal Lewis and finally to Bob.

The doctor had diagnosed stiff toe joints due to Arthritis and advised that the wearing of standard issue boots would severely aggravate the condition. He concluded that *'this soldier should be excused from wearing the aforesaid boots in order that the condition is not unnecessarily worsened.'* The corporal handed Bob a slip of paper on which all this was written, headed 'to whom it may concern' and signed by the M.O.

"So what does that mean" Bob asked Corporal Lewis. "It means you don't have to wear boots" he replied. "Yes, said Bob but what about marching, what about the assault course?" "Good point" said the corporal, "I'd better find out." Bob was wondering what would have happened if the Doctor had actually examined the foot that had a problem!

Later that day Corporal Lewis came to see Bob with the answer to his question about marching etc. Because he was excused the wearing of boots then regulations would forbid him from taking part in any 'forced marches' and also he would not be allowed to join in any kind of assault course activity. "I'm sorry" said the corporal, "But apparently it's the rules."

Bob wasn't sure if Corporal Lewis was serious in thinking that he would be upset about not doing these things any more. He decided to go along with it and said "Oh dear, I will miss

the assault course." "Mmm.." the corporal was still not smiling,
"Anyway you have to report to the C.O at eight in the morning,
don't be late!"

Chapter 23

He was stood to attention in front of Captain Smith's desk. Several minutes passed while the captain read whatever was in front of him on his desk, a sergeant who had escorted Bob in was standing just behind and to one side. He was beginning to feel like a naughty boy brought up in front of the headmaster. This was just the sort of situation that would have the effect of making him behave in a contrary or belligerent manner and he worked hard to keep himself under control.

Finally, the captain looked up, he was a striking looking man with silver hair neatly combed and parted. He had piercing blue eyes and a moustache that any RAF pilot would have been proud of. "At ease Private." He had the lazy drawl that was so common among the officer class. He dismissed the sergeant, stood up and walked round to the front of the desk where he perched on the edge. He was older than Bob had first thought and had limped as he came round the desk.

"So, you're the fellow with the dodgy feet eh?"

"Dodgy foot sir" said Bob.

"Don't split hairs with me private, or should I say split legs," He found this greatly amusing and spent some moments laughing at his 'joke.' Bob tried to maintain what he hoped was a respectfully amused face.

"Right, so you can't wear boots, is that right?"

"Yes sir"

The captain explained to Bob that in peacetime he would be medically discharged but these were very different times he said. He went on to say that there was a need for drivers, lorry drivers in particular as so much was going on now, especially with the way things were shaping up, he didn't elaborate on how things were 'shaping up'.

"Right, that's settled then, I will have some special duties for you, oh and in future you will report directly to Sergeant Collins. Have you any questions?" "Er, no sir" said Bob, wondering if he should ask about the special duties but deciding against it.

"One more thing before you leave Private," Bob waited.

"You do drive I suppose?"

Bob said yes he did drive, not mentioning that it was years earlier and nothing bigger than a van.

It turned out that 'the way things were shaping up' was that British and French troops were now retreating towards the French coast. German forces had simply bypassed the fortifications on the Maginot Line and pressed on at breakneck speed. With their far superior numbers and equipment it seemed that they were unstoppable.

Germany had invaded Holland, Belgium and Luxemburg, things were looking worse all the time. Bob scanned the papers for some more cheerful news but there just didn't seem to be any.

As far as Bob could see the only slightly positive news was that Neville Chamberlain had been replaced by Winston Churchill as Prime minister and, unlike Chamberlain, he was not in favour of appeasement at all.

The camp was a hive of activity with more men and equipment arriving every day. Rumours circulated several times a day. Sometimes they were all going off to France, other times they were going to defences on the Kent coast but nobody had any idea really and the training went on.

Bob found that almost all the training required the wearing of boots and so, being excused from it, he had quite some time on his own in the hut and used this to write some letters and catch up with some reading. He was learning to drive a lorry and was going out with an instructor twice a day in preparation for a test before being allowed out on his own.

It was a strange time for him with reporting directly to Sergeant Collins while Corporal Lewis was in charge of the section and so he was looking forward to passing his lorry driving 'test' and then, presumably, starting his new role as a driver with 'special duties.'

Only a few days later Bob joined five others in a place where they were to be tested as lorry drivers.

They were called one at a time and with the examiner sat next to them in the cab they were directed round a course. This involved a mixture of reversing, negotiating the lorry into a tight space between two barrels and finally starting on a steep slope. This last part, starting on a slope, was tested by the examiner placing a box of matches three inches behind one of the rear wheels of the lorry. Anyone allowing the lorry to roll back and crush the match box would have to start the training all over again. There were a lot of high revving engines and once or twice the examiner was thrown violently back in his seat but nobody crushed the matchbox.

It was now nearing the end of May and the news from France was very bad. British and French troops were trapped on the beaches at Dunkirk. A huge evacuation was under way with hundreds of boats of all types and sizes going across the Channel to bring thousands of troops back before the over-whelming force of German infantry reached them.

Bob was now part of a column of army lorries picking up men as they arrived back from Dunkirk and transporting them to the designated camps or barracks. Suddenly the war was no longer just something happening elsewhere. It was close and getting closer.

Bob was impressed by how calm and disciplined the return-ing soldiers seemed. Just occasionally there would be a disturb-ance as a man broke down but these were dealt with quickly and in the main things went amazingly smoothly.

For four days Bob was driving to various barracks dropping off soldiers and then returning for more. Sometimes he would hear the men in the back singing but other times he made the whole journey in absolute silence. He supposed that it had to do with their different experiences in getting away from Dun-kirk.

Finally, after bringing some men who were now to be ab-sorbed into his battalion, he was ordered take the lorry to the maintenance section and then report to Captain Smith. He drove round to the maintenance shed where there was a huge assortment of vehicles parked in rows presumably waiting for repair or servicing. Not finding anyone to ask Bob just parked the lorry on the end of one of the rows and walked off back to his quarters. The hut was empty when he got back and he dropped his pack on the floor and lay on his bed. He was pretty tired after four days of almost constant driving and soon fell asleep.

He was awakened by the return of the others and was soon telling them what he had been doing. They wanted to hear what state the men from Dunkirk were in and were surprised at Bob's description of the orderly, and mostly cheerful, lines of men waiting to be returned to their barracks. The mood was dampened when he told them that he had only come into contact with the soldiers that were fit for duty and all of the many wounded were dealt with elsewhere by the Medical Corps.

Sergeant Collins came to see him. Apparently, Bob was to be driving to London the next day and the sergeant thought it would be a good opportunity for him to see his contacts for some more bottles and maybe more. Bob knew what he meant, and said yes, but didn't quite understand how it would work. Sergeant Collins said, "Do you think perhaps you should report to the C.O?" Bob had forgotten that completely!

"At ease Chaloner," Bob was again in front of Captain Smith's desk and again the captain walked round to the front and perched on the edge, it was obviously a habit.

"Nice of you to finally get around to seeing me," he didn't wait for a response.

"Right private, you may recall that I mentioned special duties when we spoke before."

"Yes sir" said Bob.

"At seven in the morning a car will be ready for you to collect from the pool. Be here to pick me up at eight on the dot, you will take me to London, Whitehall actually, and then you will go on to collect some goods for *special delivery*, understood?"

"Yes sir," Bob did understand but decided to have some fun.

"You will return to pick me up at Whitehall at precisely four pm, any questions?"

"Yes sir"

"Right then, that's all Chaloner"

"That was, yes sir, I have some questions"

"What!"

Captain Smith sighed, "Ask then"

"Where do I go to collect the goods and where do I take them?" asked Bob, pretending not to have understood what was wanted.

Captain Smith just stared at Bob for several seconds. "I thought Sergeant Collins had spoken to you about this?"

Bob was enjoying the Captain's obvious discomfort. "I suppose all the details will be on the paperwork, won't they?"

"The sergeant will come and speak to you again later, you are dismissed" said the captain rather sharply.

Bob came to attention and turned to leave, he was thinking that maybe he shouldn't spoil what might turn out to be a good thing for him and so he turned back and said "Sorry sir."

For a while the captain just stared at him again and then burst out laughing, "Private Chaloner, you're a bastard, get out."

Chapter 24

The car was outside the maintenance shed waiting for him to collect. It was a large black saloon, an Austin 16 according to the mechanic who was polishing the front wing. "She's all ready to go, enjoy" he said. To Bob's surprise the car was already warmed up and the fuel gauge read *full*. The 'WD' marked on the front and rear of the car meant that it was a requisitioned vehicle. It was immaculate and Bob wondered who it had been requisitioned from, they would surely be missing it!

He decided to drive around for a little while to familiarise himself with the car, it was very different to anything he had ever driven before. The smell of the leather seats mixed with a hint of polish and petrol added to the pleasure of the drive. After a while he glided elegantly up to the HQ entrance and, with a small squeak from the brakes, pulled up at exactly 8.00am.

The captain just stood outside waiting and Bob thought that maybe someone else was going with them. Eventually Captain Smith came round to the driver's door, Bob wound the window down. Very quietly and obviously struggling to stay calm he said to Bob "As my driver you are supposed to come round and open the door for me and salute as I get in." Bob wasn't at all sure that this was right but nevertheless he complied and finally they were under way.

They were stopped in Whitehall just ahead of the War Office and Captain Smith showed his identification as requested but with obvious irritation as he sarcastically asked the M.P if he thought the uniform was borrowed! Giving a smart salute the M.P said, "Sorry sir, just keeping everyone safe as ordered." Captain Smith returned the salute and snapped at Bob, "Come on drive on, I don't want to be late."

He was directed to the entrance to the War office where he pulled up and waited for the captain to get out. Hearing an impatient sigh coming from the back he suddenly remembered that he was supposed to do the 'chauffeur' thing and hopped out and went round to open the door and salute. He wondered again whether this was correct procedure or was Captain Smith just having some fun at his expense.

Everything had changed since his last visit to the area, on a sightseeing trip with Angela. It looked very different now with sandbags stacked up against the buildings and manned sentry boxes by the doors. Bob noticed that almost all the people he passed were carrying gas masks and wondered if he should have been given one, Captain Smith didn't have one either, he would ask about it when he picked the captain up later.

The roads were very quiet and just thirty minutes later Bob pulled up outside Benjy's warehouse. The 'office' door was open and as he approached, he could see Violet sitting at the desk concentrating on her knitting. "Don't drop a stitch," he said and Violet did just that, actually she dropped all her knitting. She jumped up and pulled Bob into a big hug while planting a big kiss on his cheek.

Violet told him off for not telephoning to let them know he was coming and he explained that being in the army didn't give him much access to a phone. She was not impressed, "Surely in these modern times they could put a phone in your room." Bob wasn't sure that she had quite grasped the army thing.

Benjy was out all day doing his deliveries and Violet wouldn't be able to contact him. Bob was disappointed, he had been looking forward to seeing his friend again and also he needed some supplies but maybe Violet would be able to deal with that.

It was almost eleven so Violet closed up for an early lunch, it wasn't a problem because things had been so much quieter lately, she said. Bob had noticed how much less stock there was with some shelves being completely empty.

He walked Violet out to the car and opened the rear door for her, "Thank you my man" she said, giggling as she arranged herself in the back seat. They drove the short distance to the pub and Bob leapt out and ran round to open the car door for her, "I wish Benjy could see this" she said, they were still laughing when Reg opened the pub door.

"Bloody hell! Someone's doing well." Reg called Edna out and they all stood looking at the car. "It's an army car" said Bob, "I'm just driving our captain for the day." "Bloomin posh for an army car" said Reg. "Yes" said Bob, "I am beginning to wonder if there's more to Captain Smith than meets the eye."

They stopped at the pub for a nice lunch, Edna always seemed to be able to produce a meal at the drop of a hat. Later on Bob drove Violet to the shops. He suspected that she didn't really need anything but he took pleasure from her obvious enjoyment of being 'chauffeured.'

By the time they got back to the warehouse it was almost three o clock so Bob went round and quickly selected the things he thought would be best received by Captain Smith and Co. This was mostly spirits, but he also took a selection of things that were now generally hard to get, he did give a thought to how it was that Benjy could still get these things but had no time to ponder this.

Violet proved to be as hardnosed as Benjy when it came to business but Bob didn't haggle. At the very least he would be getting his money back very soon, he wasn't seeing this as a profit making enterprise.

The boot was surprisingly small for such a big car and they only just managed to get the four boxes of 'supplies' in and Violet found an old sack to over them up. Suffering another crushing hug and promising to telephone next time, Bob set off for Whitehall with not much time to spare.

It was just about four o clock when he reached Whitehall and as he approached the War office entrance, he was stopped by an M.P.

Bob had learned early on in his time with the army that you didn't mess about with the 'red capped' Military Police, it was best just to go along with whatever they said.

"Right, state your business" he looked in at Bob's uniform and added "private."

"I'm here to collect Captain Smith from the War office" answered Bob.

"Smith is it?" he was looking inside the car now.

"Not Jones then, definitely Smith is it?"

"Yes it's Captain Definitely Smith" said Bob, immediately regretting it.

"Well we'd better have a proper look at the car then eh"

Bob got out as he was ordered and went to the M.P who was now standing by the car boot, "Let's open it up then"

Bob fiddled around with the key deliberately using the wrong one first stalling for time; this was getting a bit serious. Finally he could delay no longer and turned the handle on the boot lid and let it rise up.

"What in God's name are you doing!" standing next to the M.P was Captain Smith. The M.P saluted the captain and took the paper that was being thrust at him.

"Stop messing about in the back of the car and get me back to the barracks immediately"

Bob had the boot shut and was back in the driver's seat in a flash.

"Thank you sergeant, carry on" said the captain, taking back his paper.

They left Whitehall and after a few moments Bob said to the captain, "That was a close shave."

Catching Bob's eye in the rear-view mirror and keeping a straight face, Captain Smith said "I'm sure that you mean *'that was a close shave **sir'*** but I have no idea what you're talking about and by the way, it's Major Smith now."

He really is very good at this, thought Bob.

They made it back to the Camp without incident and, as ordered, Bob handed the car with the 'supplies' still in the boot over to Sergeant Collins.

He went off to get something to eat and then returned to his quarters. After a while Corporal Lewis came and told Bob that he was to report to Captain Smith *again* in the morning. He had stressed the word *'again'* and Bob was detecting a bit of hostility. He hoped that the corporal would benefit from his delivery and that would smooth things out.

Bob lay on his bed thinking about the trip to London. He was a bit concerned because he had no idea of the whereabouts of the 'supplies' that he had paid for. Some of the spirits he had selected for himself and to share with the lads, and how was he to get them back? He decided that he would sort things out in the morning. He would question Sergeant Collins firmly and not take any nonsense.

The next morning he was back in front of Major Smith's desk and was surprised when the major didn't come round and perch on the front. The major remained seated and finally looking up said, "At ease." Bob had no idea what was coming next and just stood patiently waiting.

"Thank you for doing a little shopping for me yesterday, I must settle up with you. How much was it?"

Bob told him exactly what he had paid and, without any comment, the major took out his wallet and counted out the amount and handed it over.

"There may be other occasions when I will need you as a driver but in the meantime, you will continue with the transport section"

"Permission to speak sir" Bob thought he was getting quite good at this army stuff.

Given permission, Bob explained that he had done some 'shopping' for himself, and the lads, but had left it in the car with the rest.

The answer surprised him, "Return to your quarters Chaloner, I think you'll find that Sergeant Collins or Corporal Lewis will have sorted that out."

When he got back to the hut it was empty, the others were obviously doing more training, about which he felt a twinge of guilt, but he was excused from the training and being kept busy with driving so he dismissed it quickly.

He wondered what had been 'sorted out' regarding his bottles of whiskey, after all they didn't even know that three or four of the bottles were for him.

He had received instructions that he was to drive a lorry to a depot in the north of England. Leaving at 6am the next morning, the orders were to pick up some equipment and deliver it to a location on the Kent coast, he would be told where exactly when he had picked up the load.

Sitting on the bed and wondering what to do for the rest of the day Bob noticed that his kit bag was not in the same position as he had left it. It was an unwritten rule in the huts that no one would so much as touch anyone else's kit, so this was odd. He pulled it out and opened it up to check that everything was there and found that three bottles of whiskey had been put in. They were placed in almost exactly the same way as he had stored the first lot.

That evening there was singing in the hut and the frequent laughter was just a bit louder than usual, almost two bottles had disappeared by 'lights out.' There would be some hangovers in the morning but Bob would be saved from that 'grouchiness,' he would be on the road by that time. It was only when he was in bed later that it occurred to him that, whether by accident or design, Major Smith had actually paid for their drinks.

The next day he found that he was part of a large number of Lorries all heading for the same depot to be loaded with equipment. They were ordered not to travel in convoy and were timed out at ten minute intervals.

All the drivers came back together by stopping at a popular roadside cafe which was roughly halfway to the depot. After they had eaten a late breakfast they wandered outside and stood around for a while in groups smoking and chatting. They discovered that none of them had been given details of where they would be taking their loads.

The last lorry to arrive had a sergeant sitting next to the driver who leapt out as soon as it had come to halt. He was shouting as he came towards the drivers, "Bloody big target this is, get moving and not all in a line!"

Bob began to realise that there was actually a real danger of them being bombed or strafed by a German plane or planes. Strangely, even though he had been involved in transporting the 'Dunkirk' soldiers, the war had still seemed somehow remote but now the thought of being attacked in his lorry made him feel decidedly uncomfortable.

They all made it to the depot and lined up ready to be loaded, the sergeant fussing around making them drive backwards and forwards until they were exactly in line. *'Nice orderly line to be bombed now'*, thought Bob.

All the drivers were ordered to assemble inside the depot while their lorries were loaded. They were told to make sure that their fuel tanks were full before setting off. Six of the lorries, of which Bob's was one, would be getting an escort to their destination and had orders not to stop at all on route. To these six drivers the sergeant said, "You'd better make sure that you use the toilet before you go because you're not going to stop, even for that!"

Bob discovered that having an armed escort had advantages because just six hours later, having not stopped even at road junctions, they arrived at Deal on the Kent coast. A couple of miles further on they reached the army camp which was just a group of temporary buildings surround by a barbed wire fence.

Once he had been allowed through the gate and directed to back up behind the largest of the buildings Bob leapt out and, unable to wait a second longer, he ran round to the side of the lorry for a desperately needed pee. As he walked round to the back of the lorry he was ushered away from seeing what was being unloaded which seemed a bit unnecessary to Bob as he had already seen that everything was in unmarked crates anyway.

It was quickly unloaded and he was shown where to park up and then pointed towards the canteen. Although it had the general appearance of an army camp he had noticed that the majority of people were actually civilians.

It was mid afternoon and there wasn't much food to be had but he did find a slice of cold meat pie and took that, together with a cup of very stewed tea, to a table where a couple of those civilians were seated. He asked if he could join them and one of them just waved at him to sit and then continued talking to his companion.

Being completely ignored by the two men, Bob finished his pie and tea quite quickly and left the table. Most of what they

had been saying didn't mean anything to him but he had over-
heard enough to work out that they were discussing the design
of some sort of early warning system. That would explain the
secrecy surrounding his load.

His armed escort had disappeared as soon as he had arrived and now, leaving with an empty lorry, he was waved out
through the gates without even having to stop.

The traffic was very light and he made good time back to
camp and arrived a little after seven. By the time he had
checked his lorry back in and was heading to his quarters it
was much too late to get a meal. Luckily, he ran into Sergeant
Collins who said he would be allowed to eat in the officer's mess
as it was late and that was the only way to get a meal at this
time of day.

There were not a lot of officers in the mess but those that
were there were very jolly and making quite some noise. Bob
felt quite awkward and also being tired after a long day, he ate
his meal quickly and left.

As he walked to his hut he met Major Smith heading for
the Mess, he saluted and it was returned.

"Chaloner" said the major.

"Sir?" said Bob.

"Come and see me in the morning please."

"Yes sir, at what time?"

"Yes yes um, in the morning" said the major, and strode off
towards the Mess.

'Right I'll make it nine then' thought Bob.

The next day, after a nice leisurely start to the morning, he
presented himself at Major Smith's office at 9.0am. After a ten

minute wait he was sent in and stood to attention in front of the desk, *'This is getting to be a habit'* he thought.

"I've been receiving good reports of the way you are carrying out your duties" said the major, as he walked round and perched on the front of his desk.

"You will be doing a lot more driving over the coming weeks and much of it will mean that you will be on your own, no leave on the horizon at the moment I'm afraid, also I will need you to drive me to London again, possibly in two day's time"

"Yes sir" said Bob.

"Are you still at attention?"

"Yes sir"

"Well it's difficult to tell, at ease then," the major had gone back to his seat.

Bob was a bit hurt, he thought that his standing to attention had come on quite well lately,

"I'm approving your promotion to Lance Corporal effective immediately, you're dismissed."

Bob stood to attention, or his version of it, and saluted. "Thank you, sir" he said and left.

That evening he was congratulated by the lads and felt obliged to produce his last bottle of whiskey. They finished it off completely and later on in bed, as he drifted off, helped by the whiskey, he was wondering how on earth any one could have come up with the idea of promoting him.

Chapter 25

The news on the hut radio was that a German battleship, the Admiral Graf Spee, that had been wreaking havoc amongst British ships, was being hunted by British navy ships with orders to destroy it at all cost.

They didn't need the radio to tell them what was happening in the air. The camp was sited mid-way between the South Coast and London and almost every day now they could witness battles between British and German fighters. Even when they couldn't actually see the fighting, the sound of the engines howling and the guns firing would still reach them. Occasionally they would see one of the planes plummeting to earth with smoke pouring out behind but it was hard for them to spot whether it was British or German.

Training had been stepped up, 'call me Edward' was now the section machine gunner and Charlie Wilkins had become a radio operator. The section along with the rest of the platoon had changed enormously and, as far as Bob could tell anyway, it now resembled a proper fighting unit.

An anti-aircraft gun had been sited to the West of the camp and two 25 pounder field guns had arrived, they were stationed to the rear of the camp pointing ominously coastwards.

The next two days were both taken up with local runs for Bob just picking up supplies for the camp and dropping them off at the stores.

On the Wednesday morning, as ordered, he picked up the Austin early in readiness to take the major to Whitehall. He really enjoyed driving the Austin and that almost made up for going through the pantomime of opening the door and saluting. As usual it was full of fuel and had been warmed up ready for him. The same mechanic as before handed it over and Bob suspected that he was also enjoying a bit of a drive if only for the 'warming up.'

For weeks now the talk everywhere was about the German invasion and when it would happen, most people really were talking about *when* rather than *if*. Bob thought that he would try to find out something from the major as they would be in the car on their own for a few hours. That idea didn't last more than five minutes into the journey as Major Smith's first words were "I have a lot to think about so quickly and quietly if you please."

'*Ok*' thought Bob, '*I have permission to go quickly then.*' For the next fifty minutes he drove as fast as he could, even frightening himself a couple of times as he went into bends much too quickly. He glanced in the rear-view mirror a few times to see if the major was looking worried but it was having no effect on him whatsoever and he was just studying the folder that he had taken out of his brief case when they set off.

Bob slowed it down as they neared the city centre but they had made very good time and were going to complete the journey in little over an hour. As they approached Whitehall the major asked if he had enough money to do a little shopping and

Bob told him that he had. He now knew that he was expected to come up with another 'special delivery.'

Things looked a bit different to last time, there were even more sandbags stacked up against walls and around the sentry posts. There were even more soldiers manning the many barriers that were slowing down everyone attempting to enter the Whitehall area.

Eventually they got the War office and Major Smith told Bob he would be ready to be picked up at five, "On the dot please" he called out as he walked briskly to the entrance.

*

It was still before 8.0am when he pulled up outside Benjy's warehouse and, of course, there was nobody there yet so he just settled down, and with the car still being quite warm he was soon asleep.

Five seconds later, or so it seemed, there was a loud knocking on the side window. He was still trying to work out where he was and why. He looked at his watch, it was almost 9am! The knocking started again, he couldn't see out with all the windows steamed up and as he opened the car door to see who had the nerve to touch 'his' car, he felt a thump followed by the sound of a splash.

It was raining steadily and a big puddle had formed in the road, in the middle of which sat a policeman trying to stand up without putting his sleeves in the water. Bob got out quickly and attempted to help but the policeman waved him off and finally got back on his feet.

"I remember you, never forget a face I don't." he said stepping back into the puddle again. Bob recognised him now. It was the sergeant who had been to the warehouse searching for the stolen whiskey.

"You did that on purpose, I know your type" said Sergeant Brook.

Bob was thinking, *'I have my rifle here, I could just shoot him'*

"Told you, I never forget a face, I'll have a name in second"

Bob got back into the car to keep out of the rain, "I'm not keeping it a secret."

"Secrets is it? Well I'll have a name in a minute then there'll be no more keeping secrets"

"My name is Chaloner" said Bob. "That will be Lance Corporal Chaloner to you, Sergeant Brook"

"Where did you get my name?"

"We've met before, you never forget a face do you." Bob was looking at his rifle wondering if it was loaded.

"Is there something you want"

"We had a report of a dead soldier left in a car, had to come and check, there's a lot of funny stuff going on these days"

"Well I'm not dead so everything is ok" Bob was trying hard to stay patient.

"Yes I suppose it is, but in future don't.." The sergeant couldn't quite think of what it was that Bob shouldn't do in the future.

"Well, I've got things to do, just remember I've got a mind like a filing cabinet so mind what you're doing in future Corporal Charlston."

'Face like a filing cabinet' thought Bob.

Standing under the archway, arriving unnoticed by the sergeant or by Bob, were Benjy and Violet. Bob left the car where it was and ran to join them under the arch, they all went on into the 'office,' leaving the sergeant to race off to his next case.

*

"So, back to see us again with your posh motor, I heard all about your last visit" said Benjy. After being hugged violently by Violet, Bob brought them both up to date with what he had been up to.

They were anxious for any news from him that might tell them more than the radio or newspapers but he knew no more than they did. Later, as usual, they headed for the pub, it had stopped raining and Benjy said he would prefer to walk.

"Nothing against your posh motor" he said, "I need to do more walking the Doc said."

"Are you ill?" asked Bob.

"Nah, just need to lose a bit of weight that's all." Bob suspected that there was more to it than that but didn't pursue it.

They made it to the pub before it started raining again and were soon enjoying some food and drink with Reg and Edna, always the perfect hosts. It was raining again when, later on, Bob left the pub and ran to get the car which he drove back to collect Benjy and Violet.

"I can see why Violet was so impressed, I like this it's really nice" said Benjy.

"Very small boot though, you're better off sticking with the van" said Bob.

He went around the warehouse collecting a selection of things including 2lbs of sugar, 8oz of tea, a block of cheese that probably weighed a pound and, most surprisingly he found a whole gammon. Bob was definitely not going to ask where that came from! He added a selection of spirits and Benjy helped him to pack everything in boxes, adding up the bill as they went along.

There was so much 'shopping' this time that it wouldn't all fit in the boot and there was a box on the front passenger seat, Bob had draped his greatcoat over it and would just hope for the best.

Leaving the car running to warm it up and clear at least some of the condensation from the windows, he said his good-byes to Benjy and Violet. He asked Violet to take special care of Benjy. They had spoken quietly together earlier and Violet had told him that the problem was Benjy's heart. He had to lose some weight, drink less and avoid strenuous activity apart from a 10 minute walk every day.

Arriving back at Whitehall with fifteen minutes to spare Bob found a place to park outside the barriers and a short walk from the War office entrance. He decided to go and meet the major at the door and ask him what to do about the 'shopping' on the front seat.

At five thirty the major finally came out and, seeing Bob waiting said "Where is the car?" Once he had heard about the 'shopping' he said "Well, we'd better have a walk then eh!"

They walked off toward the car and Bob, seeing the major walk more than a few steps for the first time, noticed just how much he was limping. He measured his pace to stay beside and just a fraction behind the major letting him set the pace. Ten minutes later they reached the car and he quickly unlocked it, went round and opened the door for the major.

They had been on the road for about ten minutes when Major Smith spoke. "A bit enthusiastic with your shopping were you?"

"I just got things that I thought you..." Bob trailed off, thinking that he should continue the game.

"I just got some things that I needed but I may have overdone it a little"

"Yes well, as long as you used your time wisely eh, and by the way, I'm glad you've got to grips with driving this car at last, perhaps we'll be back a bit faster than last time."

Bob put his foot down on the accelerator.

He drove as fast as he dared but it had no noticeable effect on the major who was speaking to him about the huge challenges that they would all have to face. Major Smith continued on the same theme, they would be tested and must not be found wanting he said. Bob got the feeling that he was not really talking to him but was actually rehearsing a speech for the men.

The roads had dried up and they made good time, arriving back at about 7.0pm. They were met by Sergeant Collins and Corporal Lewis; the major spoke quietly to Sergeant Collins and then was gone. Bob ate in the officer's mess again while the others dealt with the car, he hoped that things would be shared out a little and this time, not just the spirits.

The following morning he was back in front of the major as usual and was reimbursed for the 'shopping.' Major Smith told bob to take a seat, this had not happened before.

"This is going to seem very unfair I know, but we cannot share any of the goods that have somehow appeared in the camp with any of the men. I know you would like your section to have some but when word got out, and it would, there would be a problem. Please don't think that the officers are just enjoying this without regard to your section. Of course, you may find that some bottles find their way to you again."

This was disappointing but Bob knew the major was right, it would cause so much trouble with the rest of the platoon let alone the rest of the men in the camp.

Four bottles of whiskey were in his kit bag when he got back to the hut, at least the men in his section were getting to enjoy a drink, and he enjoyed a lot of freedom that many others didn't. He also got to see his friends so there were benefits to this.

All around the camp, pill boxes were being built and further out a huge trench had been dug. More Field guns had arrived and the roads running passed the camp were now bristling with what someone told Bob were called hedgehogs, the roads had six inch square holes dug about three feet deep into which were slotted steel girders that stood up three or four feet above the road surface in a random pattern. The girders were stacked at the side of the road and would be put in when, and if, needed.

For the next five days Bob hardly had time to eat, he was part of an operation to move large numbers of soldiers from camps in the North of England to camps in Kent and Sussex. Many of these soldiers were fresh out of training and Bob was beginning to feel like an old hand.

It was rare now that he could complete a trip without being brought to halt at least a couple of times. Sometimes it would be a low flying German plane threatening to strafe the road, mostly dealt with quickly by RAF fighters. On one of these occasions all the men in the lorry had jumped out and raced into an adjacent field, it had taken half an hour to persuade them to get back in!

At other times it would be bomb craters that would hold them up, apparently the Luftwaffe bombers were trying to hit airfields and factories but some would just drop their bombs anywhere and turn for home. The roads were quickly repaired, or temporary roads were laid around the crater to keep things moving.

They were constantly warned about driving in convoy but it was difficult to keep any kind of distance with so many lorries on the road at the same time.

Finally Bob was able to enjoy a day without driving but was then forced to join the rest of his section for some P.T. Corporal Lewis seemed to take some malicious pleasure from this saying to him, "You don't need to wear boots for this so 'snap to' and join the others."

The next hour was spent doing star jumps, running on the spot, doing press ups and running around the square of concrete known as the 'Parade Ground.' Bob admitted to himself that after so much time spent behind the wheel, it actually felt quite good to be doing some exercise but he grumbled along with the others anyway.

The section was dismissed and they made their way back to the hut which now housed the whole platoon. While Bob had been away with his driving duties, bunk beds had been put in and now his section occupied one side with another section on the other. The numbers in the camp had pretty much doubled in the last two weeks or so.

He managed to have a few words with Corporal Lewis before he left,

"Did I tell you that I know your father?"

"Really" said the corporal, frowning.

"Oh yes, we've done business together" Bob was stretching things a bit. He went on,

"If I get to the shop again, I'll be sure to tell him that, thanks to me, you're getting some little extra luxuries."

The corporal just said, "Yes, right" and walked off.

He had just been reminded that being found dealing with 'black market' goods would be as bad for him as for any of them.

*

Bob was ordered to collect the car and pick Major Smith up at six the next morning for yet another trip to Whitehall. He was there on time for the major and they were soon underway.

His knowledge of the roads had improved a lot during the last few weeks and this time he chose a completely different route, bringing them into London from a different direction but hopefully, taking no longer. The major approved of this, "Good thinking Chaloner, glad to see you're taking security seriously." Actually, he just fancied a change but well...

Major Smith was talkative again and Bob's feeling that there was more to the major was proving to be accurate.

"I'm sure that you have worked out by now that I am not just the C.O, I have other duties with the Home Defence Executive, I'm sure my regular trips to Whitehall have not gone unnoticed," he said.

"Well obviously, but I never discuss our trips to London," said Bob, thinking more about the 'black market' activity than anything else.

"Right, right, of course" said the major, "Don't want any Jerry spies finding out what we're planning eh?"

'or finding out that you're having ham and eggs for breakfast' thought Bob, then regretted that thought as Major Smith seemed a decent sort really.

There was no time for 'shopping' on this trip as the major said he would be ready to return in no more than two hours. This was a briefing by General Brooke the recently appointed Commander in Chief of Defence, Home Forces. Major Smith obviously supported the change in leadership.

"General Brooke has only been in charge for a month but already we're getting some decent defences in place!" He suddenly seemed to remember that he was talking to a lowly Lance Corporal and said nothing more.

Bob stopped at the entrance and let the major out, doing his 'chauffer' thing as he thought of it, he walked round to the front of the car and stood there wondering what he would do for the next two hours.

"Oi you! Get that thing moved now!"

Bob was somewhat put out by this,

"Do you know whose car this is?" he said.

"I don't care if it's Winnie himself, it's not stopping there!"

Bob could now see that the man shouting at him was a police constable wearing a tin hat and carrying what looked to be a pretty ancient rifle.

Bob did not deal with authority well, however in the army he had managed to keep himself in check, most of the time. The

one thing guaranteed to bring out the worst in him was someone trying to use the little authority that they had, or assumed,
to intimidate others.

"What is your name constable?" Bob was speaking sharply
in his best 'Public school' voice.

The constable had lost a little of his confidence but, thinking he had the rules on his side he carried on.

"I don't think that's your business and I think you had better move now"

"Do you see any identification on this car?" said Bob.

"No, I don't," the constable was looking puzzled.

"That's because you're not supposed to, the person I am
driving has the authority not to be identified, do you understand?"

The constable was nodding his head, obviously trying to
make sense of what Bob was saying. He was going to fail, of
course, because there wasn't any.

Bob took a gamble based on past experience.

"Stand to attention when you're speaking to me and you
will address me as 'sir'!"

In spite of himself the constable stood up straight, not quite
at attention but almost. He was just about to speak again when
Bob cut him off.

"Now you will give me your name and then return to your
position at the barrier, any more insolence and you will find
yourself in front of the superintendent, is that clear!"

Bob had raised his voice and was using his most authorita-
tive tone. The tone of voice coupled with the confusion about
what or who he was dealing with was working to unsettle the
constable and he finally conceded defeat.

"My name is Roberts.... sir," the last word was said with a curl of the lip. He turned on his heel and walked, in a strange upright way somewhat reminiscent of a funeral march, back to the barrier.

Bob lit a cigarette and lounged against the front wing of the car. Ten minutes later he got in and drove away, turning left at the first opportunity he found that there were four cars parked in a line with the drivers standing in a group chatting. Only one of the cars was an army vehicle, the rest were all commandeered cars of a similar type to the one that Bob was driving. He parked behind the last car in the line and joined the other drivers.

It was while they were swopping stories about their driving and their officer passengers that Bob discovered that he was the only one that was not permanently assigned to driving an officer. The others were amazed that he was driving lorries all over the country in between driving the major. He thought perhaps he would ask the major why he was different to all the others.

Two hours later he was parked outside the War office entrance behind the other four cars, their passengers were obviously all in the same briefing. The constable left the barrier and walked towards them but, spotting Bob getting out of his car, he just turned around and went back to the barrier.

All the officers came out together and General Brooke was in the middle of the group. As soon as the general saw the line of waiting cars he marched straight over to the barrier where Constable Roberts was talking to a colleague.

"What were your orders regarding cars parking outside the War office?!"

"Well sir," the constable was looking desperately across at the drivers and Bob in particular.

"Well sir, nothing!" said the general, "This will be reported to your superiors, you just don't follow orders do you!"

Soon after this they were heading back to the camp, the major was looking very serious. Bob decided not to try any conversation and they travelled in silence, back to what was about to be a very different camp.

Chapter 26

The changes started to happen the very next day with many of the men being assembled ready to move. There were rows of lorries waiting to take them to barracks nearer the coast but this time Bob was not one of the drivers.

Sergeant Collins called his platoon together and told them that they would be staying at the camp. Corporal Lewis would remain in charge of the section and Bob would continue in his "Rather unusual role," as the sergeant put it.

The camp was to become what was called an 'Anti-tank Island.' They would be the first line of defence for this area, with the newly formed Home Guard being secondary defence at the nearby village.

During the weeks that followed, the whole area was transformed, there was a sense of urgency about everything. The trench that had been dug earlier was widened and deepened and huge concrete blocks were placed at each end to prevent anything driving around it. Even more Pill boxes were built and strategically placed and machine gunners were readied to man them. A nearby stream was diverted and a field to the east of the camp was flooded and now more like a lake.

While all this was going on Bob was driving Major Smith to a different camp or barracks almost every day. Each morning at 5.30am he would collect the car, which had been cleaned and fuelled overnight, and would be ready for the major at 6.00am.

All the places they went to were undergoing similar work and Bob assumed that they were all to be 'Anti-tank Islands.' The major was tireless and, in spite of his limp marched about shouting instructions about where things should be sited, or demanding changes to things that had already been started. Bob had little to do while this was going on and was able to eat and rest, he was glad of this because quite often they didn't get back, to what the major was now calling 'Base', until late in the evenings.

During this whole period it seemed to Bob that there was hardly an hour during the day when the sky wasn't full of planes. At times there were so many German planes overhead that the clear blue sky of the summer was obscured and the light was akin to a cloudy autumn afternoon.

By mid-September, what everybody was now calling The Battle of Britain had reached a climax, with the RAF effectively defeating the Luftwaffe and having performed miracles in the process.

The German bomber raids had pretty much ceased during the day and now took place at night when it was more difficult for the RAF fighters to defend. The newspapers were reporting massive damage in London which, of course, was the most targeted place.

Bob was worried about his friends he had not had a chance to see them for weeks. The major was travelling less and had not been back to Whitehall since the briefing with General Brooke.

Finally, in the second week of October the section was given five days leave from the Sunday and reporting back before midnight on the Friday. Bob went to the vehicle maintenance area to see if they knew of any vehicle that was going to, or near to London. He was known to the lads in 'Maintenance' as the major's driver and they looked after him, making sure that the Austin was well maintained and whenever possible having a decent lorry ready for him. They had no vehicles being readied to go out at all on Sunday, the first one that they knew of was a lorry setting off for the Croydon depot at 6.00am on Monday.

After some thought Bob decided to have a relaxing day at the camp on Sunday and cadge a lift on the lorry on Monday morning, he could get to Norwood easily enough from there. It was while he was deciding how to get to London, and Norwood in particular, that he realised that he had not actually thought about going anywhere else. He decided that next time he was on leave he would try to visit Jim and Winnie.

Apart from his brother Jim he still had no contact with the family at all, it was like they just didn't exist. From time to time he would feel quite depressed about it, once or twice he had considered making contact but each time, reminding himself that he had not instigated the rift, he quickly abandoned the thought.

At 6.00am on Monday morning, he threw his kitbag into the back of the lorry and joined the driver in the cab. The driver already knew Bob's name and introduced himself as Ron. They were off straight away and the driver was not hanging about, the lorry was empty and was quite lively with no weight in the back. An hour later they had reached the suburbs and already they were seeing evidence of the bombing that was now a nightly occurrence.

Several times they were guided round the ruins of what had been someone's home until just a few days, or even hours earlier. They came across a whole parade of shops which had been virtually destroyed by a bomb followed by the resulting fire, which was still burning. Water was still being sprayed on the ruins and people were still searching amongst the rubble. There were some women stood across the road, just watching what was going on, one of them gave a little wave and a weak smile as the army lorry managed to get through.

They passed more and more bomb damage and the many fires that were still burning as they made their way towards the depot. Bob had had no idea of the extent of the damage being inflicted by the German planes on ordinary people and was now, for the first time, feeling extreme *personal* anger towards Adolf Hitler and all that he stood for.

Ron had said that this was a nice easy run, the job was to pick up general supplies from a Croydon depot and return to the camp but Bob had noticed that they were leaving Croydon. He asked Ron where the depot was and was told that they had passed the depot a couple of miles back.

"You wanted to go to West Norwood didn't you?"

"Well I do" said Bob "But I don't expect you to take me there"

"It's not far, and anyway who's going to know in this chaos?"

"That's brilliant, thank you" said Bob.

"No problem, gotta look after the bloke that's driving our guvnor around eh."

Bob asked Ron to drop him off as they reached the start of Norwood High street, he leapt out of the cab, went to back of the lorry and climbed up to retrieve his kitbag. He gave a wave and then watched as Ron manoeuvred the lorry in a very neat three-point turn and roared off in the direction they had come from.

*

He decided to walk round to the pub first to see if Reg was up, he was often up early doing things in the cellar and preparing for beer deliveries.

Bob knew that something was different even before he rounded the corner.

There was a smell of burning wood with a strange chemical edge, it reminded him of the morning after Bonfire night. Dust seemed just to be hanging in the air. But it wasn't just that, the light had changed and a shaft of early sun was showing between the end of one terrace and the start of another. Bob had never seen that before. It shouldn't be possible.

He turned the corner and saw that where the pub had been was now just a pile of rubble, it had almost completely gone. The houses on either side were missing most of the front and side walls, what was left of the rooms was now open to the world. In the remains of one upstairs room a double bed stood right on the edge of the missing floor, it was still made up and the lamp on the bedside cupboard was somehow still on. As Bob stood and stared in disbelief the lamp flickered and went out.

He was suddenly aware that someone was talking to him.

"They really caught a big un' didn't they." An older man in blue overalls and wearing a black tin hat was gesturing to where the pub had been.

"Sorry" he said, "Are you erm, connected with, erm.. did you...?" he could see by Bob's face that he was upset but he didn't know what to say to him.

"Did you erm... know someone?" he finally managed.

"My friends own the pub," said Bob, starting to walk past the man.

"I'm sorry, you can't go any further," said the man holding onto Bob's arm.

Bob shook his arm free but stopped where he was.

After a few moments he turned and started walking away, as he did so the remaining floor holding the double bed finally collapsed raising a large cloud of dust. He arrived at Violet's house almost without having thought about it. The house was empty, at least nobody answered the door. Feeling a bit lost, he decided to go round and see if she and Benjy were at the warehouse.

In the event, Benjy and Violet arrived at the warehouse at the same time as Bob, but came from the opposite direction. Violet gave Bob a hug and then burst into tears and rushed to the office door. She fumbled with the lock for a few moments and then went in and closed the door.

Bob and Benjy shook hands and then, for the first time ever, Benjy pulled Bob towards him for a hug.

"They wouldn't let us through. Violet spotted you standing there."

"We called to you from the other side of the…." Benjy tailed off, not knowing what to call it.

"You didn't hear us calling."

Violet came back outside to join them. She had obviously been crying but was now putting on a brave face.

"We went home quickly thinking that we would find you, but you weren't there so we took a short cut through the alley ways and came here." She said.

They went into the warehouse. Benjy went over and took a bottle of brandy from a box marked as lemonade. He poured a generous measure into three mugs and they drank while he told Bob what had happened, or at least as much as he and Violet had been able to put together.

The air raid warning siren had sounded at about 5.30pm the previous day. Benjy and Violet had gone home as quickly as they could. Before they went into the garden shelter they had grabbed some food and a bottle of milk in case they were in there for a long time.

They had only just settled down in the shelter when there was a huge bang followed by some smaller ones. Benjy had said "Some poor bugger has copped it out there."

Less than an hour later the 'all clear' was sounded and they emerged from the shelter. Looking around they could see that their house and those in the surrounding area were undamaged. Knowing that the air raid siren would be going off again before too long Benjy went to investigate the big bang that they had heard. Violet insisted on going with him and they headed off towards a plume of smoke rising above the houses.

Ten minutes later they were looking at the remains of the pub. Someone was saying, "Poor devils, nobody got out of that one." A man that they vaguely recognised came over to talk to them.

"I only left a minute or two before that happened" he said.

"Reg and Edna were having a bite to eat," *'Before the bombs started'* Reg said. Al was serving at the bar, the pub wasn't open of course, there was only two of us having a sneaky drink." The man went on,

Reg had said *'it's too bloody early for the bastards to be here yet, let's finish our food.'*

The man had walked off leaving Benjy and Violet just stood looking at what little remained of the pub. There were several fires in the area and an Auxiliary fireman with AFS painted on his helmet was moving people away. He was telling everybody that there was a danger from the incendiary bombs that were dropped, some might not have gone off yet he said.

That was when Violet had spotted Bob on the other side of cordoned off area.

When Benjy had finished telling Bob what they knew he topped up their mugs and they just sat in silence. Bob was thinking about all the times they had shared in the pub and the generosity of Reg and Edna when he was down. He knew Violet, particularly, would be hard hit, Edna and her had been friends for a long time.

He spent the next four days with Violet and Benjy, mostly at their house. There was not much business for Benjy these days and he was spending less and less time at the warehouse. It was a sad time for them all. Every night they were in the 'Anderson' garden shelter for at least a part of it. On one of the nights the bombing had gone on through the whole night, only ending as daylight arrived. The explosions sounded a good way off but they were continuous and was no way to get to any sleep. He had wondered why everyone looked so tired and now he knew.

*

Bob had said his goodbye's to Violet and Benjy with the usual promises to keep safe and keep in touch even though there was really no way for them to do either of those things.

He arrived back at the camp and went to the hut where, over the course of the evening the others arrived and joined in the swapping of stories about their leave time. Bob didn't feel much like joining in but he had, on Benjy's insistence, managed to fit five bottles into his kit bag and he thought this would be a good time to share one of them.

They all lifted their mugs in a toast to the section and also to Bob for bringing the whiskey. Within minutes of this happening Sergeant Collins appeared, *'it was almost like he could smell it'* thought Bob. Several of the men were coming to attention but the sergeant told them that there was no need as they were still on leave until midnight. They weren't sure that this was right and didn't like it when the sergeant was nice. Something rotten usually followed.

The sergeant looked at Bob pointedly. Bob turned so that none of the others could see and held up three fingers while nodding towards his bag. Sergeant Collins smiled and nodded before leaving the hut. He would be collecting them at some time the following day. Bob was not altogether happy about this but he supposed there would be some benefit as time went by.

Things had settled into a bit of a routine at the camp. Training and defence practice continued and there was still some movement of men and arms but the threat of an invasion had diminished and nothing was expected to happen in the immediate future.

Bob was still driving Major Smith around and there was still the occasional trip to London when he could go on to do some 'shopping.' The range of things that he picked up were in even shorter supply generally and he was amazed that Benjy could still get them, albeit at some very high prices.

He enjoyed seeing Benjy and Violet when he could but his visits seemed to just bring up the memories of their lost friends. There was no longer the banter that had always been there between him and Benjy. Violet had stopped pretending to seduce him, things would never be the same again.

The 'supplies' he bought back were apparently appreciated even more and there was never a problem getting his money back. He was concerned about the amounts that they expected him to get hold of. He wondered how things would turn out if he were ever caught with the 'black market' goods as they were now known.

Time went by and Bob, like the rest of the platoon, slipped almost unnoticed into what seemed more like a civilian job than a soldiers. There was news from the various 'fronts' and apart from a few setbacks it was agreed by most people around the camp that the war was slowly being won.

After Pearl Harbour had been attacked and the Americans were drawn into the war it seemed like just a matter of time for the German army to be defeated. That had been some time ago but nevertheless progress was being made.

News came of Lieutenant-General Montgomery's victory over Rommel in the dessert and, in common with the rest of the country, the camp celebrated what was described in the press as a *Great turning point in the war!*.

Apart from two occasions when they had been ordered to a state of readiness to 'ship out,' and then almost immediately stood down, they had just remained where they were. They were the defence against an attack that they were fairly certain would never come. From time to time rumours would go round that they were to be moved to the coast but nothing ever happened.

They were all getting leave more often and for longer now and Bob finally made it down to Weymouth to see his brother. He was greeted warmly by Winnie. Jim was not there but had written home to say that he would start his leave and be home in a week's time. Bob had three weeks before he had report back so luckily, with Jim arriving in week that would still give them two weeks together.

Bob enjoyed being with Winnie and the children, and for a week they managed a walk on the beach at some point every day.

Jim arrived and was thoroughly welcomed by Winnie and all the children. Then at his suggestion, he and Bob went outside for a smoke. Things were a little strained for a while but before long they were chatting away and swapping stories about what they had each been up to since they were last together. There was a lot to tell.

That evening Jim brought his almost empty kit bag into the living room, "You might think that there isn't much in here but you will be amazed" he said to Winnie and Bob.

When he was sure that he had their attention, he started pulling some material out of the bag and then just kept on pulling the material out. It was parachute silk and it seemed like it had no end! Finally, it was all out in a pile on the floor, it didn't seem possible that all that material had been folded into less than a quarter of Jim's bag.

Jim told them that he thought he would be able to use this material to make some luxurious items of clothing, maybe some dresses or skirts or even men's shirts. After throwing around various ideas Winnie came up with the idea of making ladies knickers. She told them that this was an item that would be snapped by women who had been deprived of decent quality underwear for a long time now. Also, they would be able to make a lot of them out of the material.

Using the oldest of their girls as a model Winnie soon had some samples ready. She had included in the design a gusset which, she said, would make them into real luxury items. Bob just couldn't resist the opportunity to be selling again and midway through the second week in Weymouth he was calling on some local shopkeepers and taking orders for silk knickers.

The time in Weymouth flew by and all to soon Bob was saying goodbye to Jim, Winnie and the family. He had really enjoyed his visit and hoped he could see them all again soon. He knew now that he and Jim would never be partners again as they had been before, but it was good that they were reunited as family.

He reflected on the fact that he had not made a very convincing silk knicker salesman.

Maybe his future didn't lie in that area. Anyway, he was due back in camp the next day and there was no sign of that 'job' coming to an end yet.

Chapter 27

On his return to the camp he was straight away in front of Major Smith.

"You have been very steady in your duties and appear to be respected within your section. You are now promoted to corporal, this will in no way alter what you are doing and you will continue in exactly the same way." The major continued, "You will still report to Sergeant Collins and Corporal Lewis still has the section, do you understand?" "Yes sir" said Bob.

He didn't really understand why he was now a corporal but he thought it was not bad, having the rank and the pay but having no responsibilities.

Bob had seen no German planes overhead for a long time now and had even stopped wearing his tin hat when driving lorries, although regulations still actually required him to do so. The roads were no longer suffering with bomb damage and there were fewer roadside security checks, driving was a lot more straightforward at last.

He enjoyed the freedom of his longer drives to depots in the North of England. At the very least he was out of the camp all day and often had to stay overnight at the depot. They always provided a meal, a bunk bed and some breakfast before he set off on the return trip.

This was very welcome on his current trip because it was February and although there had been no snow so far, it was bitterly cold, particularly so in the north.

It seemed that more and more supplies were being moved to the South of England and it didn't take a genius to work out why. Everybody was agreed that this year, 1944, would be the year that finally, the Nazis would be driven out of France.

He finished his breakfast and walked round to the depot loading bays. His lorry was parked in a row of others but was sticking out about twelve feet in front of the others. Going to back of the lorry he found out why this was. Not only was his lorry absolutely filled to the top with crates but it also had a trailer attached with a canvas cover stretched tightly across the top.

The large trailers were the same width as the lorry and could be seen easily while being towed. The trailer attached to Bob's lorry was the smaller type and while driving, the only time you got a glimpse of it was on a really tight turn. Being out of sight they were notoriously difficult to reverse.

In common with most loads these days all Bob had in the way of paperwork was a sheet showing the number of crates on the lorry and a sheet showing one trailer. The exact details of the load were in a sealed envelope which would be given to the storeman on arrival. The only thing that the drivers knew was that if you didn't have an escort then the load wasn't ammunition.

He drove for two hours or so until came to a roadside café that he had used a number of times before. He saw that if he went in to the parking area he would have to reverse out so he drove on. He would rather go thirsty than be embarrassed.

Further on and being on a straight stretch of country road he took the opportunity to pull up and pop behind the hedge for a pee. Much relieved, he was back in the cab and away in no time. About twenty miles or so further on and now on one of the many routes that he used to skirt around London, he was brought to a halt by what looked like a bomb disposal team blocking the road.

The man holding up his arm to stop the lorry came up to the cab, "You had better stay where you are for a while" he said, "We've got a live one here."

"How long for?" asked Bob, not that it made any difference, there was nowhere he could turn the lorry round even if he wanted to.

"We'll have on your way in no time," said the man.

Ten minutes later the road was cleared and Bob was waved through.

'*Blimey*' thought Bob, that was quick. He noticed that road surface was intact and briefly wondered where the bomb had actually been but was soon lost in his thoughts about life in general, as was his habit when driving long distances.

There were no other hold-ups and an hour or so later he was at the camp gate. As usual the sentry was there to check him in. Detailed checks were taken care of in the stores so all the sentry had to do was sign that the vehicle was in the camp.

The sentry gave Bob back his signed sheet for the lorry but not the one for the trailer.

"Excuse me" said Bob. "Have you got the trailer sheet? I will need to hand that in at the stores"

"You taking the mickey?" said the sentry.

"No, I really should have it," Bob was wondering what was going on with the sentry.

"Look," the sentry was getting impatient. "I don't what your game is but why would I sign a trailer sheet if there's no trailer"

Bob got out of the cab and walked to the back of the lorry. There was no trailer!

Things happened quickly after that and in no time at all Bob found himself being questioned, rather aggressively by two Military policemen. They were in a room with just a table and two chairs and nothing else, one of the M.P's kept walking around and each time he was behind Bob he would lean in and ask Bob what he had done with the trailer.

The other man who was sat opposite was taking notes and occasionally asking questions. The questions were very much the same, just phrased in different ways. Bob had described his journey in detail three times and, although the seated man took some notes, they continued as if he hadn't said anything at all. They repeatedly asked him who he had arranged to take the trailer and where they were going to take it to.

He spent the next two weeks as a prisoner which was particularly unpleasant as when he wasn't on latrine duty, he was locked up. Nobody came to see him and even though he had asked several times there was no sign of anyone being appointed to defend him. It seemed to him that a Court Martial was the next thing to happen and surely he was entitled to a defence. *'For crying out loud,'* he thought, I have done nothing wrong. *Well...lost a trailer but.....still.*

On the Monday morning of what would have been the third week of his detention Bob was collected by two very serious looking M.P's. He was taken to a room where his uniform was waiting, folded on the table. He was left to put it on and having done so he felt a lot better, even though he didn't know what was to happen next. The M.P's came back and, still refusing to say a word to him, marched him to the C.O's office where they left him standing to attention in front of Major Smith.

Twenty minutes later he was back, sitting on his bed in the hut reflecting on what had just happened.

Major Smith had delivered a 'bollocking' of giant proportions, he had gone on and on trying, Bob thought, to find as many ways to say 'idiot' as he possibly could. Finally running out of steam, the major told Bob that he would be a Private soldier again and would be continuing as he had before. Apparently, only the major's influence and Bob's previous good record had saved him from any further action.

Later on that week Bob learned from Sergeant Collins that a group of men had been using various methods to stop lorries on country lanes and then steal from them while distracting the driver. He also found out that the trailer that he had 'lost' was full of army greatcoats. He felt a little better knowing for certain that it was not guns or ammunition.

His duties had not changed at all. It was not long before he was dropping the major at Whitehall again and going off to see Benjy and Violet and, of course picking up as much as he could to take back to the camp. Things had changed a little in this area, now he was being quietly asked for specific items rather than just getting what he thought would be enjoyed. Of course, all things that were requested were those that were in the shortest supply.

Benjy always had the things that were in short supply, he never seemed happy about it. Ever since the hundred and fifty cases of whiskey had been forced on him all that time ago Bob had known that he was being forced to move things on through his warehouse. He never spoke about it directly and even if he had Bob would not know what to do about it.

As well as getting things for the major and sergeant Collins it seemed that Bob had become the supplier of 'luxuries' to the officer's mess as well. He wasn't overjoyed at this turn in events but could do little to change it. It had helped him with the 'trailer business', he supposed, and he did seem to be getting a fair bit of leave.

*

The movement of everything, including troops had reached a very high level and Bob was driving the lorry every day. Sometimes he would be part of a convoy and at other times he would be picking up from depots and delivering to various places on the south coast. Now they always had a co-driver in the lorries and although it was tiring, driving all day every day, at least there was someone to talk to.

A few days into June everything came to a stop, at least as far as Bob was concerned. He remained in camp with no orders to do anything or go anywhere, which felt odd after the previous weeks of almost non-stop driving.

And then, on the sixth of June 1944, the Allied invasion of France started and for those soldiers left in defence of England there was not much more to do than follow news of the invasion as it unfolded.

During the following months Bob was involved with some strange jobs. He had helped to deliver parts for Gliders to a nearby airfield. He had spent three days driving strange half-tracked armoured vehicles to the docks ready for shipping to France, each time having to scrounge a lift back to collect the next one.

The news coming from Europe was mostly good, apart from some setbacks the Allies were pushing the German forces back all the time and it was accepted by most people now, that the end was in sight.

There were still shortages of so many things but in spite of that the mood everywhere was lighter than it had been for a very long time. There was a sense that things were returning to normal, or soon would.

Bob and the rest of the section were getting out to the local pub a lot more now. They were even finding their way to the NAAFI when they could beg a lift there, five miles was a long way but if it was just walking back, especially with some beers inside them, it didn't seem too bad.

It was on one of these visits that a group of Land Army girls came in, obviously familiar with the place, they soon had drinks in their hands and were chattering away to each other. While this was happening Charlie and two others had discovered a piano that had been covered with an old blanket. They were now banging the keys in a random way and laughing at their efforts.

'Call me Edward' suddenly remembered that Bob had been coerced into playing the piano for a camp concert some time ago. In spite of Bob's efforts to keep him quiet he managed to let everybody know, including the Land Army girls who were now insisting that Bob should play something.

They dragged the piano into the middle of the room and Bob found some sheet music inside the piano stool. While he was looking through the music for something cheerful the barman came over carrying a pile of music, all of popular songs. He had no idea why it had been under the counter, no-one had played the piano in ages he said.

Gradually everybody had gravitated towards the piano and before long they were all singing loudly and laughing together. As soon as Bob had finished one pint, another appeared on top of the piano as if by magic. It took him straight back to another time and the memory brought a rush of sadness that caused him to stop playing. There was shouting for more music and someone said, "I think the piano's broken down!"

One of the girls had perched herself on the edge of the piano stool next Bob and stayed there all the time that he was playing. Now that he had stopped playing, he turned towards her, she was not joining in the shouting and as he looked her way she just smiled and touched his face lightly. "Are you going to play some more?" she said.

He played for another hour until they had all sung themselves hoarse. When he stopped this time, everybody went to sit down. They dragged the chairs from other tables and sat in a big circle round one of the tables. Except for Bob, who stayed where he was because the very pretty girl had now moved round to sit on the stool properly and was now right next to him making no attempt to move.

For all that had changed over the years, the one thing that stayed the same was his inability to say two sensible words in a row when trying to talk to a woman that he was attracted to. He was certainly in that situation now.

"Hello, I'm George" he said. '*Why the hell am I saying that?*' He thought.

"I thought I heard them calling you Bob?" Said the girl.

"Yes, that's my name, well it isn't really, but everybody calls me Bob"

"Well, I'd better call you Bob then."

"I'm Iris," she said, offering her hand.

'*Well, that's odd*' he thought. '*Maybe she is teasing me*'

"I hardly like to say this, but surely they were calling you Chris, weren't they?"

"They were," she said. "There are two of us called Iris and I never liked the name so I changed to Christine, now everybody just calls me Chris.

"So, let's see" she said. "You are George but everybody calls you Bob and I am Iris but everybody calls me Chris"

"So, we are Chris and Bob, Bob and Chris. She was trying it out and it sounded good to him.

They spent the rest of the evening talking and laughing and for Bob, the time far too quickly.

The only thing that had distracted Bob slightly was the sight of 'Call me Edward' trapped in a corner being kissed passionately by one of the girls. '*Well*' he thought, '*You just never really know about people.*' He really should stop thinking of him as 'Call me Edward,' it had been used so much when the section first met up that now some of them just called him 'Call me.' He didn't seem to mind this anywhere near as much as being called Eddie.

Bob stood up from the piano stool and called out to the others. "We should be making a move, we've got a long walk back."

Charlie wandered over to them and Chris said to him "Is he the boss then?" looking at Bob.

"Nah, but he looks out for us, some of the lads call him Uncle Bob," he went on. "He was a corporal once mind, til' he lost a bleedin' trailer." They all laughed, far too much as far as Bob was concerned. He was still a little hurt by what he thought of as an injustice.

They made arrangements to meet at the NAAFI again three days later, well at least Bob and Chris did and the others just went along with it.

He thought a lot about Iris, who was called Chris, she had certainly got under his skin. There had been a few chance encounters with ladies over the last four years or so but for various reasons, mostly to do with him, none that survived beyond a second meeting. The only person he had thought about in this way at all was Angela, his 'show girl' as he thought of her, but he was beginning to think, or hope, that this might be something more.

They all met up again as planned, all that was except Charlie, who had cried off at the last minute with stomach ache. As they greeted each other he realised that there were five girls and now five men, and now they were seated, each with a girl next to them, he wondered about the real reason that Charlie had decided not to come with them. Had he been so engrossed with Chris that he hadn't noticed that Charlie was not really being included in the fun?

Bob bought a round of drinks and then he and the lads sat and listened while the girls described what they had been doing for the last few months. It all sounded to the men to be a damn sight more dangerous than anything they had done lately, but they were not about to say that. They'd also been told very firmly that they were not with Land Army girls, they were with girls of the Timber Corps!

Before the next round of drinks was bought, and to Bob's surprise Chris quietly suggested that they, just the two of them, should go for a walk. It was a lovely clear evening and they both had warm coats, she said. They left, with calls of "don't do anything I wouldn't do," and lots of laughter from the rest.

Chris looked back at them and poked her tongue out and then, turning to him she said "Now you can tell me what you did with that trailer."

Two hours later they were back outside the NAAFI. They now knew a great deal more about each, other including the fact that with Chris being 'nineteen on her next birthday' as she described being eighteen, there was more than twenty years between their ages. Chris had said almost immediately that it was not going to make any difference to her.

They were still kissing when the others came out and then they suffered lots of teasing before they parted and the two groups went their separate ways. As he walked back to the camp he couldn't help grinning every time he thought about Chris's reaction to their ages. She had been so positive and definite in her response and what pleased him even more was that she had just assumed that they would keep seeing each other.

It was all arranged that they would meet up at the NAAFI the following weekend. Bob was going to try to scrounge some transport for them all to maybe get to the pub and even stay out a bit later.

*

Timber Corps was part of the Land Army and as such was a civilian operation. The Land Army and all it's various branches and forms was run on military lines and discipline was seen as important, not only to the success of the operation itself but also to the welfare of the girls who had volunteered. Overseers as they were called looked after each squad, or group of workers, and mostly although quite fair in their ways, they were very strict.

Chris and her group were billeted in a large old house which had been divided up to give them a room each and a common room in which they could meet up and relax, as well as a kitchen and bathroom. The overseer had lodgings in the village and used an old van to get to and fro.

Without any real knowledge of any others they were all convinced that their Overseer, Neil Hutchinson was the worst and they might have been right. He threw orders around like an Army officer might have done and kept insisting that they call him 'sir.' Not one of the girls ever did, and once they had found out his Christian name they always answered him as Neil which made him grimace every time.

The girls all flopped into the common room chairs the end of a long and tiring day. Usually they would be left to get cleaned up and have something to eat. If they weren't going to the NAAFI they would just listen to the radio or chat about their plans for life when the war ended. Today was different. Neil Hutchinson followed them into the common room and placed himself in the middle.

"There have been complaints from some of the people in the village about your behaviour," he looked around at them all.

"Nosey bloody parkers, what we supposed to have done anyway" Ruby had got to her feet and now had her hands on her hips. She was thinking, *'ok I might have been a bit passionate with Edward but who would have seen that?'*

"I don't have to explain in detail to any of you but I will tell you that it concerns you all coming in late from the NAAFI on more than one occasion, and one of you was seen walking out with a man on your own." He stared at them each in turn but none of them were as intimidated as he had hoped.

"I am responsible for your welfare as well as the reputation of the Timber Girls and so I have decided that for the next seven days you will all remain in the house after your duties, after that I will review the situation and make a further decision." He hurried from the room before any of them could respond.

"Pompous old fart," said Ruby. "He just doesn't want anybody to have fun thats all." She was cross with the Overseer but not unduly upset about a week without going out.

The one person that was really upset was Chris. They hadn't noticed until he had left, but now they did and tried to comfort her. She told them that Bob was going to risk getting hold of an army vehicle so that they could all go somewhere other than the NAAFI. How were they going to let him know that they would not be there?

That particular problem was solved the next day when Neil Hutchinson took it upon himself to visit the camp to furnish the commander with the details of the soldier's outrageous behaviour in and around the NAAFI.

He actually only made it as far up as the duty sergeant who, after tracking down who the culprits were, passed on his 'complaint' to Sergeant Collins. The sergeants only words to the section, apart from telling them about the Overseer's curfew, were that they were "Very naughty boys," delivered in what he thought was a school teacher's voice.

The following evening Bob discovered that Hutchinson had left a number for the telephone at his lodgings, "In case you need my help," he had said. Much to the amusement of the duty sergeant. The sergeant didn't take much persuading to give up the number and to leave Bob and three of the lads alone in the gatehouse while he went and had a smoke.

"Remember, you lot, I don't know anything about this and don't be long, it's bloody cold outside."

They all crowded round the telephone and Bob dialled the number. He was just about to give up when it was answered by what sounded like an old lady.

"Hello, may I speak to a Mr Hutchinson" he said. There was no answer and he just waited. The lads were all looking at him expectantly, they had no idea what he had in mind and at that moment he had no idea either.

"Hello, Neil Hutchinson speaking," even on the telephone there was a slightly pompous edge to the voice. It may have been that which led Bob to his response, almost without thinking.

"Hutchinson!?" Bob had adopted his 'senior officer' voice.

Without waiting for a response, he went on. "Brigadier Thomson-Smythe here, I understand that you are the officer in charge of the Timber Corps." He had moved the voice up to its most autocratic level.

The lads were trying their best to keep quiet but not quite succeeding.

"Well not actually all of it,"

"Let's not be splitting hairs eh?" Bob continued, "You and I have to take actions that are not always popular with the troops eh, but discipline is crucial to proper control don't ya think"

"Er, yes absolutely," said Hutchinson.

"As soon as I heard about your visit to the camp, I knew we were alike." There was a burst of laughter and Bob quickly covered the mouth piece and shushed them.

"Where are you speaking from?" asked Hutchinson, he had obviously heard something.

"I can't divulge my whereabouts to anybody I'm afraid, and that is part of why I have contacted you."

"I see," said the Overseer, although he clearly didn't.

"Look, what I can say is that I run certain ops that don't get reported in the newspapers. Know what I mean?"

"Ah, yes"

"Right. Some of my lads are off on a bit of a caper in a few days, and getting back is not guaranteed."

The others were now having a great deal of trouble keeping quiet, every time they looked at Bob, who was now pretending to twiddle a moustache, they started to laugh again.

"I'll get to the point, you have, quite rightly ordered one of your units to remain at base but I'm going to ask you as one officer to another if you will do me a favour. I would like you to allow the 'gels' to meet with my chaps on Saturday night. I'm sure you understand why I would like them to have a little fun before they….well I can't say any more."

"I understand and of course we must do whatever we can for the chaps, if they are at the NAAFI on Saturday evening, I will make sure that they have some company"

"Thank you, Hutchinson and England thanks you as well." Just before disconnecting, he said "Oh and by the way, there will be six of my chaps coming." And then, finally he started laughing himself.

They went back to their hut and spent the rest of the evening laughing and talking about how Neil Hutchinson might try to sort things out. The next day Bob would have to try to organise some Saturday night transport for possibly as many as twelve people. Why did he always feel that he was the one to organise things?

He managed to 'borrow' a lorry from the maintenance shed, it was booked out as being road tested but had to be back in the shed before the morning. The lorry had been used for moving people and so in the back it had hard benches bolted down each side under the canvas cover. It was pretty uncomfortable and very cold, but it was better than walking.

The Timber girls were at the NAAFI and still talking about what could have happened. In less than twenty-four hours an outright ban on leaving their Billet had turned into something only just short of an order that they go out and enjoy themselves.

Their best guess at the moment was that Neil Hutchinson had a mental problem. When a couple of the girls had said that they no longer felt like going he had practically begged them to go! He had also asked them to take another girl with them, they didn't know her but were happy for her to go along, albeit as totally mystified as the girl herself.

The noise of the lorry pulling up outside brought the girls out to see what was happening. As soon as they saw the lads jumping out there was lots of good-natured teasing and a lot of joking about the 'luxury' transport.

The girls were soon helped up into the back except Chris who climbed into the cab with Bob.

"Hold tight everyone" yelled Bob. And they were off round the country lanes. There were plenty of bends and plenty of bumps on the way and there were squeals and laughter coming from the back all the way.

In the cab Chris had moved as close to Bob as she could and because of this had started to change gear, each time he shouted a number she would ram the gear stick in the direction that she thought best. The grating noise coming from the gear box only made everybody laugh even more. He headed for a pub about ten miles away. He had passed it many times before on his travels but, being on his own, had never stopped.

The twelve of them almost filled the bar in the little pub and with a log fire burning in the corner fireplace it was very cosy. The lady behind the bar was pleased to see them, her takings had probably just doubled for the week!

Once they had all got their drinks and sat down the story of how they came to be allowed out was told by Edward, insisting that Bob did the voice when he got to that bit. Chris told them how worried Neil had been when it looked like some of them wouldn't go. Then finally she introduced Mabel to the group. She explained that Neil had insisted that Mabel be included but neither they, or Mabel had any idea why.

"We've interrogated her and she is definitely not a spy," said Ruby. "But at least we're six a side now." Nobody gave it another thought except Bob, who was watching Charlie, who was watching Mabel.

Nobody was in any hurry for the evening to end and the landlady was happy for them to stay in the warm as long as they liked she said, "After all no one's going to bother you out here."

The evening eventually wound to a close and it was after midnight when Bob coasted the last fifty yards towards the girl's house with engine off but, having done that, brakes screeched so loudly when he pulled up it must have woken everybody within half a mile! Lights were going on all over the place. Neil was going to be handling some complaints tomorrow!

Bob and Chris were going to meet again as soon as they could and he promised to find a way in which they could get messages to each other. Christmas was coming and they had decided that one way or another they would spend it together.

Much to Bob's relief they got back to the camp without incident, the roads had frozen and were deadly in places but the amount of driving that Bob had done in recent years meant that he could cope well with it. He dropped the lads off and took the lorry round to the maintenance shed and parked it up next to the doors.

He took his time walking back to the hut and thought about his time in the army and what he would be doing this time next year. It was a fair bet, he thought, that the war would be over and so would his time in the army. He smiled to himself because what he had actually thought was, *what will **we** be doing this time next year,* he was now including Chris in his long-term thinking.

Chapter 28

With a bit of persuasion at both ends, Bob and Chris were now able leave messages and even have the occasional chat by using the gatehouse telephone and the telephone at the Timber corps billet. They saw each other as often as possible and, now that Bob's Christmas leave was confirmed, they planned that he would join Chris when she went home for the break.

Bob's leave started the week before Chris was released for the Christmas holiday and so he travelled to Norwood to visit Violet and Benjy for a couple of days. He had arranged to meet with Chris in Willesdon on the Friday before Christmas. They would meet up at a café in Church road at mid-day and it was only a short walk from there to her parent's home.

He arrived at Violet's house and she and Benjy were surprised and pleased to see him. He told them his plans for Christmas expecting that they would try to persuade him to stay with them. They were genuinely pleased about his 'new girl,' as Violet called her, but made no effort to change his plans for Christmas which surprised him a little.

"We are planning to have a nice quiet Christmas on our own" said Violet.

There was a sadness about them and Bob realised that they were still greatly affected by the loss of their friends. He was sad, but being out of the area and also being kept busy had enabled him to deal with it much better. They were still right there, where it had happened.

Violet went off to make them a cup of tea and while she was in the kitchen Bob asked Benjy how the business was doing. Benjy told him that he was hardly going to the warehouse at all now. He had got rid of anything that wouldn't keep indefinitely, and the rest of the stock was just sitting there. If someone wanted a specific item, he would take them round there to get it but was not actively selling and definitely not delivering any more.

Before Violet came back with the tea and biscuits Benjy told Bob that he wasn't too well, his 'ticker' was playing up a bit he said. He could no longer do any lifting and definitely couldn't drive the van any more.

They sat and chatted while drinking their tea and Benjy explained that he was looking for someone to take over the business. Bob must have looked a bit surprised because he went on quickly to say that he and Violet had talked a great deal about Bob and the business.

Benjy described himself as a London Spiv and a bit of a 'wide boy' who dealt with some very dodgy types. He and Violet, he said, didn't see Bob in that role at all. They felt that Bob was well educated, intelligent and would go on to be successful at something that was not as 'iffy.'

He didn't know whether to be upset or not, after all he'd just been rejected for the role of a 'wide boy.'

Bob enjoyed his couple of days at the house, whether by accident or design he was sleeping in his old room and although tinged with some sadness, it reminded him of some happy times and it was warm and cosy. The weather had turned very cold.

The newspapers were reporting on what was called the 'Battle of the Bulge.' The German army were pushing back and had created a bulge in the front line of the Allies advance. On Friday morning, over breakfast they listened to the news on the Home Service. Although bitterly cold, the skies had cleared and Allied planes were now able to join the fight which was helping to turn the German forces back.

"They thought it would be all over by Christmas" said Benjy, "But the buggers are still fighting."

They finished breakfast and Bob helped Violet to clear the table and wash the dishes. She had suggested to Benjy that Bob could use the van while he was on leave and Benjy had agreed. There was plenty of unused petrol in it and he was sure that Bob would be 'buying' some things from the warehouse for his new girl and her family.

Bob left, wishing them a Happy Christmas and promising to get the van back, in one piece and before the New Year.

He loaded the van with the things he had chosen from the warehouse which included packets of tea, several bags of sugar, some jam and marmalade. There were also some bags of sweets and a few bars of scented soap, but best of all were the stockings. He had found a box sitting at the back of a top shelf which contained four pairs, he didn't know anything about sizes but they were stockings!

With everything secure and covered up in the back he set off on the drive to Willesdon.

Arriving in plenty of time, he drove round for a while mainly to keep warm. The van had no heater but he pulled up every so often and the engine heat was just enough to keep his legs and feet warm. There was an old towel in the passenger side footwell and he had soon found out what it was for, using it to wipe the condensation off the inside of the windscreen every few minutes before it turned to ice.

He parked right outside the café and went in. Chris had seen him arrive and stood up to greet him with a big smile. For some reason he had thought that she would be in civilian clothes and was surprised that she was still wearing her Timber Corps uniform. The reason for this, he found out, was that she had not been home yet and had waited to see him so that they could arrive together.

Chris cleared a small patch in the condensation and looked out of the café window at the van, she laughed, "What have got there, Bob? Are you sure it's not going to fall apart?"

Bob put Chris's small case in with his kitbag and the rest of the stuff from Benjy's and once they had cleared just enough ice to see out, they set off.

It was only a five minute drive to Chris's home, in fact two left turns and they were there.

Dick and Lil lived with their three children, Iris who was the oldest and her younger brothers, John and Peter. The flat was above a parade of shops and was accessed by a very sturdy steel staircase leading up to a small balcony and the main door.

They struggled up the stairs, Chris with her case and the box containing the stockings and Bob carrying two boxes with all the other 'goodies.' In spite of Chris's insistence that her parents would want him to stay, he decided that carrying his kitbag in first would appear a bit presumptuous. He would go down and collect it once he had definitely been invited to stay.

The door was opened as soon as they reached the top of the stairs and Dick came out to give Chris a hug.

"Get yourself in the warm girl, and this bloke looks like he could do with a warm as well" he said, taking her case and waving them both inside.

"Lil, Iris is here!" Dick was shouting, as he reached to take the boxes from Bob.

"Hello Iris, your looking a bit thin, have you been eating properly?" Lil was moving her into the next room.

The outside door opened directly into the kitchen, a door from there led straight into a large living room. Chris and her mum had moved into the living room leaving Bob and Dick in the kitchen.

Bob could hear Lil questioning Chris about what she had been up to as Dick was saying to him, "Nice of you to help her up with this lot," he was looking at her case and the boxes next to it on the floor.

"Lord knows what she has got in them but I suppose we'll find out soon enough. You will stay for a cup of tea, won't you? I hope my daughter hasn't dragged you too far out of your way."

He called out, "Lil are you going to make this bloke a cup of tea, I expect he wants to get on to where he's heading," turning to Bob he said, "Have you got far to go?"

Bob had hardly said a word up to now, "Err no, not far" he said.

He called out in desperation, "Chris!" It came out louder than he intended and had a slightly panicky sound to it.

"Who is Chris?" said Dick.

"That's me" said Iris.

"Why does he think you are Chris?" said Lil.

"Because I am Chris" said Iris.

"Hold on, everybody!" said Dick loudly.

"So, this bloke has helped you with all your luggage, whatever it all this is, and for some reason you've told him that your name is Chris, is that it?

"No dad" said Chris.

"Can we start all over again?" she said.

They started again and introductions were made, Bob couldn't help noticing the looks that were exchanged between Dick and Lil when Chris told them that they were courting. Courting was not a description that Bob had thought of before, but he thought now, yes that's exactly what we're doing.

They all sat and drank tea, the conversation was a little bit stilted and when Dick asked Bob where he was staying Chris jumped in and said, "I was hoping that Bob could stay here."

"I suppose we could make a bed up in the top room," said Lil.

The atmosphere was suddenly changed completely by the arrival of John and Peter. They came bundling in, bringing a lot of cold air in with them and were yelled at to get their shoes off before they left the kitchen.

"Hello sis!" said John with a grin. Peter said hello quietly and went over to his mum.

"We've been looking at the guns in Roundwood park" said John.

"I told you not to pester the men, didn't I?"

"We didn't ask, they just showed us," said Peter.

They finally noticed Bob and Chris said to them, "This is Bob and we're courting." The boys looked at each other and John said, "Oooh, courting," that started fits of giggling while they put their shoes back on.

"Don't go near those guns again and be back at before dark!" shouted Lil.

They all sat for while in silence and then Lil said, "Iris mentioned that you've just had a birthday, none of us getting any younger, so what did that make you?"

Bob was getting a little fed up with feeling like he was being assessed, and failing.

"Yes" he said "My birthday, it made me a year older, that's what they do isn't it?"

Chris heard the slight edge to Bob's voice and decided that she should do something.

"Let's wrap up warm and go for a walk" she suggested to Bob, "It will be dark soon but I can show you some of Willesdon before that."

Bob knew that he was being rescued and agreed quickly, getting up and heading for his coat which had been hung up by the door.

When they got back things seemed a little more relaxed, the boys arrived shortly after them and before long they were all sitting down to a meal. Once they had finished and he and Chris had washed up Bob opened the boxes and unpacked the things onto the drop-down shelf on the larder cabinet.

Lil was very pleased and said, "Gawd, best not let the neighbours see any of this, Dick you can have some marmalade at breakfast!"

Dick was not showing any pleasure and just said "As long as we're not all arrested before then."

*

Christmas passed without any unpleasantness although Bob could sense it being near the surface. He listened to Dick as he was 'taken to one side' and told about their concerns regarding the age difference. They still didn't know exactly what that difference was, in spite of repeated and ingenious attempts by Lil to get his age, he had not yet divulged it.

Dick had told him that apart from the 'age thing' his only concern when it came to Iris was that she should be happy and *stay that way* he said, staring in what Bob imagined was supposed to be a threatening way. Being a good six inches shorter and slightly built was not helping Dick, but he carried it off well enough and Bob was not about to spoil his day.

Bob had to leave before Chris and she came down and sat in the van while he let it warm up. They had managed very little time on their own and the sleeping arrangements had done nothing to help that. They made a date to meet at the NAAFI on the Saturday following New Year. If for any reason they were unable to make contact before then they would have something arranged.

Finally, Bob said that he should go and Chris got out and stood waving as he drove off. He got the van back to Benjy's warehouse, there was no sign of him or Violet so he put the car key through the flap in the office door.

Walking as quickly as he could he was round at their house in less than ten minutes but they were not there either, it was disappointing as he wanted to thank them for the use of the van and wish them a happy New Year, but he had to go.

When he got back to the camp, he was surprised at how much had changed. The field guns and the Anti-aircraft guns had gone and the roads outside had been returned to their previous condition. The hundreds of sandbags that had surrounded anything remotely considered as important, had miraculously disappeared.

The biggest change though was in the numbers of men in the camp. As far as Bob could make out about half the men in the camp had gone. Over the following days he learnt that men had been transferred all over the place, mostly in a northerly direction. Corporal Lewis had gone, Sergeant Collins was to be moved shortly, he said.

Bob found out more when a few days after returning he was ordered to drive Major Smith to London. On the drive up the major was quiet and thoughtful and Bob made no attempt to talk, they had got to know each other pretty well over what was now some years. As they arrived in Whitehall, he said to the major that he doubted that he would be able to do any 'shopping' but he was concerned about a friend who had helped with it.

Major Smith told Bob that he had no idea how long he would be and suggested that he go and check on his friend as quickly as he could and then come back and wait outside.

He drove off towards Norwood, the Austin was running as well as it ever had, it was still undamaged and had been well polished. Whenever he was in this car, and more so when he was on his own, it gave him such a good feeling. He had so often wished that he could just drive, going wherever the car might take him. Those thoughts were still with him when he arrived at the warehouse, he was a bit concerned because he couldn't remember too much of the journey there!

Just like the last time he had been, there was no-one there and the place was locked up and looking a little uncared for. He drove on to the house, parked outside and went and knocked on the door. He still had a key but it didn't feel right just to go in. While he stood there wondering what to do, one the neighbours came out and called to him, "It's Bob isn't it" she said.

He recognised the woman but they had never spoken before, "Violet asked me to keep an eye on the house, she is spending so much time at the hospital."

"The hospital?" asked Bob.

"Yeah, it's her fancy man" said the woman, pursing her lips disapprovingly. "Heart attack they reckon."

"Do you mean Benjamin?"

"Oh, is that his name?"

"Big man, moustache, check suits?" Bob was getting angry.

"That's the fella, fancies himself a bit."

"That man is a good friend of mine, and is Violet's *husband!*"

"Well, she never told me that."

"No, I don't suppose she asked you to keep an eye on things either, so go back indoors you old witch."

Bob used his key and went in. He had no idea where Benjy might have ended up, most of the hospitals had evacuated out of London because of the Flying bombs. He had get back to Whitehall, so the best he could do for now was to leave a note for Violet with the camp postal address on it and hope that she would write.

As he came out and got into the car the curtains twitched at the house next door, he glared at the window for a few seconds knowing that the 'old witch' was watching, and then drove off.

When he got back to Whitehall, he was met by a young Private who, after establishing that he was there to collect Major Smith, told him that he was to wait outside the barrier and the major would be informed that he was there. Apparently, there had been some sort of incident and absolutely nobody was allowed through.

Eventually the major came out and limped down the road to the barrier. Bob jumped out and went around to open the car door but the major just waved him away saying, "Just drive me back to base please." During the drive back he told Bob that the camp was to be used as some sort of transitional facility for returning soldiers. "There'll be thousands of them, I suppose they have to be processed somewhere."

It was clear that Major Smith was not happy. He confided to Bob that he had felt useless in this war and was definitely not looking forward to commanding a 'processing' unit. Bob reminded him of his role in the Home Defence Planning Group and the work he had done helping to create the Anti-tank Islands.

"Damned nice of you to say these things" said the major, "And thank you for….," he hesitated. "The things you have done."

When they arrived back at 'base' Bob went around and opened the door for the major, standing to attention and giving a smart salute. The major smiled and returned the salute. Just as he was about to walk away, he turned to Bob and asked, "Have you really got dodgy feet?" Bob replied, "No, not dodgy feet. Just a stiff toe, it's called Halex Rigidus."

That was to be the last time he drove the major anywhere. The major no longer warranted having even a part-time driver and so Bob would not be driving the Austin 16 anymore. There was no delivery this time for Sergeant Collins to spirit away, so it fell to Bob to return the car.

On an impulse he decided to take the car and visit Chris at the house, it was getting late in the afternoon and would soon be dark so, hopefully the girls would be back.

They were back and, with a bit of help from some of the others he found his way to Chris's room. He had been fairly miserable when he arrived and told Chris all about his trip to London and his worries about Violet and, particularly Benjy. There was also the fact that this was his last time with the car, driving the major about had come to an end. Everything was changing and very quickly.

It wasn't too long before Bob was feeling much more cheerful and it was later when he and Chris were lying together enjoying a smoke that he suddenly sat up and said "Will you marry me?" He didn't leave until well after mid-night by which time they had decided that they would get married the next time that Bob was on leave.

He got the car back to the camp and took it round to the maintenance shed where he left it for the last time.

There seemed to be nothing for Bob to do, he had a couple of trips out in a lorry picking up supplies but that had been all for two weeks. His request for leave had been granted and he was looking forward to it starting at the end of March. Just one more week to go.

A letter from Violet had finally arrived. She wrote that Benjy had never really recovered after collapsing at the house one morning. He had passed away a week later. She was staying with a friend in Southend and was not returning to London. She finished by saying that Bob had been a good friend to both of them and she hoped that they would meet again at some time.

For the first time Bob and Chris were able to travel to London together. They stayed with Dick and Lil who were less than enthusiastic about the wedding plans, but did their best not to show it. Chris seemed totally oblivious to any disapproval by her mum and dad and everything went ahead as planned.

They managed to find a house to rent, not too far from where Chris's mum and dad lived, which was not the reason that Bob liked it. The man who owned it had long since given up any hope of selling it and was now very happy to rent it, especially as not knowing quite when they would be moving in, Bob paid three months in advance.

The wedding was held in Willesdon registry office with Dick and Lil as the witnesses. Bob wondered if that would be a problem but in the event they just signed where they were asked to. They all went to the local pub for a drink and then on to Dick and Lil's for a meal. The day went by without incident and Bob and Chris left as soon as they could for the first night in their own home.

The end of Bob's leave was approaching and Chris would have to go back soon so they left together and their train and bus journeys were quiet and sad affairs. Bob was surprised at how upset Chris was at their having to part for a while. He supposed it was something to do with them being married now, it certainly seemed to have changed their relationship to something more serious.

Just two weeks later they were back in London. They arrived in Willesdon on the 7th May and it seemed that almost everybody they passed was smiling. The atmosphere was almost like there was a Carnival taking place.

They thought that Willesdon was a much happier place when they arrived, but the following day the whole place just seemed to go crazy! It was V.E day. People danced in the streets. Pubs opened their doors all day and there was a seemingly endless supply of beer. They partied all day and most of the night, linking up with one group of strangers for a while before drifting off and linking up with another. It was like one huge party and at 2.00am, when they finally headed for home, there were no signs of it finishing.

The end of Bob's leave was nearing and Chris had to return to the Timber Corps, but only for a short time.

Somehow, although he didn't qualify on the points system for being demobilised, Bob was 'Demobbed' at the start of June. Chris had already left the Timber Corps and had started making a home for them at the house. There was some furniture already there and they had got hold of a few things before leaving in May. It didn't matter if you had the money or not, there just wasn't much of anything to be had.

It took nearly two weeks for him to get through the seemingly endless process of being 'demobbed.' Bob finally set out for Willesdon to join his wife in their new home.

He had his new set of clothes which included a suit and shoes. As luck would have it, his Burtons suit was a very good fit, unlike a lot of men he had seen with suits that were either much too big or painfully too small. Most of them, he thought, looked like they were about to appear in a comedy film.

During the journey he thought about his farewells to the few that were left at the camp, they were all going off to very different and mostly unknown futures. With a decent amount of money still in the bank and his back pay and 'demob' money still to come, he had no immediate money worries. Lots of ideas about a new business had been buzzing around in his head for months now and with one idea in particular he could hardly wait to get started!

With all that, a home to go back to and his new wife waiting, he was feeling like a very lucky man.

Bob arrived at the house just after lunchtime, he put the key in the door and opened it as quietly as he could. He was going to surprise Chris and was looking forward to her reaction. The house was cold and quiet and as he went in it was soon clear that there was no-one at home. He went from room to room, ending up the kitchen where looking around it was clear that Chris had not just popped out.

He was disappointed but not unduly worried and was reasoning that Chris had felt lonely and was staying with her parents until he came home. He walked round to Dick and Lil's flat and was surprised to find them both in, Dick was not well and having a day off work. As soon as he entered the flat, he could feel that there was an atmosphere.

"Is Chris," he corrected himself, "Is Iris here?"

"No, she's with her friends, one of them is going back to America"

"Oh, I see" said Bob, "Did she say when she would be back?"

"I should think she'll be a good while, she's going to miss that lad. Such a handsome *young* man and lovely manners"

"He has been here then?" Bob was getting a bit upset but trying not to show it.

"A few times, I thought they looked such a lovely *young* couple." The stress was on the word '*young*' again.

"That's enough Lil." Growled Dick. "Just leave it now, Iris is married to Bob or did you forget?"

Dick told Bob to go home, if Iris went to them first, they would let her know that he was back.

"She'll be home in no time" he said, almost kindly.

Back at the house Bob opened some windows to let some fresh air in and turned on the radio. He was attempting to cheer himself up but it wasn't working. After a while he went out to buy some cigarettes a newspaper and luckily, half a loaf of bread. On the way back he convinced himself that Chris had returned and was waiting for him, but she hadn't.

She didn't come back that evening and after mid-night Bob finally fell asleep on a chair downstairs. He hadn't closed the curtains and the sun coming up in the morning woke him up.

It was a few seconds before he got his bearings and then he decided that Chris had returned in the night and, not wanting to disturb him, had crept upstairs to bed. Even as he climbed the stairs, he knew really that it was nonsense, but he went and looked anyway.

Suddenly feeling hungry, Bob made some toast under the grill and then, finding absolutely nothing to put on it just ate it as it was.

He re-read the paper, wandered about the house for a while and then headed off to see if she had arrived back at her mum and dad's flat. When he got there Lil just opened the door and told him that Iris was not there, obviously there was no invitation to go in so he left.

As he walked slowly back to the house his head was all over the place.

He was angry with Iris, her parents and this American, did they think he was stupid to be treated like this? He wouldn't put up with it.

Then he was sad and couldn't understand how Chris could have changed so much since they were last together.

Then he decided it was all a mistake, she was just staying with friends, her parents had got the wrong end of the stick and there was no more to it than that.

His thoughts were just going round and round in circles, he would have to find some answers soon.

All through that day he wandered about lost in his thoughts most of the time. At mid-day he went to the café in Church road where he had a cup of tea and some kind of soup that he didn't recognise. They had met here before Christmas on their first time in Willesdon together, being here was upsetting him so he finished quickly and left.

That evening at about 8.00 he was sitting listening to the radio when he heard the front door slam. He sat up straighter in the chair and waited for Chris to come into the room but she didn't. The next thing that he heard was someone running up the stairs and slamming the bedroom door.

Bob got up from the chair and went slowly up the stairs, he could hear sobbing coming from the bedroom and after a few seconds thought, he went in.

They didn't shout or scream at each other, that was not in Bob's nature anyway. Hours later he knew what had happened, well at least as much as Chris wanted him to know was how he thought of it.

She had met the young American airman with a group of friends and something had just happened between them. In no time at all their feelings had grown and even though they both knew it was wrong they just couldn't help it she said.

Bob had asked where they were to go from here. Chris told him that her feelings toward him had not changed and this 'thing' with the American was just a 'slip-up' that was over. Bob was just feeling that he could possibly accept that when Chris said "He's gone back to America anyway."

He slept downstairs again that night and for two nights that followed. Gradually they began to talk in a more normal and relaxed way and seemed to be getting back to what they had been before the 'thing.'

On the third night following her return Chris had kissed Bob and asked him if he would please go upstairs with her. It seemed to him that this was the moment that would decide whether they were to go on together or not. He went upstairs and that night Chris was more passionate than he had ever known, it was almost like she was a different person. He could not have said it was anything but enjoyable but afterwards, with her asleep beside him he lay wondering what exactly had just happened.

The summer went by with them getting on with making their home. They made new friends and took their turns at hosting parties, most of which went on into the early hours and, if they didn't get at least two complaints, were not considered a success.

Bob had been developing his idea for a new type of sign that would be made from plastic and not wood or metal as had always been the case previously.

Two Jewish men had fled from Austria to England in 1937 just in time to avoid the Nazis and managing to get their money out with them. For years they had just waited hoping that they would one day return to their homeland but by the time the war ended they had decided to stay in England and resume the business of manufacturing.

Before the war they had been experimenting with plastic moulding and they used that knowledge now to set up a small factory making plastic 'spoon and pusher' sets for young children. They had known at the start that they would need to expand into more products if they were to survive and grow. So, one day when a smart well-spoken Englishman came to them with his prototype sign and the drawings of what would be plastic moulded letters and numbers, they knew that this was for them.

Three months had passed since Bob's eventful return to the house, he and Chris were back to the way they had been before, in fact Bob had barely thought about the 'thing' for weeks. Chris had been a little off colour for a while and had been to the Doctor "for a tonic" she said. He was a bit concerned but she assured him it was nothing serious.

A few days later she broke the news to Bob. He was to be a dad was how she put it and after a few seconds while it sunk in, he held her and told her how pleased he was. The baby was due in the middle of March.

That night Bob lay in bed and, despite telling himself that he wouldn't, he counted back the weeks. The result was not reassuring and as he lay there, thoughts of Lucy and the boy he had met in the shop came, unbidden, into his mind.

The next day Chris looked radiant, she kept glancing at Bob and smiling and he couldn't help smiling in return. Each time he held her now he was overwhelmed with a protective feeling that was totally new to him.

That evening he went for a walk on his own. There was a calmness in him that he not felt before. He thought about a lot of things as he walked, all the people he had known and those that he had lost. There was his time as an Estate agent and there was Lucy, of course. He recalled his time with Benjy and Violet, he hoped that she was ok, and there was 'Trixie' his show girl. It was as he was recalling his time in the army that he arrived back home having not consciously thought about where he was going. That was new.

The next morning, he was up early, the sun was out it was a lovely September morning. He made some tea and toast and took it up to Chris who was just waking up.

"What's all this about" she said.

"Just because" he replied, and sat on the bed while she had her breakfast.

He went downstairs to the kitchen, put the dishes in the sink and then just stood.

'This is the start of a new time for me'

'I have money in the bank.'

'I have a new product which is already selling well.'

'I have a home.'

'I have a lovely wife and soon I will have a child.'

'I must start just enjoying things, after all what can possibly go wrong?

He bent down to start clearing up the pieces of the plate that he had just dropped.